Surrender

APHRODISIA BOOKS are published by

Kensington Publishing Corp.
850 Third Avenue
New York, NY 10022

All Kensington Titles, Imprints, and Distributed Lines are available at special quantity discounts for bulk purchases for sales promotions, premiums, fund-raising, and educational or institutional use.

Special book excerpts or customized printings can also be created to fit specific needs. For details, write or phone the office of the Kensington special sales manager: Kensington Publishing Corp., 850 Third Avenue, New York, NY 10022, attn: Special Sales Department, Phone: 1-800-221-2647.

Aphrodisia and the A logo are trademarks of Kensington Publishing Corp.

ISBN: 0-7582-1526-6

First Trade Paperback Printing: August 2006

10 9 8 7 6 5 4 3 2

Printed in the United States of America

Surrender

Vonna Harper

APHRODISIA

KENSINGTON BOOKS

http://www.kensingtonbooks.com

Contents

The Dance

1

"So, how does it feel to be canned?"

Because she was the only one in her bedroom, Asia Drake didn't expect a response. Instead, she lifted her glass of wine and toasted her image in the dresser mirror. The polished image of a successful professional woman saluted back.

"What the hell are you smiling at?" Asia challenged. "Your audience is gone. You don't have to pretend anymore."

Nodding in acceptance and defeat, she put the glass on the dresser and removed her heels. Relief at being rid of the damnably uncomfortable things briefly distracted her. Straightening, she again faced herself. After a momentary appraisal, she shrugged and started unbuttoning her new teal jacket. The jacket had set her back a couple of hundred dollars but was a necessary part of how she projected herself to her employers at Maximize Enterprises.

"Amend that. Soon-to-be ex-employers."

Her hand shook as she finished with the buttons and pulled off the garment. After dropping it on her bed, she picked up the wine again and took a hearty swallow. Then she acknowledged that she hadn't been fired so much as been a casualty of what the company's board members called outsourcing.

"Big fucking deal. Bottom line, girl, is that you're out of a job. Services no longer required."

But I created the marketing department. My campaigns put the company on the map. Doesn't that account for something?

Apparently not.

Deep-down weary of the whole thing and more than a little scared, she focused on removing the rest of her work clothes. By the time she'd hung up her jacket, silk shell, and slim white skirt, she'd polished off the wine and replenished her supply. Now she stood facing her underwear-clad form.

"You aren't even thirty yet. And you're not hard on the eyes." Head cocked to the side, she cupped her breasts and lifted. "No sag . . . Tight ass, flat belly, runner's legs." Shifting direction, she ran her fingers over her pantyhose-clad thighs. "The package isn't bad. You won't have any trouble selling it to another company."

Wait. Was she really thinking about using her physical assets to get herself a job? It had to be the wine talking. But . . . hell.

"What can I say? Sex sells. And I know how to make it work."

Ridding herself of the pantyhose without snagging them took concentration. Still, as she slid the sensual material over her skin, she couldn't help but admit that being young, female, and attractive had gone a long way toward helping her achieve career success. Just because her current employer's bottom line and priorities had robbed her of a job didn't mean she'd soon be selling pencils on the street corner.

"Hell, no. If worse comes to worst, I'll sell myself. And no street corners either." She slipped a hand under her bikini panties. "This package deserves to be a kept woman."

Kept? Hmm. Now there was a possibility, a damn intriguing one.

All right, so what was the life of a kept woman like? Sure there was the sex part, always available, willing, appreciative, grateful, a happy little energized bunny. But the rest of the time would be hers, as would a generous allowance and credit cards she wouldn't get the bills for, right?

Yeah, but other than spending money on herself and spreading her legs at the snap of a finger, how would she fill her life?

A joyless laugh ended in a near sob, startling her. She hadn't cried for so long she'd all but forgotten what it sounded like. And although the question of how long she'd be able to afford the payments on her luxury condo had to be faced, she wasn't about to mire in self pity. Feeling sorry for herself, like giving into heartbreak—something that had nearly destroyed her twice—never changed reality.

She switched off the overhead light and reached for the nightstand lamp but didn't turn it on. Instead, she lit a trio of candles and let the scent of vanilla and spices waft over her.

In a precious few days, she wouldn't be waking to an alarm clock before the crack of dawn so she could get in some exercise before going to the office. As long as she was unemployed, gaining a few pounds wouldn't be that big a deal. She wouldn't need her power suits, would have no reason to choose between her twenty-some pairs of heels. Would no longer spend too many evenings hunched over her briefcase. Instead she'd, what? Have a pleasure-fest? Come until she couldn't come anymore?

Wine in hand, she opened her nightstand drawer and contemplated her sex toy collection. As she recalled, the pearlized lavender vibrator had fresh batteries. She couldn't say it was her favorite. It was just one of the precious few that still worked. Maybe that's what she'd do with some of her spare time. Replenish her supply. And prowl the Internet for more sites specializing in sensual reading and viewing material.

Well, not just sensual, she admitted to herself. She reached under the toys for the folder she hoped to hell no one ever saw and placed it on the bed. After another swallow of wine, she opened the folder and began spreading out the photographs she'd downloaded. In the uncertain light, some were hard to make out, but she'd seen them so many times that she went by memory.

Every one portrayed naked or nearly naked women in various stages of bondage, ranging from rope spiderwebs circling their lush bodies to metal restraints that allowed only minimal movement. For the most part, the men responsible were photographed in shadow, which left a lot to her imagination. Too much. And unfortunately, she'd never been able to come up with an image of the perfect Dom. Big and strong, of course. Sure of himself. Dark and dangerous, but not over the top in that department.

Sighing, Asia put down her glass, removed her bra, and returned to her drawer. Selecting a pair of gold nipple clamps, she ran the metal over her breasts. As she did, she felt her pussy loosen and soften. The familiar, safe fantasy took hold. It would work. It always did.

In her mind she stood naked and exposed on an auction block. Because a bright light was directed on her, she couldn't see the audience, but she could sense their presence. Powerful men had come to bid on her. The details of how she'd come to this place were always vague. What she'd been before she'd become a sex slave didn't matter. Only the chains securing her arms over her head did. Only the large, elaborate clamp the auctioneer was placing on her nipple did.

Panting, she steadied her right breast as she settled a clip over her hard nub. Sensation raced through her from breast to crotch. She closed her eyes and imagined knowing eyes raking her flesh and deep, approving voices as the auctioneer demonstrated how much nipple play turned her on by pulling on the clamp. Then he swept his hand over her pussy and held his glistening fingers up to the light.

"The current offering comes to us from a flesh trafficker who prefers to remain anonymous," the auctioneer in her mind announced. "She's well-trained in the art of pleasing a man and is truly submissive. See how easily she accepts everything I do to her."

Although Asia attached the second clamp, in her mind she stood still and heated while the man in charge of her sale did the deed.

"However, because she was born free," the auctioneer continued, "she still has spirit, which will provide her new owner with endless entertainment and possibilities. She fights her nature. See how she can be made to struggle to try to free herself."

Arms reaching for the ceiling now, Asia twisted from side to side. The gesture sent her captured breasts into motion. Moaning, she imagined her possible owners leaning forward so they could closely study her performance.

"She is a slave to her sex."

Asia ran a hand under her panties. She didn't stop until she'd reached her hot, wet flesh.

"See how quickly she becomes excited. Although she fights herself, she orgasms easily and hates being denied. Hunger and frustration make her docile and compliant and eager to please. Use her instinct and what she learned at the hands of the trafficker to your advantage, gentlemen. Now, who wishes to start the bidding?"

Trembling, Asia slipped her wet fingers into her mouth and sucked.

A sex slave. My existence revolving around my pussy.

Fantasy pulled her in even deeper and took her back in time to when she'd been captured by the slaver who'd prepared her for her life as a sexual object. He'd run her down, cornered her, lassoed, and hog-tied her before cutting off her clothes. Then he'd knelt beside her helpless body and pushed a hard rubber dildo inside her.

Imagining her fingers were the dildo, she rammed them home. Despite her desperate attempts, she couldn't move as her captor continued his invasion. She begged and pleaded until he silenced her by securing a large ball gag in her mouth. The dildo remained buried in her pussy.

He gripped the large, firm rod again, sliding it rapidly in and out of her vagina. The pace quickened, ignited hidden flesh, insisted on surrender and subservience. "That's it, slave! Rock and roll. Let's hear you whimper."

She did, the helpless cries muffled by the ball that forced her mouth to remain open.

The dildo continued to work her. Tireless, relentless, frenzied now, it powered its way not just into her cave but throughout her. Her mind seized and froze. No longer distracted by rational thought, she rode the invasion.

"Scream, girl. Scream!"

"Ahhh!"

"Beg for it."

Please, please!

"You love this, don't you? Say it!"

Please, please, let me come!

"What will you do for me?"

Anything.

"I can't hear you, slave. If I let you explode, what will you do for me?"

"Any . . . thing," she whimpered around the gag.

Her captor drove the artificial invader home, impaled her on it, demanded. Wave after wave of sensation ripped through her. And she screamed again into her gag.

As her shudders weakened, Asia's fingers slid out of herself.

Her hands hung at her sides, and she panted. One clamp had fallen off. The other still pinched.

Silence enveloped her, and as she stumbled toward her bed, tears blurred her vision. There was no slaver, no auctioneer, no masterful owner. And despite the powerful and vital fantasy, she couldn't imagine ever taking it beyond her lonely bedroom. So there never would be one.

2

At a little after six the next morning, Asia parked her leased Buick near the entrance to the county park with its miles of jogging trails. She got out, and after checking the laces on her athletic shoes, she stretched her leg muscles, then took off at an easy pace. The conditions of her generous severance package called for her continuing to work for the firm through the end of the month, but she had no meetings planned for today. She'd get to work when she got there. When she'd extinguished the hot frustration that had stalked her restless night.

As she lengthened her stride and let the familiar pattern take over, she struggled to put her mind on what she should do—since she hadn't been bought by a new, wealthy owner, after all.

She could start her own company. Her experience with Maximize would speak for itself as she made the rounds of corporations. But the idea of knocking on doors made her stomach knot; she wasn't looking forward to having to switch gears from what she'd done for Maximize to dancing to other employers' tunes.

Although she risked getting sucked right back in by the tide of desire, she allowed her mind to return to last night. As climaxes went, that one had barely merited a blip, but it was better than nothing. Still, she always felt uneasy as she put away her bondage pictures—not because she was a prude, but because sometimes her imagination and secret dreams surprised her. After all, what was a nice, professional woman doing getting off on dominance and submission?

Well, she'd been horny as hell last night and in need of some serious stress reduction. She couldn't remember the last time she'd been on a date, let alone had a living, breathing fuck.

Looking around, she realized she'd already run a mile. Most mornings, she quit at three so she could get cleaned up and to work on time, but today she could go as long as she wanted. As long as she needed. And with everything that was happening . . . she *needed* to run.

Under her practical sports bra, her nipples still ached from the clamps. What was it the auctioneer of her imagination had said? That she was a perpetually horny piece of flesh who'd do anything for satisfaction? Well, not *anything*. But if necessity called for masturbation and a dose of playacting . . . so be it.

Thanks to the Internet's exploitation of the kinkier aspects of sex, she'd had plenty of material to feed her BDSM fantasies. Unfortunately, reading fiction about the submissive lifestyle and looking at staged videos hadn't told her much about what being dominated was really like. Fantasizing was one thing, reality probably quite another.

Still, as long as she was pretending, what would she want in the way of a Master?

He'd be big and strong, of course. Supremely confident and in control. That much she knew. What else? Well, naturally, a fine, firm ass, shoulders and arms made for carrying her. Deeply tanned with dark, dark eyes—mandatory. He'd understand how weary she was of assuming responsibility for her life and body. And he'd know exactly how to wrench that responsibility from her and make it his own. She'd want and need nothing more than to please him. When she did, he'd reward her with his tireless, oversized cock and mind-scrambling climaxes.

When she displeased him, he'd bring her back in line, much as a dog trainer turns a puppy into a well-behaved pet. The idea of being strung up to a post while he laid into her ass with a stinging but carefully crafted lash made her wince. At the same time, she wondered if the sound, like the pain, might turn her on. And the discipline. Sometimes she got off imagining having to wear a metal collar only he had the key to. Of course he'd keep her naked unless they were out in public, and he'd chain her in the bedroom or maybe in a basement to make sure she stayed where he wanted her. Sometimes he'd plug both her holes with remote-controlled vibrators and secure them in place via a chastity belt. Even if he was off at work, he'd periodically remind her of his dominance via random jolts that kept her sexually on edge.

No! What was she thinking! She had no interest in being someone's pet.

Like you'd have any say in the matter if you were a slave, some perverse alter ego pointed out. *Slaves have no rights.*

And no responsibilities. No bills. And all the sex she could handle as long as she earned it.

A sex slave?

An odd trickle of alarm yanked her back into the here and now. There were several other joggers out this morning. A trio of teenage males far ahead, an older couple she'd just passed. And hadn't she recently moved over to the side to accommodate a bicyclist? The park was safe in daylight.

Still . . .

Looking around, she spotted a man coming up behind her. He was shirtless and way too muscular for a distance runner. Not one of those yuppies who suck down endless designer coffees and buy their expensive running clothes at specialty shops, but a real man. Real and raw. Like the Master she'd been day-dreaming about. For just a moment she wondered if her imagination had conjured him up. But no.

Judging by his pace and long, strong, naked legs, he'd overtake her in a few seconds. Because she had to juggle judging his powerful, confident stride with making sure she didn't fall, she couldn't be sure, but his gaze seemed to be settled on her. She always carried pepper spray in her shorts pocket, but she'd never come close to needing it.

Tall, strong, deeply tanned with long, windblown, dark hair. Breath-stealing shoulders and lean hips. Firm-as-rock ass. Bare feet silent on the cement path.

Bare feet?

Closer he came. Closer. She felt his presence in her bones and muscles, sensed his touch on her nerve endings. His impossibly dark eyes threatened to suck her in.

I've come for you.

Even as the words settled over her, she felt her world shift.

3

Dense, heavy vegetation pressed in on Asia. Her breath came in ragged gasps as she half-ran, half-stumbled, down what couldn't really be called a trail. Panic came at her in waves and rendered rational thought impossible.

She knew only one thing—to flee.

Arms pumping, legs straining, she leaned forward and dodged to the side in a desperate attempt to avoid an overgrown, head-high bush. She managed to keep her footing, but with her next step, her heels sank into damp earth.

Heels? What had happened to her jogging outfit?

Don't think! Don't think!

Shaking her feet free of the damn useless shoes, she plowed on. Too soon, she knew she'd made a mistake. The feet of her pantyhose were already shredded. Her soles were being cut by rocks and tree roots. Sobbing, she willed herself to dismiss the pain and disconnected sensation. She had to run, to escape!

Escape what?

It didn't matter. If whoever was pursuing her caught up with her, she was doomed. If she knew nothing else, she knew that.

Running had always calmed and centered her, but this was different. Instead of a paved path, she was on uneven and treacherous land, and time had buckled in some incomprehensible way. Not only didn't she have a clue where she was, the contrast between light and shadows made anticipating her next move impossible. Panic again clawed at her throat.

Unexpectedly, she fell. She managed to turn so she landed on her shoulder instead of her breasts, then struggled to get to her hands and knees. Her straight-line skirt clung to her legs much as ropes would. She started to pull the fabric up over her thighs so she'd have more freedom of movement, but a sudden weight on her back slammed her belly to the ground. She smelled wet earth and struggled to look over her shoulder. The weight shifted until the pressure was between her shoulder blades.

Oh, God. Someone's foot was holding her down.

"Give it up!" a man ordered. He punctuated his command by shifting his weight to the back of her neck.

Her legs and arms remained free, but what good were they if all they could reach was the ground? Even worse, she couldn't breathe! The burning in her lungs became more and more intense. She tried to reach behind her, to get free, but couldn't grasp anything. As her consciousness faded, she wrenched her body to the side. Gasped for breath. Before her attacker could adjust, she struggled out from under him and onto her hands and knees, ripping her hose even more. Instead of trying to stand, she forced herself to look at the threat to her freedom and maybe her life.

Because she was staring up at the sky, she saw little except a massive, dark, nearly naked shadow.

"Like the feeling of a little freedom?" The shadowy figure taunted her, voice deep, and husky, and knowing. "It's not going to last." With that, he leaned down and pressed his large hands against her shoulders.

Although she tried to scramble away, his greater weight forced her to the ground again. This time, instead of putting pressure on her neck, he straddled her and settled his hips over her buttocks. He yanked off her blazer, popping buttons as he did and exposing her sleeveless silk shell. Then he wrenched her arms down against her sides.

Before the threat fully penetrated, he ran a rope around her right elbow and pulled it toward him. He grasped her left arm. Propelled by desperate strength, she managed to briefly free it. Grunting, he pinned the arm to the ground with his knee, then slowly and deliberately looped rope around that elbow. He leaned back, pulling on the ropes to force her arms as far behind her as they would go. He secured the bonds so her elbows nearly touched.

Handcuffs wouldn't have done a better job of rendering her arms useless, but he obviously wasn't satisfied because he grabbed the long, thick hair she'd always been so proud of and lifted her head. He ran more rope around and under one shoulder, and then the other. Once he'd tied that off, he released her hair and ran yet another rope from the one over her shoulder blades to her elbow restraints. Even if she'd been able to force her elbows closer together to loosen the tie there, the latest rope effectively prevented her from freeing herself.

Caught!

Her eyes burned, but she wouldn't cry. No. She could get out of this. She would.

When she'd fought off the surge of panic, the man was no longer sitting on her. He pulled her up by the rope harness, first to her knees and then to her feet. Then he turned her toward him and released her.

The man she'd seen in the park!

Except . . . instead of shorts, he now wore what appeared to be a loincloth, which ended just shy of his knees. He needed a shave. His dark hair was long and wild looking; his eyes black and deep set and strangely beautiful. Mesmerizing. His skin tone made her guess he spent much of his life out-of-doors.

"Didn't expect this, did you?" her captor asked, but he didn't seem to care if she answered. "You should have been careful what you wished for."

Wish? She couldn't think beyond this moment. Her awful helplessness.

Her legs trembled so much that she had to put effort into keeping her knees from buckling. Technically, her hands were free, but it didn't matter because she couldn't use them. She who had never felt any kind of restraint in the real world was acutely aware of every strand and knot binding her body. His handiwork forced her to arch her back, which emphasized her breasts. True, she wore a top and bra, but the covering now seemed transparent. How could it be otherwise with the way he was staring at her breasts?

Her nipples had become erect. Certainly she wasn't turned on!

But this man was like no other she'd ever been in contact with. There was nothing civilized or restrained about him, nothing soft. It was as if he'd stepped out of some private and sensual recess of her mind.

"Fear isn't far from eroticism. And you're feeling both." He flicked a finger over a nub. She jumped back. "Predictable reaction, just as I know what you're going to do and feel from now on. Turning your back on everything you've ever been or believed about yourself won't be easy. That, in part, is why we took you back in time to your professional life—to make the contrast clear." He made a show of reaching out. Although she back-pedaled, he easily kept pace and closed his thumb and forefinger over her nipple. Despite the two layers of fabric, he held her in place with his grip. "Lots of lessons ahead of you, Asia Drake."

"How—how do you know my name?"

"You'll find out in good time, *my* time."

Apparently finished with his ominous pronouncements, he stepped back, folded his arms over his deeply tanned, naked chest, and regarded her. In some respects, his expression reminded her of the look she'd seen too many times on the faces of the company's brass as she gave her presentations. She'd always hated those "keep her in her place" glares but had never imagined it reaching this level.

This was about survival and freedom. Not a job.

Her arms already ached from unnatural confinement. Did he think the pain would make her beg? Twice she'd groveled before a man. Twice, but never again. The mere idea made her stomach clench.

"Shorter than I thought you'd be. Small bones. Big boobs." He grabbed her blouse's hem and yanked it up over her breasts, then reached behind her. No doubt, he intended to unhook her bra.

"No!" Whirling away, she ran.

Her heart felt as if it might burst, and her childhood nightmares of monsters closed around her. She ran as if her life depended on it, but not being able to use her arms had her at great disadvantage. What did years of running matter if her restraints held her awkwardly upright?

Though in her soul she knew she couldn't outrun her captor, she still plowed through the strange vegetation. For a few brief and wonderful moments, she found herself in a relatively open area. The ground-hugging weeds under her feet felt soft, and she could almost believe she smelled fresh-mowed grass.

Too late, she found her flight had propelled her into a canopy of vines and low-hanging branches. They closed around her, caressing and abusing at the same time. She twisted one way and then the other, but although she managed to make some small progress, it was as if she were moving in slow motion. Thinking to protect her face, she tried to lead with her shoulders. Through it all, and despite her contortions, her blouse remained bunched under her armpits.

A weight, maybe a presence broke through her panic. She denied it. Fought her living prison. But when the thick growth closed around her, she stole a glance back over her shoulder.

Him!

She screamed, the sound tearing at her throat, the noise like a wild animal's. She hated him. She *hated* him. Desperate, she attacked the vegetation with her nearly useless body. Bit by reluctant bit the brush gave way. By the time she was in the open again, she was coated in sweat.

Run, run her mind chanted. *You* have *to!* As for how she'd free herself from the bonds—

"A fighter. Good."

Disbelief clamped off her breath. At nearly the same instant, hands closed around her waist. She was lifted off her feet and shoved forward, landing with such force that she might have been knocked unconscious if he hadn't tossed her at a bush. The growth gave way, and she sank into the thick growth. Leaves and branches settled over and around her. Legs higher than her head, she couldn't regain her balance.

She hung helpless in her living prison.

4

Blood rushed to Asia's head. Because her face was surrounded by greenery, she was as good as blindfolded. She expected her captor to pull her out, but he obviously wasn't in any hurry. Instead, he pushed her skirt over her hips and bunched it around her waist. Then he pulled off what little remained of her pantyhose and patted her ass. To her disbelief, she felt herself respond to the gentle, intimate contact. *I'll be taking you places you've never been*, the touch seemed to say. *The journey will change you, and I'll be there the whole way.*

"Nice ass. Firm. I'm going to enjoy training it."

"Training?"

"What do you think this is about?"

I don't know! I don't know anything!

He continued running his fingers over her buttocks. Although he didn't slip them under her nearly nonexistent panties, he easily could if he wanted to. "I'm calling the shots. You belong to me, every inch of you." He ran his hands down her legs, as if gentling a skittish horse. Or checking it for soundness.

She tried to kick him but only succeeded in burying herself

farther in the bush. His fingers slid over her flesh from knee to calf and back up again, the touch gentle but take-charge. Her muscles jumped under the light pressure.

"No! Damn you! I'll have you arrested!"

"The rules are different here, Asia. They exist for those like me, not you and your kind. Eventually you'll understand. Embrace."

Nothing made sense. How had she gotten here, wherever *here* was? What was going to happen to her?

His fingers stilled. A heartbeat later he removed them. Despite her nearly upside down position, she struggled to get a glimpse of him. Did he mean to hurt her? She froze when she felt ropes circle her ankles. *This isn't happening!*

The strands around her left ankle tightened. "No!" She kicked wildly again, dislodging the loose rope around her right ankle. But the other remained in place. She continued to thrash, frenzied, until he yanked on the bond and held her left leg suspended behind her. In spite of the undeniable message in his firm grip, she lashed out again and again. At length her muscles threatened to cramp, and she couldn't catch her breath.

She prayed he'd release the grip on her secured leg and lessen the strain in it. Instead, he easily held her in place while he once again looped rope around the ankle she'd managed to free. Patient and persistent, he finished the too simple task of tying her ankles together, as if all of her struggles meant nothing. The bonds were so snug that her thighs pressed together and trapped her wet and warm core.

Wet? No, she couldn't possibly be turned on.

Oh, God, my fantasy come true.

"Now you're not going to hurt yourself or wear me out." He punctuated his remark with yet another possessive pat of her buttocks.

Almost gently, he pulled her out of the brush and set her on her feet. She swayed and would have fallen, if he hadn't steadied her by grabbing an arm. Because she had no choice, she leaned against him. The sun and the hunt had heated his skin. She smelled his sweat. He was a rock, a mountain, pure strength and power. After a moment, he shifted his hold to her waist, lifted her off her feet and over his shoulder and carried her to a tree. *Shoulders wide enough to easily support me.* He righted her, propped her against the tree, and stepped back.

"An A package. That's one of the benefits of having been here for awhile. I get first pick of the new *recruits.*"

"Here?" Her voice squeaked. She couldn't bring herself to ask what he meant by a recruit.

"Surrender Island."

"An—an island?"

He again folded his arms across his big, naked chest and stared down at her. She felt small. "Feel it. Experience it. Understand. You won't find it on any maps because it doesn't exist in the dimension you're accustomed to. Everything will become clear. Eventually."

"Why?"

"Because deep down it's what you want. Your *bedroom activities,* toys, imagination, and secret needs helped spawn your transportation here. Right now you won't agree, but you eventually will." He gave a languid shrug that made her all too aware of his athletic build. His chest, biceps, triceps, and thigh muscles reminded her of a body builder's. Although she'd drooled over such specimens at the gym, she'd always been more than a little intimidated by the jocks' power and potential. It was one thing to dream about having one in her bed, quite another to actually do it.

His midnight eyes trailed down her body, raking her flesh along the way. Despite their disconcerting intensity, she found she didn't want him to hurry his study of her. "Your time with me will be memorable. You'll never forget our *relationship.*"

"How—how long . . ."

"How long will we be *working* together?" He reached out and lightly stroked her throat. If he wanted, he could encircle her neck and rob her of air, but like some dumb animal being hauled to the slaughter house, she just stood there. Waited. Besides, despite everything that had happened so far, she didn't believe he intended to kill or even harm her. When he closed his fingers around her throat, it felt as if he was taking her pulse. "Suspense is a large and vital part of the experience. For the record, I've made arrangements to have your belongings placed in storage and the condo put on the market. As for the Buick, it'll eventually be repossessed."

"No!"

"Yes."

Asia's breasts and chin pressed against her captor's back. Her bound legs hung over his chest, and her waist was draped over his shoulder. Although she occasionally lifted her head so she could glimpse her junglelike surroundings, mostly she simply let him carry her. She was dimly aware of an unexpected roughness to his back, ridges where the flesh should be smooth, but lacked the will to try to determine why that was. Everything in her screamed that she should fight her helplessness, but even if she managed to free herself from his grip, what was the point?

Most of the time he held her in place with a muscled arm around her middle, his free arm swinging in time with his long, smooth stride, but occasionally he slipped his fingers between her legs much as the auctioneer in her last sex fantasy had done. When had that been? Had she actually clamped her nipples and masturbated or had it been a dream, something he'd programmed?

Pressure against her pussy served as a reminder of how little protection the hot-red panties provided.

Before he'd hoisted her over his shoulder and they'd taken

off, he'd informed her that, for now, he wouldn't bother gagging her because if she cried out, no one on Surrender Island would pay attention. No one would come to her help. In addition, he'd finished, his decision to allow her to breathe freely and speak would change if she did anything to displease him.

What did he mean by "displease"?

The farther they went, the more helpless she felt. Nothing that had happened since she'd been spirited away from the park was within the realm of her comprehension. Obviously her captor was using her ignorance to his advantage, but she had to have answers if she ever hoped to get back to where she belonged—wherever that was.

Her condo was being sold . . . Someone was boxing up her clothing, toiletries, bed and other furniture. Crude and barely literate men might be laughing, even now, when they came across her treasured supply of sex toys.

And, oh, God, what about her bondage picture collection? Was that how he'd found her? Was her captor a pervert with a nose or an eye for women with healthy libidos and limited opportunity for getting certain itches scratched? So far, like the man who'd caught her in her fantasy, he'd run her down, removed a few articles of clothing, and tied her up. As they say, the ball was in his court. Hell, she was in his court!

You want this. You've always wanted this.

Where had the insane thought come from? If she hadn't known better, she would've sworn that the island itself had spoken.

She had no way of gauging how far they'd come when he stopped and stood her up. The blood that had pooled in her head during her upside-down journey meant she looked out at a blurred world tinged in red. She felt dizzy and weak. Helpless. Waiting.

"Arms getting sore, aren't they." He made it a statement.

"Yes. You don't need to—I can't get away."

"What will you do in exchange for me taking off a rope?"

"Do?"

He slapped her right breast. Slapped it! She tried to step back, lost her balance, and fell, landing on her buttocks. Thank goodness for a carpet of weeds and grasses. He positioned himself so he straddled her outstretched legs and shook his head. "Think before you move. You don't need to make things worse than they're going to be."

"Please let me go. I—I have some money, a severance package. You can have it all." Though she bargained for her freedom, the shock of the slap had worn off, leaving a hot awareness, an erotic stinging, in its place.

Eyes all-knowing, but not unkind, stared down at her. "I don't need money here."

If he took another step closer, she'd be able to see up his loincloth, not that she needed to because she'd have to be blind not to realize he had an erection. And his cock was large, huge even. *Lordy, Lordy!* "You—you can leave."

"I don't want to. As long as I'm on the island, I'm supplied with what I've been prepared for, specifically subs like you."

"You mean a submissive? No! This is all wrong! I'd never want—"

"Yes, you do."

"How can you say—"

He silenced her by placing a foot against her crotch and applying just enough pressure to grab her full attention. Although she warned herself not to, she couldn't stop herself from trying to scoot away. He let her slide out from under him, but just as she rolled onto her side in preparation for trying to get to her feet, he leaned down and forced her onto her belly.

"Don't!" she protested. "God damn you, stop it!"

Ignoring her, he removed the rope from her shoulders and the one connecting her elbows to it. Instead of freeing her elbows, though, he grabbed her hair and pulled. When her face was off the ground, he forced rope between her teeth and looped the length around her head twice, gagging her with it. Then he secured the gag behind her head.

"It's time for you to think about everything I can and will be doing to you—time to start acknowledging what you are beneath the surface. I know more about your sexual nature than you do—as does the island. It's my job to introduce you to the truth about yourself."

She whimpered into the gag as he tied her wrists and finally freed her elbows. Although she still couldn't use her arms, at least she no longer felt as if she was in danger of having her shoulders dislocated. *Thank you, thank you.* Next he did something to her ankle restraints that made it possible for her to separate them by several precious inches. She might even be able to walk, although running was out of the question. But did she want to?

When he brought her upright and turned her to face him, she thanked him with her eyes. "This is only the beginning, slave. From now until I decide different, you don't have a name. I'll call you whatever I want, do whatever I want, and you'll accept it. You have no choice. You'll come to crave my mastery of you. By the end, you'll fully understand what it is to be a submissive." He patted her cheek. "To embrace what you've always wanted."

No, she wanted to scream. But she *had* fantasized about becoming a sex slave. And he knew.

She was still trying to come to grips with her new reality, when he pulled a knife from the leather tie holding his loincloth in place. Her eyes widened, but this time she didn't make the mistake of trying to avoid his reach. He fingered her skirt, which had remained bunched around her waist. "You aren't going to need this any more." He began cutting. All too soon he'd split the fabric from hem to waist. He pulled it off her, slowly and deliberately. Hot humid air stroked her now naked middle. As for her bra and top—

"Anticipation's part of the game. I could get rid of these, right now—" He slid a finger under the hip-hugging panties. "But I'd rather have you think about the when and how. No suspense about the blouse, though."

The flimsy silk garment had set her back close to a hundred dollars, but he handled it as if it was a rag when he pressed the knife blade against it. Not long ago, she'd have charged him with destruction of personal property. Now she accepted that was beyond her control. He started at the neckline and slowly worked his way down. Once he'd fully opened it, he slid what remained down her arms until the fabric rested against her wrist bonds.

"For the foreseeable future, you're going to be naked. Eventually I'll allow you to wear something, but you have to earn the privilege. And the timing has to be right."

Something about the way he said *timing* made her tremble even more. He distracted her by yanking up on her bra and exposing her breasts. He made no move to remove the garment but left it to press down on her mounds. He didn't touch her breasts, but she had no doubt it was only a matter of time—*his* time—before he did. When he stepped back to study her, she gathered her courage and glanced down at what his loincloth covered.

He was still aroused. And what bulged under what seemed to be soft leather hinted at every red-blooded woman's fantasy. Would he let her touch his cock? Hold it? Suck it?

He cupped a hand under his cock but left it covered. "You'll get a feel of it in due time, a feel and a taste, but it isn't going to happen until you're in heat."

In heat? Was that a threat, or a promise?

He patted her arm. "I'm not going to rape you, slave. It

won't be necessary because you're going to want it. Want to fuck and be fucked as you've never wanted anything before."

Never!

But even as she silently protested, she fought the urge to thrust her pelvis at him.

He'd nearly stripped her naked. Eventually he'd finish what he'd begun and touch her everywhere, claim every inch. Her cunt belonged to him. Her legs and breasts. He could tie her in endless ways, slide a dildo into her pussy and a plug up her ass and secure them. Control them. Force a climax out of her or deny her if he wanted.

Hadn't she cruised the Internet for pictures of women with tight ropes circling and distorting their breasts and more bonds pressing against their pussies? Hadn't she printed out some of those images and studied them while masturbating because the pictures heightened her self-pleasure? Because she wanted to feel what those women had?

He's seen them. This time, she was sure of it.

Asia plodded as rapidly as her ankle ties allowed through dense trees that kept them in deep shadows and turned her captor into more specter than reality. He'd loosely tied a rope around her neck and used the extra length as a leash. She had no choice but to follow like some obedient dog. She tried to study the man so he'd become more human, but concentrating was nearly impossible.

The need to focus on her footing gave her scant opportunity for it, or to think about where they were going. But in those rare moments when she wasn't struggling to remain upright, she questioned what lay ahead. What had he meant by saying the island was a force? He'd been trying to scare her, that's all.

Was he taking her to a dungeon? Maybe he had a hut or cabin somewhere. It was possible they were going where there'd be other people who'd take pity on her or let her pay them for her release, people who knew him for the demented Tarzanlike beast he surely was. That was it! He was crazy. He had to be.

Would he be locked up? To her shock, she realized she didn't want that.

What had he called this place, Surrender Island? Did that mean she wasn't the only captive here? Oh, God, what if he took her to some prison? Would there be bars and locks on the doors, handcuffs and metal collars, chains securing her to rings cemented in stone walls?

She too easily imagined herself being thrown into some cold, damp cell. She'd huddle naked in a corner while forced to listen to unseen women beg and cry and scream. Faceless men would haul her and her fellow sex slaves out of their cells and drag them into large, dark rooms where Masters and Doms waited. Driven to their knees with chains dragging on the cement flooring, they'd be whipped as they groveled at their owners' feet. They'd know to always be available and ready for sex and willingly take any number of cocks in their pussies, asses, and mouths.

Not long ago she'd headed a creative group and had developed the art and skill of leadership. Surely she could put those talents to use in engineering a mass slave break for freedom—but what if he kept her in isolation?

What if, as he'd hinted, he knew how to make her so horny she couldn't think of anything else? Already she responded to him. He might know how to make her a slave to her need for a climax—to willingly do whatever he demanded in hope of release—to grovel before him while she begged him to fuck her—no, anything but begging! Nothing he could do would ever reduce her to that again.

An impatient jerk on her leash forced her to pick up her pace. When she'd accomplished that, she went back to studying what she could see of the man. She had to, because her survival and sanity depended on understanding as much as she could about him. Because of the shadows, she couldn't be sure, but it looked as if someone had decorated his back with strange and random symbols, lines really, but even so in another time and place and situation, she'd definitely be attracted to him.

If she spotted him at a bar, her cheeks would flush, and she'd feel more than a bit tongue-tied. She'd send out an unspoken message designed to let him know she was interested.

A look, a smile, a wink maybe and he'd get up and walk toward her. There'd be no stupid "Where have I seen you before?" No inane "What's a nice girl like you doing here alone?" Instead, he'd simply say, "Do you want this to go anywhere?"

"Yes," she'd answer. *Yes.*

He'd ask her to dance. She'd put down her glass of wine, slide her hand in his and follow him through the minefield of bodies. He'd put his arms around her and hold her close and she'd smell soap and denim.

"I'm not going to ask anything else," he'd say. "Unless you walk away, right now, I'm taking you to my place. You'll stay there until I say you can leave. I'll do what I want to you when I want, and you'll beg me for more. My terms."

"I understand. I want."

"I know you do."

"I've never done this before."

"Doesn't matter. You're doing it now. With me."

"What—will you do to me?"

Silent, he'd grip her wrists and position her hands behind her. Then he'd lean over her, forcing her off balance. She'd widen her stance to keep from falling. He'd slide his legs between hers and thrust. His insistent cock would prod, demand, promise.

So far she hadn't met anyone she could imagine taking command like that, but she'd fantasized about letting a man, the right man in on her secret desire to be tied up and have a climax forced out of her. To actually come out and tell someone that, however, she'd need to know him well enough to trust him with her deepest secret.

Now she was under the control of a man who knew that secret, who'd already demonstrated his domination of her body. A man bent on turning her into a sex slave, a slut, a whore, a submissive. Just the thought of becoming those things heated her.

Give it up. Surrender. Let the surrender you crave happen.

But if I do, will there be anything left of me?

There's only one way to find out.

I'm scared.

"We're almost home," he announced. "You're curious about where you'll be staying, but you'll have to wait. Wait for a lot of things."

She forced herself to stand motionless as he cut what remained of her blouse off her. And when he fashioned a blindfold out of it and robbed her of sight, she shuddered but managed not to struggle. Nothing, not the world, not even the island, existed anymore. There was only him. When he tugged on her leash, she fought her instinct for self-preservation. As he led her down what her feet told her was a sanded path, she bit into the ropes in her mouth and tried not to think about how thirsty she was or contemplate where he was taking her.

She belonged to him. Unless he released her, she would remain *his*.

No! Not going to happen!

What choice do I have?

I'm scared.

Deal with it. Embrace it.

When he abruptly stopped she strained to see but remained locked within her world of thought and reaction and instinct. Something sleek and sharp touched her throat. His knife. "Feel it, slave. Feel and accept."

She trembled as he slid the blade down her body. He didn't

break her skin, but she knew how easily he could make her bleed.

He lowered himself to his knees, then untied her ankles. Because she didn't know where she was or what was around her, she didn't move. Couldn't. Standing, he again kissed her throat with the blade. What would his mouth feel like? What would she do if he touched her there with his tongue instead of his weapon?

"Take off your panties."

How, she wanted to ask, but of course she couldn't speak. Fighting her helplessness and deep-rooted focus on his every word—and her reactions to him, she squared her shoulders. She imagined herself as he surely saw her, a gagged and blindfolded woman with her hands tied behind her, naked except for her underpants, trapped in his world. Alone. Completely vulnerable and dependent. Scared and excited and desperately trying not to let him know.

"The panties. Now!"

Propelled by the sharp command, she gnawed at the ropes in her mouth. Heat coiled low in her belly and flickered throughout her pussy.

An object. A piece of meat. *His* to do with as he wanted. His gift to himself.

Although the reality of her situation washed over her in heated waves, she managed to push the scant fabric over her buttocks. Then she leaned to the side and guided the panties down, down, exposing her crotch. A warm breeze feathered over her recently-shaved flesh. When the sleek fabric reached her knees, she straightened and twisted from side to side until it slithered to her ankles. Caught in the erotic symbolism of the gesture, she stepped out of what little had stood between her and his plans for her. She was all but wrapped up in a neat gift bow for him, scared shitless and barely able to stand the wait for whatever he had in mind.

"That's a good little slave."

Don't call me that, please. I don't know how to handle it.

"I'm going to release your hands so you can remove your bra," he said. "You don't want to make the mistake of reaching for your blindfold, do you?"

She shook her head.

"Good. Maybe you aren't going to be as hard to train as I'd been led to believe."

Who had told him about her? Was this some cruel joke on the part of her former employers? But no, she hadn't been abducted off the street or kidnapped from her condo. Instead, she'd been sucked out of her world and deposited into whatever this was. What was it he'd said, that the island itself had chosen her?

Sensing he'd stepped behind her, she waited breathlessly for him to free her arms. Instead, he surprised her by lightly stroking them. The longer he ran his fingers over her skin, the more she relaxed. He was deliberately disarming her and undermining her defenses, but, in an elemental way, it pleased her. When was the last time she'd been treated like something precious and desirable and malleable?

Had she ever?

When he slid his arm around her neck and pulled her against him, she sighed and let him support her. She imagined her body arched toward him, full breasts jutting out, toned legs spread to help her balance. He tightened an arm around her shoulders and easily held her in place. With the other, he began circling her exposed breasts. Fingertips and palm laid claim to her, the unending contact soft as the silk he'd cut off her. *This is mine,* the touches proclaimed. *You are mine.*

Her head fell back and rested against his chest. This man was so strong, so powerful. He could and would turn her into whatever he wanted her to be. By the time he'd finished with her, he'd have remolded her, fundamentally changed her. She almost believed she could hear his heart beating, but maybe she was responsible for the sound.

"So lonely," he whispered. "So hungry."

She didn't care. Nothing mattered except being locked in a sightless, wholly tactile world. His fingers laid claim to every inch of her breasts, the touches telling her that he now owned them but promising to be a kind, if demanding, Master. She moaned into her gag.

"Not fighting me, are you, slave. That's the last thing you're thinking of right now, isn't it?"

Incapable of lying, she shook her head.

"There are two sides to every human," he went on in a low and seductive tone. He closed his fingers over a nipple but with none of his earlier punishing grip. "Yin and yang. Push and pull. I have you on my hook. Sometimes I'll let you play with the line. I'll insist you fight and give you all the line you crave. Just when you think you can't take any more, I'll let you rest and regroup so you almost believe you're free." He rolled her nub from side to side. Heat wrapped around her, and she tried to thrust her ass at him. "You'll forget there's a hook in you. Then I'll reel you in, I'll net you and haul you into my boat. You'll feel my hands all over you as I remove the hook, but you won't know whether I'll keep you or throw you back."

She couldn't concentrate. How could she with her nipple between his fingers and her back pressed against his naked chest? His toy. His possession. His everything. A moan fought for freedom, and the heat between her legs became a flame. She felt fresh moisture gather around her labia.

"I'm not throwing you back. By the time I'm done with you, you'll beg me to keep you. Use you. Work and reward you. Sometimes punish you. No matter what I do to you—and it'll be more than you can imagine—you'll embrace it because it's your nature."

My nature? To beg? No!

But before she could protest, he shifted his hold and began a slow journey down over her belly that nearly had her screaming. She opened her legs farther and tilted her pelvis toward him. He repositioned his restraining arm so it flattened her breasts and turned her toward him a little, increasing his access to her pussy. Panting into the gag, she widened her stance. If only he'd let her see! And yet blindness forced her deep into herself where sensation simmered and grew.

"Hunger and feeding. Sometimes I'll starve you." He demonstrated by first lightly slapping and then removing his hand from her mons. Leaving her untouched where she needed it the most. "Then when you believe you'll die if you have to wait another second, I'll feed you." He closed his palm around her offered cunt. "But you'll never know what is going to happen when. What buttons I'll push and when, or how." A finger flicked her clit, and her legs shook. "That's the beauty of what's ahead for you. And the hell."

Still, she thrust her sex to him. Her hips moved from side to side. His thumb and forefinger closed around her labia. Hit with an almost-electric jolt, she jumped. Instead of releasing her, he pressed the hot and sensitive flesh together, sealing her opening. "Don't like this, do you," he muttered when she fought to shake him off. "You want to be full, not empty."

Trembling, panting, hating him and fearing herself, she waited. When he loosened his hold on her, she prayed he'd plunge his cock into her weeping opening. No. She didn't want him, damn it! He had no right, no right! But if he cast her off, she'd go insane.

Perhaps he'd read her splintered mind because a long, thick finger slid into her. Pressed against her. So good. Not being able to anticipate what he was going to do next heightened her reaction, that and the bold, demanding intimacy. The dark and dangerous stranger of countless fantasies had become reality. He existed, had substance, understood so much about her.

"Wet. Drenched and hot. You're a hungry little piece, aren't you?"

Beyond caring, she nodded and tried to close herself around him so she could hold him inside her. His finger fed some of her hunger. It was better than nothing but not enough. With the heel of his hand, he pressed against her inner thighs—a wordless order to remain open and accessible to him. Willing to do whatever she had to for the climax she needed more than she needed breath, she remained as still as she could. *But soon, please! Quick and hard! Before I lose my mind.*

His finger explored and retreated, circled her inner recesses, branded her there and made her core his. Her leg muscles felt like jelly, and she could barely keep her feet under her. Couldn't find the boundaries between them.

He slipped another finger in to join the first.

Don't! I can't handle—

"Experience. Don't think. Feel."

Don't want! Don't dare.

"Stop fighting yourself, slave. Your cunt is speaking to you. Let yourself hear it."

Hear. Feel. With terrible clarity, she now understood why he'd robbed her of sight and speech. The senses he'd left her with took over, and despite the terrible danger, she gave herself up to sensation. His fingers filled her, invaded, possessed, owned. With her other senses, she'd have been able to tell herself that she was a modern professional and embrace everything she'd spent her adulthood becoming. But now, the firm pressure and movement throughout her pussy took her beyond those petty concerns.

She was a slave, not just to him, but to her own sexuality.

"You don't yet fully understand what I'm doing and what you want to happen. You just know you need what I have, or rather, what you pray I'll give you." The dance of retreat and advance increased, fingers fucking, teasing, taunting, owning, promising but not yet delivering. "This is what will turn you into what you're destined to become. Not ropes or chains and leather although that's going to be part of it. Not even whips. But your own body. Your nature."

He rammed his fingers in as far as they would go. She gasped, struggled to breathe, couldn't. Her teeth clenched down on the gag. She fought her blindness. *Can't take! Can't take—*

The pressure held, impaling her. She felt him in her belly. Her entire awareness centered on his hand, on the relentless gift. He lifted her by her cunt, stood her on her toes and still he pressed harder, deeper, dared her to expel him. Challenged her to try.

Climax waited. Her muscles clenched, and she sucked in air. Raced toward the edge.

"No." He pulled out of her. "No. No. No."

Her pussy muscles clenched again, this time in frustration. She thrashed her head about and cursed into the gag. Compelled by her inner heat, she thrust out her pelvis and blindly searched for him.

"Not going to happen, not yet," he said from somewhere to her right.

Please, please, please!

"You're calling me a bastard, aren't you?"

Yes!

"I am. I'm also your salvation. But before that happens, I need to prepare you for your next lesson in relinquishing ownership of your body, and soul."

Body? Soul? Sanity was starting to return along with the feel of damp jungle air now mixing with her juices. Fluid ran down her fevered thighs.

At least a minute passed before she felt rope around her waist. At the first touch, her muscles clenched.

Ropes symbolized a loss of freedom, of helplessness, manipulation.

Ownership.

She counted three loops around her waist followed by a quick tie. A length of rope hung down her legs in front. *What are you going to do with that? Please, tell me something, anything.* When he pressed his palms against her breasts, she braced herself.

"I'm not going to knock you down, at least not now. I just needed to see if you remembered what I'm capable of. You understand, don't you? If I shove, you'll fall, right?"

She nodded.

"You can't stop me, can you?"

She shook her head.

"I can punish you any time and in any way I choose, right?"

Another nod. Tears brimming. She squeezed her eyes shut, grateful for the cloth over them.

"I'm in charge of everything. It's my role. What and when and if you eat or sleep. Your body." He abruptly released her breasts, snatched the loose rope, and threaded it between her legs. Although she struggled to close her stance, he easily tugged the cord against her labia. He briefly held and then wrapped it around the coil circling her waist. He knotted the crotch rope in place. "Now not even your cunt belongs to you any more." He proved his point via a quick, hard tug that left her panting. When he released the rope she discovered that it tightly hugged her labia but wasn't what she'd call painful—yet. Everything centered around that part of her body.

"What I've just done is pretty basic." He lightly tugged. "Nothing sophisticated about a rope chastity belt, or trigger if that's how I decide to use it." A third jerk left no doubt of his intention. She stood on her toes. "From what you've seen and experienced so far, you probably believe the island is peopled with savages. That we live in caves."

He grabbed her shoulders and turned her in what felt like a circle. "I assure you we have all the amenities you're accustomed to, and more. In time I'll introduce you to the refinements we've developed for our purposes." He gave the crotch rope another breath-stealing tug that brought her back onto her toes and ignited another unwanted heat flash in her clit. "The *refinements*, the *techniques* are inventive and effective. You'll beg me for demonstrations. Whatever it takes for your rewards, you'll comply. First, you'll have to earn them."

A wave of libido-fed confusion washed over her. Hot tears stained what a short time ago had been her blouse. She who'd vowed to never cry or beg again would have done anything to regain control over her responses.

Once again he let a full minute pass before he touched her. This time he untied her hands and briefly rubbed her wrists until circulation had been restored. Despite her gratitude, she wanted to claw out his eyes. Instead, she remained docilely in place because he'd demonstrated how easy it was for him to impose his will on her. And because sexual frustration continued to chew at her nerves. If she complied with his every command, would he grant her a climax?

"Do you remember what I told you?" he asked.

No. How can you expect me to think?

"You have two seconds."

For what?

He slapped one breast and then the other. Gasping, she tried to turn away. He grabbed her hair and held her in place. Another stinging slap had her struggling again. His grip tightened, pulling her head to the side. He repeatedly struck her right breast until the pain centered there became everything.

"I'm sorry." She prayed he could understand her. "I'm sorry. I—"

"I can't hear you, slave. Make yourself clear."

He continued to force her off balance as he gripped her newly punished nipple and squeezed. She yelped into the gag.

"Think! One simple command. What was it?"

"Bra!"

"Bingo." He released the throbbing nub. "Do it, now."

Her nose ran and her clumsy fingers shook, but finally she managed to unhook the back fastening.

"Hand it to me," he ordered before she could drop the useless garment.

Chastised and defeated, she held out her hand. She saw herself as he doubtlessly did, a trembling captive robbed of sight and speech standing naked and defenseless and compliant before the man who'd proclaimed himself as her lord and master. Surely she wasn't the only one who smelled her sweat and need.

After making her wait, he took the bra from her. Then he draped it over the back of her neck next to the rope he'd placed there. When he'd arranged it to suit himself, he snagged her right wrist and tied it behind her again by securing it to the waist rope. She expected him to repeat the process with her left. Instead, he closed his own large, strong paws around it, trapping it. He applied pressure.

"A pretty little thing. Slender fingers. Manicured nails. Unfortunately, you've had your last manicure."

Why that statement sent her over the edge she couldn't say. All she knew was that she could no longer hold up her head. "Pleez," she muttered against the gag. "Pleez."

Her cry earned her a harsh jerk on her untethered hand, which brought her head up again. Her just-uttered plea filled her with self-loathing. His breathing was harsh as he yanked her arm behind her and secured it against her ass as he'd done with the first.

He slapped each breast in turn. "Don't beg."

Awash in emotions both new and old, for a while she stood where he'd positioned her, but at length she couldn't take the unknown. Step by tentative step she walked in a exploratory circle. Packed sand felt warm under her feet. Although being nude made her feel unbelievably vulnerable, she loved the damp warmth on her flesh. The breeze caressing her skin felt gentle and soothing. She heard birds singing. At least she assumed they were birds. She'd never heard quite that sound before. She'd always loved getting as far from exhaust fumes and skyscrapers as possible. It was why she ran in the park.

Maybe there weren't any spirit-crushing prisons, dungeons, or cages here.

Wherever *here* was.

When she thought she'd returned to approximately the same spot she'd been standing in when her captor deserted her, she stopped and strained to hear more. Because she couldn't see, she relied on her other senses but didn't learn anything she didn't already know. Maybe one thing. Every step she took caused the crotch rope to rub against sensitive flesh and remind her of how close he'd taken her to the release and reward of a climax. Her arousal had faded but remained. Undoubtedly he knew how to re-ignite the flame.

"On your knees."

Swallowing a squeak, she froze. Then, prompted by reminders of his ability to inflict pain, she did as he ordered. Kneeling tightened the rope's grip on her pussy. She struggled ineffectively to lessen the impact.

"Got your attention, did it?" She had no doubt he was referring to the pressure he'd imposed on her abused sex. "Get used to it. If I so decide, there's never going to be a minute when you aren't being stimulated—and frustrated. Maybe I'll let you climax. Maybe I'll keep you on the brink." He patted her on the head. "Studies have shown that unrelenting sexual frustration can drive a person crazy. You don't want that. Not that you can do anything about it."

He continued patting her. Although she felt demeaned and diminished by the gesture, that too she couldn't do anything about. Besides, not that she'd ever admit it, his hand on her was comforting—and more. From the moment he'd run her down, he'd tapped into and commanded her sexuality. He dictated her responses. He knew which buttons to push, where her triggers were, and how to keep electricity flowing through her. In his hands, her most secret dreams might become reality.

A dildo. An ass plug. Clamps on my nipples. I'll grovel before you, lick your feet, take you any way you want.

"Time to see your prison."

He untied her blindfold and yanked it off with a flourish. At first everything was a blur. Then she made out a stonelike structure a few feet away. It wasn't as large as her condo and had no windows. Instead, bars *decorated* several small openings. She couldn't see a door. The jungle grew right up to the stone and looked as if it could easily swallow the man-made structure.

My prison.

She had no idea what material the roof was made out of. It resembled palm fronds except that it looked more substantial. From what she could tell, there were no other buildings around. The *prison* seemed to be part of the vegetation, isolated and inescapable. Locked in it, she'd be as helpless as if she still wore ropes.

At his disposal.

His to play with and command.

"Looks are deceiving," he said with his hand still on the top of her head. "The interior is quite innovative. There's a porch on the opposite side, at least *porch* is as good a name to give it as anything. You'll be spending time there, too."

Too.

She told herself she should have gotten a grip on her emotions by now, should have steeled herself against waves of fear, but ordering and doing were proving to be worlds apart. Even though she hated doing so, she wilted toward her captor's legs. He must have anticipated her need for reassurance. Anticipated and denied because he gave her a rough shove, which sent her sprawling onto her side. The crotch rope bit into her and sealed itself around her core. She remained where he'd forced her and stared up at him.

"I'm not your protector."

5

Her captor—she didn't dare think of him as her Master—forced her to remain where he'd placed her for maybe a half minute before using the crotch rope to again haul her to her feet. Being controlled by pressure against her labia made it difficult for her to think about anything else. Still, she struggled to obey his unspoken commands.

The effort left her both spent and feeling diminished, proof she didn't need that he more than held the upper hand, and had no hesitancy in using it against her. What he didn't understand was the depth of her resolve to retain her pride.

He hauled her by that intimate leash around the stone building to what she suspected was the only door. She was so intent on the massive, metal door and the sensation of being led that she could only take in the basic details of the porch. It was no more than ten feet square, maybe two feet off the ground and enclosed by what looked like cyclone fencing, only thicker. It wasn't a porch so much as a cage. He'd have no problem forcing her to live within its confines.

"Down," he ordered as soon as he brought her inside.

She obeyed. This time she refused to look up at him. He released the leash and stepped back. She felt his gaze rake over her exposed body but continued to stare at the floor. Even when he circled her, his bare feet slapping on the flooring, she did everything within her power to ignore him. Encouraged by her small victory, she straightened her spine. The effort tightened the rope imprisoning her labia. The thoroughly soaked rope.

"Up."

Because she had no use of her hands and he wasn't helping, it took several awkward attempts before she got her feet under her. The labor heated her cheeks and throat, and the strands between her legs clung to her.

Earlier she'd been intimidated by the jungle's deep shadows, but that was nothing compared to her prison's gloomy interior. No lights, if there were any, were on. The walls closed in around her and trapped her within her imagination and her dependence on the Tarzan-man who'd roped her.

Tarzan? Funny how she hadn't thought about the fictional jungle god since she was a girl. Young and impressionable with a just-budding sexuality, she'd wondered what living with Tarzan would be like. He'd be the ultimate hunter of course and always provide her with fresh meat. He'd also bring home delicious fruits along with just-picked wildflowers. No dangerous snake, panther, alligator, or other wild animal would dare threaten her, and whatever savages lived in the jungle would leave them alone. They'd live in the ultimate treehouse complete with an awesome view. Her days would be leisurely and peaceful. He'd cater to her, giving her massages and keeping her in comfortable clothing. She didn't get as far as the nights or what sleeping in the same bed entailed.

At that thought, her attention went to her prison's bed, or

rather what passed as a bed, in the too-small room's far corner. It obviously hadn't been designed primarily for sleep. Not only weren't there any covers, but what served as a mattress was so thin, she could tell it lay on a metal platform. It stood waist high to a tall man, which her captor was, with enough space between it and the smooth, gray wall that he could easily walk around it. The multitude of metal rings bolted or welded to the frame's edges, some with chains dangling from them, left no doubt that she wouldn't be spending much time on her feet.

Flitting images of what he intended to do to her while she was confined to the bed filled her with an equal mix of fear and anticipation she wasn't sure she succeeded in keeping from him. Hell, she'd often fantasized about being chained and toyed with and had then rewarded herself with semi-satisfying, self-imposed climaxes. Having her dreams about to become reality, having a living, breathing Dom running things felt unreal and yet preordained.

Her mind shied away from the nerve-racking thoughts and she returned to a survey of her surroundings. Instead of carpet, she was standing on what felt like a rubber mat. Looking around, she discovered that the entire floor was covered with the dense substance. It had some give to it but not much. There were two small openings to the outside in addition to the door, and they were heavily barred—just like what she'd seen during her tour of Alcatraz. Not even a small child could squeeze through the bars.

She didn't want to think about what she'd find in the large cupboard that had been built into the wall opposite the bed. Neither was she brave enough to contemplate what might be beyond the closed metal interior door. It took all the self-control she could muster to accept the reality of rings, chains, and ropes.

This is really happening! Fantasy turned into reality—overwhelming reality.

"I don't live here." His powerful voice interrupted her thoughts, knocking her off balance again. "You'd like my home. By earth reckoning, it's about a mile from here, not far from the village, although you'll probably think of that as a compound or fort—for reasons you'll understand when you're ready to be taken there to be sold."

Sold?

"I'll explain that when I'm ready." Once again, he seemed to read her mind. "The island boasts a number of training facilities such as this one, each equipped to meet the needs and wishes of individual trainers and subs. Although I'm in the process of designing another more suited for an effective indoctrination, this will do."

If she hadn't known better, she'd believe she was a client being shown what he hoped she would consider adequate office space.

"I'm going to briefly remove your gag." His intense gaze never left her. "The pros and cons of allowing a new slave to speak have long been debated, but I've learned that the more one knows about her future, the sooner she accepts it."

Future? He made it seem dire and desirable all at once.

He again erased the distance between them. It took all her self-control not to back up. He gently yet possessively stroked her temple, before tugging on the ropes in her mouth which forced her to open it. He made her feel like a horse with a bit in her mouth. He could mount her and crop her buttocks until she broke into a gallop. And when she'd finished the race, he might steer her into a barn and lock her within a stall. Maybe he'd rub her down and feed and water her. Maybe he'd switch from bridle to halter and tie her to a post. What if he brought in a stallion to service her?

What if he was that stallion?

"Your ability to comprehend the nuances of my training

methods and your position are key to your progress. I deliberately used the word *briefly*. You need to learn what you are and aren't allowed to say. One wrong word, and it's time for a true gag. I have a sizeable collection, each with its own purpose. I prefer not to use them but sometimes they're more effective than other techniques. All are effective. Highly effective."

With that, he grabbed her shoulders and spun her away from him. A moment later the strands in her mouth loosened. She licked her dry lips but didn't try to look back at him. Neither did she speak. If only she could stop trembling. Despite everything, she loved the feel of his hands on her.

"You've made progress, and you haven't made the mistake most new slaves do of trying to bargain for their freedom, since I first captured you. I appreciate it. Now, one question. If I find it acceptable, I'll let you ask another."

Her thoughts were already so tangled she didn't know if she was capable of speech. At the top of her list was the question of what the training would entail, but she was certain he wouldn't tell her. She wanted to please him. She had to! She could again try to bribe him, maybe throwing in her body this time, but he could take it if he wanted to. Whatever happened, she didn't want him thinking less of her than he did.

"Nothing?" He turned her back around. His features remained stern as he closed his fingers over her nipples and squeezed. "So you're ready for a gag that'll truly silence you?"

"No! No." The second time the word didn't sound quite so close to panic, and she prided herself on not fighting his intimate hold. "Ah, please, what's your name?" She refused to look at what he was doing to her breasts.

Surprise flickered in his deep eyes and his grip slackened. "My name?"

"Yes. I want to know who you are."

"I'm your Master."

Only in my dreams. "You know so much about me."

"Not everything." The pressure on her nipples returned. "But by the time I'm done with you I will."

To her relief, he again backed off on his breast-hold. Although he still held her in place, the pain had receded enough that she was able to think. From his expression she wondered if none of his captives had asked him his name before. Perhaps they'd been too self-absorbed.

"I've become Zemar."

"Zemar?"

"The lion."

He was a lion, wasn't he? Proud and confident, strong, afraid of nothing. King of this jungle at least. And maybe hers. "You've become?" she blurted. "What were you before?"

"A man hell-bent on killing himself. Self-destructive. Filled with demons."

"Why?" Staring at him, she felt as if she was looking deep into a cave.

"Too damn many reasons." He pulled her hard against him. *You're hiding yourself from me. Why?*

Perhaps he sensed her questions because he wrapped his arms around her and tilted his pelvis toward her, not that she needed proof of his erection. He repeatedly thrust at her. If not for his loincloth, he might have penetrated her. Would he throw her on the bed or floor and force himself on her? If he did, she'd stop fighting her responsiveness, her compassion for his complexity and simply hate him.

But no. Instead, breathing hard, he abruptly shoved her away. She managed to keep her balance, but the effort caused the crotch rope to tease and torment.

She refused to be distracted. "What reasons, Zemar?"

He briefly closed his eyes. "I'm not going to answer that."

"Why were you trying to kill yourself?"

"I didn't say I was."

"Weren't you?"

The question earned her several sharp slaps on her breasts. Tears stung her eyes. He closed a hand around her jaw and tilted her head up so she had to stare at him.

See my tears. Know what you've done to me.

As if reading her mind, he wiped them away. "In some respects I was like you, Asia. Driven by my demons."

"I don't have any demons!"

"Yes, you do. And when I've learned everything about them, I'll turn them into your greatest weakness."

"What—what is your weakness?" *Please don't lock yourself off from me. Be human.*

His mouth twitched. "I don't have any."

"The hell you don't!" He had to. If he didn't, there was no hope, nothing to use as leverage.

Her outburst earned her something she took as a nod of respect. "What you don't understand is there's nothing I'm afraid to tackle. I courted death as an adult because I'd already been close to it as a child. There wasn't anything left to fear."

"I don't understand." She wanted to. Needed to. It seemed so important, as if it would make this somehow more bearable if she could grasp what made him tick.

"It doesn't matter. The man I was then no longer exists."

You're wrong. It wouldn't have just slipped out if that were true.

"Before I was brought here, I waited for the Grim Reaper to strike. Hell, I courted him, but he just stood there watching me self-destruct. I stayed as sane as possible by imagining what I'd do if I was the one with power."

"With women?"

"In part, yes."

"How? By fucking them?"

"That and tying them up and doing whatever I wanted. Feeling my strength, making it work. But I was a law-abiding man back then so all I did was dream. Whenever my world felt out of control, I wrapped my fantasy around me. I'm sure you understand. Then one day fantasy became the real thing."

"Like you're saying it is with me?"

"I wasn't prey. I was predator. By the time my education was complete, I had a new career. A new mission."

"Mission?"

"Transforming women into slaves."

"Why?"

Even in the dim lighting, his expression left no doubt that she'd gone too far. "Stay there," he ordered and stepped back. Mouth dry, she studied his every move as he walked over to the cupboard and opened a drawer. There indeed was a great deal of the lion in him, a smooth meshing of muscles, pride and confidence. Power and strength. Something about his back once again caught her attention, but she couldn't see it well enough to know what that was.

When he turned around, she noted he was holding an item that resembled a bridle only it was too small for a horse. "No more questions, slave. You're going to remain silent until I decide otherwise."

Even though it might earn her punishment, she couldn't stop herself from back-pedaling as he approached. Displaying no emotion, he easily caught up to her and grabbed the crotch rope. She struggled to break free. He yanked up.

"No!" he commanded. Trembling so much it made her breasts jiggle, she widened her stance to keep her legs from buckling. When he shoved a thick wooden bar into her mouth, she meekly accepted it. The bar was connected to two metal rings and lengths of what felt like leather were attached to the rings. He positioned the leather behind her head and tightened the lengths. She heard something click. The rings pressed against her cheeks, the bit held in place by the leather. The rope gag had been bad enough but this contraption had been designed for a single purpose—silencing the wearer.

6

When Zemar returned to the cupboard, Asia warned herself to concentrate on his movements so she could anticipate and maybe formulate a plan, but she couldn't wrench her mind free of what he'd admitted. Despite letting her know his goal was to tap into something basic and primal about her, to make her his creature, he'd reached out and begun the threads of a conversation between them. But then he'd forcefully severed that connection.

Finished with whatever he'd been doing, he faced her again. Knowing that he'd named himself for a killing jungle beast should have terrified her. Instead, somehow his choice humanized him. It made him no longer just her powerful captor but a man. A man with substance, weight, and emotional burdens. With an effort, she shifted her gaze from his face's sharp, dark features and focused on what he was carrying.

Metal. A single large circular band with two smaller bands attached to it via a metal chain no more than three inches long. The large band was some two inches wide, the outside hard and gleaming, the inside padded with something soft looking. The same was true of the smaller bands. She had no doubt that these were handcuffs.

He placed the large band around her waist with the smaller ones behind her and snapped it shut. The contraption hugged her skin, but what felt like fur kept it from hurting her. She supposed she should be grateful for the small consideration, but metal had a permanence missing from rope. She might be able to sever a rope if she could rub it against something. Hard steel, however, would remain around her until her captor chose to free her. Sweat again coated her. What did he need with this building when he had such restraints?

He freed one hand but only long enough to transfer it to the handcuff. A moment later he'd done the same with her second wrist. True gratitude flooded through her when he removed the crotch rope, but when the pressure against her cunt no longer claimed her attention, helplessness again licked at her nerves. Her arms were secured behind her with her wrists at the small of her back, elbows bent, breasts and pussy exposed.

"On your knees."

She dropped to the ground. Only when she was staring up at him did she acknowledge how easily he'd commanded her. Damn it, she was a thinking, feeling human being with rights.

What rights?

"On your back. Legs spread."

No, she said with her eyes. *I'm not ready for this!*

"On your back. Now!"

By way of answer, she pressed her legs together and glared up at him. At the same time, she steeled herself for a slap, maybe a hard blow. Instead, he gave her a long look before he stepped behind her, grabbed her hair, and pulled her down. Grunting into the bit, she struggled to get her feet back under her, but he stood on her hair and kept her on her side on the flooring.

"We can do this hard or easy." Leaning down, he stroked the

valley between her breasts. Her shock at his rough treatment faded. How easily he switched her from one emotion to another, from wishing he'd die to needing his touch. "But either way, the outcome's going to be the same." When he straightened, his stance afforded her her first unobstructed look at his cock. The man was indeed huge, hard, potent. He'd fill her as his fingers never could. With him buried deep in her, she'd share in strong thrusts and her fluids would blend with his, making their movements smooth and natural. Right. How long would it take for her to climax? Maybe she'd come before he did. Over and over again.

"Today you're getting your first lesson in being a *productive* member of the island." He glanced down at her and shrugged. "If you fight me, it'll take a little longer, and I'll enjoy the process more. In fact, I prefer a *trainee* who battles. But you may as well know, I've already won."

Won what? She desperately wanted him to tell her but suspected she already knew. Her body's surrender was the prize. And he was right. Her shackled hands, the gag, and the rope around her neck existed as vivid proof of his superiority.

Should she simply give up and let him demonstrate what he had in mind for her? Prepare her to be "sold."

Surrender her will, her body.

No! Twice in her life she'd experienced a man's ability to reduce her to a sobbing, heartbroken creature. She might dream of being a sub, but it would never happen in the real world.

If she wanted to beat him, she would have to pick her battles well. She couldn't win this one, not now when he was at full alert, so she forced her body to relax. Let him believe she was beaten. The only thing she wouldn't do was cry. She'd rob him of his so-called fun.

He lifted his foot off her hair but didn't step away. When she continued to lie there, he nodded what she took as approval. "Legs straight and spread."

She complied.

"Stay like that. Don't move."

Remaining splayed while he returned to the cupboard she already despised, put her in mind of a dog being kept at its master's side during a training session. Obviously he didn't give a damn that much of her weight now rested on her tethered hands. This time when he returned, he didn't let her see what he'd selected.

"Bend your knees and turn them out so your cunt's exposed."

You can't be serious! If you think—

"Now!" He slapped her belly.

She tried to tell herself that she'd done something close to this during physicals and spreading her legs to invite a man in for sex was part of a heady experience, but neither of those experiences had anything to do with today. She tried to remember to be docile and pick her battles. But this was so—

He slapped her belly again, forcefully recalling his earlier treatment of her breasts. Cursing behind the gag, she revealed herself. She'd been keeping her head off the rubber mat but could no longer do so. Now she stared at the awful ceiling with implements of imprisonment dangling from it and fought to divorce herself from her body.

His fingers tugged her labia. Her cunt heated in mindless reaction. Once again her juices flooded her, and the wonderful hot knot signaling the potential and promise of a climax clamped onto her. He'd have to be a fool if he didn't notice the signals, but he didn't say anything.

How far could he take her?

What would remain of her by the end?

He was sliding something inside her. It felt as large and long as a well-hung cock but lacked softness. A dildo! Did it vibrate?

Shit, how much do you know about my secret desires?

Sweat drenched the small of her back. Her toes dug into the flooring, and she tried to shove herself away from him. He stopped her miniscule movements by pressing his splayed fingers down on her belly. Heeding the inescapable message, she struggled to relax as the invasion continued its way into her, spreading delicate tissues and promising a mastery that excited her on a deep and primitive level. Excited her and terrified her.

Although she'd never been crazy enough to do it, she'd imagined placing a remote control bullet in her pussy and wearing it at work. Occasionally triggering vibrations that would bring her dangerously close to coming, and even when it simply rested inside her, she'd be aware of it. That, like the heady fantasy of having a Dom do it for her, had remained a figment of her imagination. Until now.

Only when she felt a flared base made from the same material cup her labia did she wrench her mind free of her images and focus on the reality. The dildo filled her, commanded her attention, spoke to her of size and mastery and mystery.

Out of her hands. Everything that was about to happen would be out of her hands. At his control and direction, his. She hadn't been auctioned and sold, but close, so close.

What was coming next? She didn't dare look.

She bit her lip when she felt something being placed around her hips. Battling the instinct to cry out in protest took incredible effort. Oddly, it also increased her awareness of how turned on she was. Strange how closely related helplessness and the need to be fucked had become.

She flinched when he snaked what she thought was leather between her legs and fastened the crotch-binding to the hip harness. Securing the crotch restraint against her, he trapped the large dildo inside her. The pussy invader became as much a part of his domination as the wrist restraints. And like the handcuffs and gag, she'd remain wedded to it for as long as he wanted.

"Back on your knees!"

Uncertain and trembling, she fought her way off the ground. The intrusion had no give to it, forcing her to modify her movements and position to accommodate its bulk. Again, tears threatened to film her eyes. He held something the size of a cell phone. Oh shit, someone, maybe he, had been reading her mind, maybe for years.

No doubt, fantasy was about to become reality. Her nostrils flared. She locked her eyes on his and felt herself begin to shrink, becoming less. At the same time, anticipation gripped her.

"High tech," he informed her. "On the Earth you've spent your life on so far, vibrators are run by batteries or electricity, but here we've designed toys run by solar energy."

Not on Earth? Where are we? Does it matter?

"Solar energy outperforms batteries hands down. Let me demonstrate." He pushed something on the object in his hand.

Asia immediately felt movement in her pussy. The object was rapidly swelling and contracting. No longer rigid, it began flexing as if multi-hinged. A cock, one hell of a cock! One hell of an improvement on the standard model vibrator, too. "Mmmm," she mumbled.

"Just getting started." He let her see him push again. The vibrations stepped up a notch. Moaning again, she straightened and tried to distance herself from the sensation. But of course she couldn't. And didn't really want to. Another push resulted in vibrations so intense she could no longer think of anything else. Frantic to anticipate the pulsations, she began rocking back and forth. *Oh, God, oh, God!*

"It gets better, much better. Although you might not agree with that particular word."

The internal gyrations ignited tissues both in and around her pussy. Movement radiated out to her belly, hips, thighs, even her heart. Each vibration prompted a short-circuited reaction in her clit, almost as if she was being assaulted by electrical currents. Because she couldn't jerk free, she endured, felt, experienced.

Although she'd wondered what losing her sanity via sexual stimulation would feel like, she'd never let a man take the lead. She'd always been an equal partner when it came to foreplay and intercourse. Not an object. Not helpless. She'd only dreamed. Pretended.

Zemar changed everything. As effortlessly as he controlled the incredible power locked inside her, he controlled her nerves and flesh and robbed her of intellect. For a brief and confusing moment, he stopped all movement, and she panted out her attempt to manage her body's reactions. Surely she could weather this! Surely she controlled her system, not he!

Then he added heat and rolling waves that forced her head back and her legs wide. *Holy shit!* Sweat ran between her breasts. Her nipples tightened and clamped. She felt the same relentless tension in her cunt. No escape. No relief.

Torture. Ecstasy.

Her eyes bulged, and although she hated herself for it, she couldn't stop from shooting him a desperate plea for relief. He ignored her stare and hit yet more buttons. The invader became hotter, the waves more intense. At the same time it pulsed, promised, demanded. She rode out the fantastic assault. She felt no pain. Instead of fear, her overloaded system bellowed in anticipation.

Go, go, go! Oh shit, please, now!

Kneeling, tied, and mute, stripped naked in a room with no way out, ripped from her life and world, sweating and gasping, under a determined and relentless man's control, she raced up a mountain and stood ready to catapult into space. She had no parachute and didn't give a damn. A chasm yawned.

She fell into it, fell and fell and fell. He continued the assault, even kicking it up until she felt as if she was at the epicenter of an earthquake. The tremors went on and on. She heard herself scream. The gag muffled much of the sound and shoved it back down her throat. The trapped scream helped fuel the explosion and kept it going.

Rollercoaster. No brakes. No end. Nerves firing and misfiring.

Stop! Please stop! She started screaming but only useless grunts and sobs tore at the air. The instrument of torture and delight continued to work her. Even the base was in motion. She dimly acknowledged something hard like rubber clamped around her clit.

Can't take—oh shit! Can't take any more!

Yes, you can. You have no choice, a voice in her head insisted. Heat licked at her flesh. She wondered if she might catch fire. Maybe she was already burning.

Heated waves rolled over her, tossing her higher and higher. Suddenly and deeply terrified, she rode the relentless surges. *Too much! Too much.*

"Enough?"

Yes, yes, yes!

"For now anyway."

The instrument of her undoing started to quiet, brakes being applied. She loved sex, loved the sweet, hot feeling that accompanied a climax. But this had been—been what?

Not been. It still was.

She was being brought down slowly, her system returning to her bit by bit, and yet changed. She felt her tingling toes and fingers. Her clenched jaw ached. Her belly remained knotted and electrical charges nibbled at her thighs. Her pussy sobbed sex-tears, drenching the dildo and flowing out to slick her legs.

"Live in the moment, slave. Don't try to be anything else."

No choice. No choice. Still melting. Finally, thankfully, all movement stopped. *Thank you. Holy shit, thank you.*

Weak as a newborn, she slumped over her knees. If she'd

dared, she would have collapsed onto her side. But she had to remain alert, try to anticipate. Relief might not last.

"A lesson," he said. "A hard one but far from the last. When I said you belong to me, this is what I meant. By the time I'm done with you, you'll do whatever your Master wants." He cocked his head as if waiting for her to agree. "As for whether, when, or under what circumstances you'll be granted another ride like this one or even a fraction thereof, that's up to your Master. You'll have to earn it."

My Master? Earn? How?

"You're a strong woman. Healthy. That's good because you're going to need all your strength to get through this. Now, stand up."

Her muscles didn't know how to respond, and her brain—what had happened to her ability to think?

"Stand!"

Her pussy spasmed.

He'd shocked her—or something close to it.

Teeth clamped down on the wood secured in her mouth, she struggled to obey. Because she couldn't use her hands, the first time, she lost her balance and fell onto her side. The dildo filled her, moved with her. Until he removed it, it would follow her everywhere. Demonstrating his lack of sympathy, he lightly shocked her again and followed up with short, jerky vibrations.

Mumbling, she managed to do as he commanded. But even so, moderate vibrations continued. Now that she'd had a respite in which to put things into perspective, she couldn't deny that the protracted climax had been the most incredible experience of her life. If she could market this magical toy, she'd be a wealthy woman—unless it killed those who used it. Despite her fear of its power, did she want him to remove it? Not that she had any say in the matter.

He laid the remote on the floor. A green light flashed in time with the random vibrations. She struggled to count them, to find a pattern, couldn't. Neither could she move. He stepped to her side and wrapped his arm around her shoulder, letting her know she could lean against him. She did. His strength now supported her, his arm and side sheltering her. His lips brushed her sweaty forehead.

"What was it, slave? Torture?"

Wanting to be honest for him, she shook her head.

"Something you've always wanted?"

Although she'd never imagined a climax could all but shatter her, she nodded.

"Then you're thanking me?"

Another nod.

He kissed her again and his arm kept her safe. The pussy vibrations continued.

7

Asia lay curled up in the dark with a blanket over her, listening to her heartbeat. Zemar had carried her outside and removed the vibrator before ordering her to squat and relieve herself. The contrast between being cradled in his arms and then having to pee while he watched was so confusing. Did he see her as a human being, a woman, or simply a subject to be worked with?

Then he'd returned her to the prison, slid the vibrator back in place, and ordered her onto her knees. Once she'd positioned herself to his liking, he'd freed her hands and placed a plate of strange-looking food on the floor next to her. At his command, she'd eaten the cold, tasteless concoction. When she was done, he'd handcuffed her wrists in front and connected them to her pussy harness. He finished her confinement by chaining one foot to a ring in the floor. Just before leaving, he'd tossed the blanket at her.

The door had slammed behind him.

Despite her discomfort, she'd fallen asleep and had dozed off and on through the rest of the day, making her wonder if he'd drugged her. When she woke up, it was night.

Alone.

But not really, she amended as the vibrator made its presence known. It rested unmoving but large and full of potential inside her, and she wondered if he might be able to trigger it from wherever he'd gone.

He'd return. He had to! Otherwise, she'd starve in here. Starve with a full-to-bursting cunt.

The rubber under her had almost no give to it, and without use of her hands, she couldn't make a pillow out of them. She supposed she should be grateful because he'd removed her gag, but she was still uncomfortable, so rolled over onto her back so she could rest her head on the flooring. He'd positioned her hands over her belly, the bonds preventing her from reaching her crotch.

Not that she wanted to of course. Not that mentally reliving what he'd subjected her to via the supercharged vibrator was making her horny all over again.

Liar.

How tame her fantasy of being a sex slave had been! How naïve. In contrast, the real thing had just about taken off the top of her head.

Sex slave? Her exploration of the lifestyle had led her to believe that everything was about pleasing the master, but so far Zemar had simply lived with his hard-on. Would that continue or would he eventually fuck her?

Did she want him that close? Did she have any choice?

Her pussy clenched, and she pictured her muscles clamping down around the unshakable invasion that served in his cock's stead. Even silent, it commanded so much of her attention.

But not all.

Despite what she'd mentally called him, there were differences between Zemar and Tarzan. If there really had been a boy raised by apes, he would have grown up ignorant and uncivilized. He'd smell like a gorilla and fuck like an ape, things she didn't want to think about. He'd have fleas and unashamedly scratch his armpits and crotch. A stranger to toothpaste, he might have a mouth full of cavities, if he still had his teeth. His speech, well, he certainly wouldn't be speaking fluid English, would he? And he wouldn't have a single, solitary clue about what human females wanted and didn't want.

Zemar knew.

Staring at the ceiling she couldn't see, Asia pulled her memories around her. Because she'd been incapable of thinking past sexual stimulation, she didn't know what Zemar's expression had been as he manipulated the remote. She hated thinking that he'd been clinical and distant, a pro objectively studying his subject's reactions and responses and taking mental notes for his files. His erection, damn it, his erection said something, didn't it? But maybe his response had been nothing more than an unimportant byproduct of a necessary procedure in her training.

What about when he'd let her rest against him, when he'd kissed her head? Carried her.

She had no intention of letting him know, of course, but in many respects after what he'd *treated* her to today, she could die happy.

Die? Her heart hammered. If he didn't come back, she would.

Telling herself that her dependence on him was mind-play on his part did little to return her heart rate to a normal pace. They were, after all, playing in his ballpark and by his rules. And if she broke one, even one she didn't know about, there could be hell to pay.

So she'd have to do whatever it took to please him in order to come out of this sane and alive. But how? What, really, did he want from her? How far was she capable of going to give it to him? And what would be left of her?

* * *

She was walking in the middle of a line of naked, silenced, and handcuffed women. Ropes from one neck collar to the next kept them in a single-file procession. She couldn't be sure where they were being led, but it seemed to be a large tent. A hooded man held the tent flap open and as each woman disappeared into the enclosure, she became more and more unnerved.

Finally her turn came. When she was inside, she stopped and tried to look around, but someone yanked on her neck rope, propelling her forward. She was being led to a platform already crowded with her fellow captives.

No, not captives. Each woman wore a sign between her breasts, which identified her as a slave and included a number. Reading upside down, she discovered that she was number thirteen.

"A fine batch this time," a male voice announced as she trudged up the stairs. "A real herd. There's a lot of bidding ahead of us, so let's get started, gentlemen."

For the first time, she noticed that the platform was ringed by folding metal chairs, all occupied by men. Some wore suits and ties while others looked as if they'd just gotten off construction jobs. Many puffed on fat cigars.

As each slave's moment in the limelight came, she stood with her head downcast. Despite the slaves' subservient postures, their nipples were erect and juice ran down their inner thighs. The auctioneer used their arousal to tease their potential masters to increase their bids. Once a slave had been purchased, she immediately passed through some kind of gauzy curtain and disappeared. As if she'd been sucked out of existence.

Then it was her turn. Although she was already standing on the red X in the middle of the platform, the auctioneer prodded her ass with a short, thick stick. "A fine one here, gentlemen. A little over educated for her new career, but eager to learn. She's *wanted to become a sex slave for many years but kept taking the wrong classes."*

Everyone laughed.

"Fortunately, none other than our own Zemar became both her advisory counselor and instructor. As a result of his dedication, she's ready to be of service. Zemar has assured me that there's nothing about the lifestyle we all love and enjoy she isn't willing to embrace. She can hardly wait to begin her new career, can you, slave?" He punctuated his question by prodding her ass again.

Because she had a gag in her mouth, Asia couldn't answer. But she knew how to demonstrate her enthusiasm. Head high and shoulders back, she turned in a slow circle as if she were a model showing off the latest Paris fashions. She smiled behind her gag, tossed her hair, batted her eyes, and spread her legs to give her potential new owner a clear view of her sex. At the same time, she did a little bump and grind. Much to everyone's delight.

"What can I say, owners? A real prize. Let's begin the bidding at a hundred grand."

Men kept yelling, but Asia couldn't understand what they were saying. Her body was a product, merchandise she was committed to marketing. And as a former advertising specialist, she knew how to present to the public. She'd begun thrusting her pelvis at the crowd when someone bellowed, "Ten million dollars."

Open mouthed, she stared down at her audience. Zemar, naked as she was, stood on his chair. He smiled.

8

"Time for part two of your education. Outside."

Desperate to demonstrate her compliance, Asia opened her mouth to speak but couldn't. He'd regagged her. At least he'd allowed her to eat more of the tasteless food and drink a glass of water before putting yesterday's contraption back in her mouth and securing her arms with the metal restraints. When he'd first come in, he'd positioned a bucket near her and briefly removed the vibrator that now felt as if it was a part of her so she could go to the bathroom. He hadn't asked about her night, and of course she hadn't brought up his. Something about the way he carried himself, less wary and tense, made her think he'd found his own sexual release. Did he have a wife, a significant other? Maybe his own compliant and well-trained slave. *No! Don't think about that.*

Because his hair was damp and he smelled like a spring morning, she assumed he'd had a shower, something he was denying her. But although she resented his uncaring, nearly silent treatment this morning, gratitude at knowing he hadn't abandoned her came before everything else. Well, almost everything. The hours apart had allowed her to regroup at least some of her sense of self. Despite the most body- and mind-blowing climax of her life, she'd be damned if she'd ask for a repeat performance.

Another round of him commanding the dildo and she might never find herself again.

"Outside," he repeated and shoved her forward. She started toward the closed door. As soon as she reached it, it opened as if reading his thoughts, giving her a second look at the caged-in porch.

The porch door opened just as mysteriously. With the vibrator dancing softly but relentlessly, she had to concentrate on keeping her footing as she went down the three steps. And if she relaxed her guard, her over-stimulated system might rocket off into a climax.

The jungle waited just beyond the small opening, promising freedom. A chance to be alone. Birds sang. A trio of pale green butterflies hovered around a lush bush alive with large yellow flowers. She'd never seen such translucent butterflies or vibrant flowers before, and had she ever looked up at such a crystalline sky?

"I want you to think about something." He joined her. "I blindfolded you when I brought you here for several reasons, one of which is because I wanted this location to remain a mystery. You don't know what creatures live here, which are predators, which aren't. Surrender Island has its own society with its own rules, and rulers who control every aspect of a submissive's life. Most live in the village but not all. Some Doms have their own settlements dotted throughout the jungle. Some of those are surrounded by high fencing to keep the subs in, while others rely on what I'll call force fields. The only way a slave knows she's gotten too close is when she's sucked in. You don't want that to happen because each Dom has his own way of running his domain. Any woman who gets too close becomes fair game."

He pushed a button, and the vibration increased but not so much that she felt overwhelmed. Still, anticipation kept her on edge. "If a slave tries to run away and is caught by another Dom, her master has to pay to get her back. And that makes him angry."

A stab of sensation in her pussy punctuated the word *angry*. Desperate to let him know she'd gotten the message, she nodded vigorously. At the same time, she wondered if he had any idea how much she loathed him. Probably.

But did she?

"I want you to get some exercise today. And I want you tired tonight so you'll sleep of your own accord. You're going to run until I tell you to stop. You won't try to escape because it won't do you any good with your arms useless, and this inside you." A powerful, brief jolt brought her onto her toes. "Its range allows me to control the impulses from anywhere on the island. Piss me off and I might never turn off this little training tool locked inside you. I know about your jogging routines and what you're capable of, so start running. Circle the building."

A vibration a notch above the one he'd just hit her with propelled her forward. She gave fleeting thought to impressing him with her running ability, but although the vibration backed off a little, it didn't stop, and she couldn't put her mind to anything else. So much for telling herself yesterday had been a fluke. No way was she immune to the impact and possibilities, the promise.

The object he'd plugged her pussy with didn't feel quite as large as it had during the night, which reminded her that he could also control its size. Having it smaller made it easier to run, but knowing he could change its contours and movement to fit his monstrous whim unnerved her. She'd run where he wanted her to run, sweat and stretch her muscles. She wouldn't fight. Didn't want to.

She dutifully circled the stone structure. If her former bosses could see her, would they take pity on her or laugh at her? It didn't matter because she might never see them again. Never return to her old world.

Who was doing her job? Was anyone looking for her or had everyone concluded she'd taken off to lick her wounds? Was someone new moving into her condo? What had happened to her clothes and toiletries? At least she hadn't had time to stock up on fresh sex toys so they weren't being wasted.

When she reached where she'd left him, she discovered that a lounge chair had mysteriously appeared. He sat in it, legs up, body relaxed. He'd become the center of her universe.

You've always wanted this, a force whispered. Perhaps the island itself was speaking to her.

"Faster." Another behavior-modifying shake of her pussy punctuated the order. She picked up the pace, but the vibrations didn't decrease. Her legs felt numb, her clit alive.

Always wanted this. Needed.

The heat and tension in her clit increased. The jungle became a tangle of vivid colors. She tasted damp, fragrant air. The sun beat down on her head, shoulders, and jiggling breasts. Her feet slapped on packed earth, creating a drumbeat in her mind.

Wilderness. Wildness.

By the time she'd completed her second circuit, her heartbeat had quickened. Thank goodness she was running. Otherwise, she might already be close to coming. She'd climax before the day was over. Unless he refused her, it would happen. But not yet. Not until she'd been submerged in tension, flames, taste, touch.

"Not fast enough," he said as she passed him. The internal assault became even stronger. The gag made breathing difficult. Her thigh muscles trembled. Her arms ached from being held in this damnable position, and her back felt strained. She couldn't settle on a stride that felt anything close to familiar. The jungle flashed by, colors bleeding together. And her clit hummed, heated, begged.

Every time she passed Zemar, she was treated to another jolt of energy. She came to expect it and anticipate the heightened awareness. At the same time, although her legs threatened to cramp and her feet burned, she embraced the sensations because they helped remind her that there was more to her than what was between her legs.

She'd been wrapped in a world which didn't exist beyond her body. Wrapped in sensation. Everything was about her, her journey into slavery and what she was learning about action and reaction. Zemar the lion had tapped into layers of her being she hadn't known existed, and unnerving as his mastery was, she'd never felt more alive. More in heat.

More desperate for a climax. In this time and place of his choosing and control, she'd do anything. Anything! Grovel before him if that's what he demanded, shame herself, fuck him, masturbate, run past him the one final time that would send her into the stratosphere.

But he continued to deny and play. Instead, her cunt remained on fire, a ravenous beast clawing at her sanity, kept a half step from leaping into release. He knew her limits and potential—knew and held her suspended over the ledge. She rounded the prison's corner and focused on him. *Relaxed*, his body language said. *Removed. In command. Owning everything about you.*

No, you bastard! No more dancing to your damnable tune. And no begging! That's behind me. Damn it, behind me!

This time instead of racing past, she pulled up and faced him as best she could. Dripping sweat and breathing hard, she struggled to hold up her head.

He studied her from his oh-so-comfortable chair. He held a

frosty drink in his free hand and saluted her with it. While she tried to work moisture into her dry throat, her gaze didn't stray from the control monitor in his other hand.

"Did I give you permission to stop?" He jolted her.

I hate you, she told him with her eyes and refused to move. She was so tense she wondered if she might shatter. Hard vibrations nearly took off the top of her head.

She rocked from side to side. Her pussy clenched against the dildo. Her feet beat a tattoo on the ground. She remained in place.

"I didn't expect that." He sounded, what, confused? "Not going to keep on running, are you?"

She shook her head. Her legs felt like hot rubber, but the need to take pride in who and what she was gave her the motivation to dismiss them. Her self-control was so fragile, so vital.

"Last chance, slave. Get going or pay the consequences."

I already am. How much worse can it get?

He showed her, the lesson pounded out in a fiery internal explosion. How stupid she'd been to believe the instrument of torture and delight locked inside her had reached its capacity. Instead, it suddenly and relentlessly began expanding and contracting. At the same time the pulsations turned into intimate earthquakes that caused her entire pelvic area to shudder. As if that wasn't enough, he *treated* her to the extremes of heat and cold. One instant she truly believed he intended to burn her. The next he turned everything into ice.

But she couldn't, wouldn't, run! Wouldn't grovel or beg even though he'd tapped into her every muscle, nerve, tendon, and vein. She needed all her intellect, courage, and determination and more to try to stay on top of the unbelievable sensations. Alive, on fire, scared, anticipating, she sunk deep inside herself. She found nothing but exposed nerves.

Screaming "No!" into her gag, she collapsed. There was nothing graceful or planned about her fall. Her knees took the initial impact, but then she sagged until she'd folded over herself, a captured ball of humanity.

Something shook her and separated her from the terrible tension.

Coming, coming, coming.

She dimly realized he was standing over her but didn't try to acknowledge him. How could she, with one climax after another rolling over her? Her pussy felt as if it had been beaten, satiated, vanquished, and gifted beyond comprehension all at the same time, and still he forced her to weather more assaults. She was flying, falling apart, shattering.

"Who owns you? Who?"

She couldn't answer, couldn't even cry out any more. Incapable of moving, she remained a rag doll caught in an angry dog's mouth. The dog shook her relentlessly, wonderfully. It didn't matter that no real fangs had penetrated her flesh, that she wasn't bleeding but instead was experiencing her deepest desires. Helplessness and relentless climaxes at his hand became everything.

Then it ended. How long the vaginal plug had been stilled she couldn't say. She trusted nothing, not him certainly, but also not her own body. Giving birth couldn't possibly serve as a greater demonstration of her system's primitive mechanism. Despite her exhaustion, she remained tense.

"Which of us won that round?"

You, she said with her eyes.

"You're an amazing woman."

Woman, not a slave?

As the moments ticked away, she struggled to ready herself for the next assault. Instead, Zemar knelt and removed her gag. He rubbed the sides of her mouth until she could feel it again. She lacked the strength to lick her lips but managed to shoot him a look between gratitude and fury as he held her head and placed the icy glass against her mouth. She drank greedily, noisily. And when she couldn't drink any more, she sagged against him while he massaged her shoulders, throat, breasts.

He'd done something like this last night when he'd tended to her exhausted body and shown her he was capable of gentleness. And while he'd been doing that, she trusted him. Just as she did now.

"You've earned this."

Keep touching me, please. "Because—because I came so many times?"

"No." He shook his head, looking, what, confused? "You're strong. Filled with pride. You stood up to me."

"No I didn't. I collapsed."

"But you refused to continue running. That took determination and courage."

Determination. Courage. Taking his time, he released her wrists and pulled the steel off her waist. After massaging where the restraints had been, he took her in his arms and stood, bearing her weight as if she were a newborn. He started walking, his strides slow and fluid, prompting her to wonder what it would feel like to walk beside him, hand in hand, as he showed her the island? Right now he was taking her to the cage he called a porch, but she didn't care.

He held her.

9

Zemar had deposited her on a lawn chair made of something that felt like satin and was designed so her legs were outstretched, her body supported. Rolling her head toward him, she watched him come back into focus. The masterful man was beautiful, handsome in a wild and powerful way, nothing like any other man she'd had anything to do with. He'd never belong in an office as part of an organization. Did she anymore?

She longed to run her fingers through his tangled hair, to slowly and lovingly wash and comb it while the sun dried it. He might think she was trying to court his favor with her gestures, but it wasn't that at all. He'd become her everything. Despite the risks, she needed him to know that.

"Interesting," he muttered. "Not what I expected."

What?

"Tough." He patted her cheek. "Not given to panic. No blubbering. Not even a tear." Frowning, he straightened and studied her naked body. His loincloth did precious little to shelter proof of his arousal. As her sex-induced lethargy faded, she half expected him to force himself on her, but the man had incredible self-restraint, either that or having a hard-on was nothing more than an occupational hazard to him.

Maybe. And maybe there was something beneath the surface in his smoldering gaze that could change their relationship. She tried to tell herself that she was reacting like a prisoner of war who has forgotten who and what she once was, and was emotionally aligning herself with her captor.

But maybe it wasn't that at all. This wasn't war because on some level she'd long craved what he was handing her. And he was what she'd dreamed of, a soul-deep Dom. Powerful. Knowing. Supremely sure of himself. Yet even those well-defined roles didn't seem to go far enough. Could there be a deep-seated connection between them, similar weaknesses, needs, and dreams?

If he gave her a sign that he wanted her as a woman and not just a sexual object, how would she respond?

The question continued to resonate as he turned away. Her attention was drawn to his broad, strong back, and she saw it clearly for the first time. Instead of a bodybuilder's flawless flesh, his tanned back was marred by a large number of stripes that weren't decorations after all. Scars! Whip scars.

Oh, God! Who did that to you? I'm sorry, so very sorry.

Were you a small child when someone brutalized you? Did anyone come to your aid or were you alone, scared? As helpless as I am?

Will you ever tell me?

If he was aware of her scrutiny and thoughts, he gave no sign. Instead, he left her where he'd deposited her while he went inside. The door to the cage had clicked shut after he'd carried her through it, but even if he'd left it open, she wouldn't have tried to run away. All he'd have to do was energize the vibrator still housed in her vagina and she'd be brought to the ground.

But now more than his possession of her kept her in place. She *had* to learn the truth behind his scars and know if he'd escaped the nightmarish memories.

Her fingers trembled as she touched the leather harness holding the amazing instrument inside her. It fastened behind her, though she had no doubt that he hadn't constructed it with hooks or snaps she could operate. Instead, like the dungeon doors, this *thing* was his to open or keep locked around and in her. The vibrator had deflated to the point where it no longer pressed against her still-burning tissue, but she'd be a fool not to realize how quickly that could change.

If he removed it, she'd be ready to receive his cock. She'd welcome him into her, not because she *had* to, but because despite the unrelenting climaxes she'd recently experienced, she wanted to feel a living and hot cock buried deep and full inside her. *Him*.

She'd wrap herself around him, holding on and being held while they fucked. He'd give her vital hints of who he was, and she'd lose herself in the act of sex. Turn chunks of who she was over to him. She'd climax, not because he'd plugged her with a toy no female could resist but because she was a woman and he a complex man, blatant sexuality wrapped in a pantherlike body. Howling, she'd call him magnificent. He'd proclaim her *his* and she'd believe him. Want the word and everything it meant. She'd press her lips against his scarred back and take away ancient pain. And when they were too exhausted for anymore sex, he'd tell her how he'd gotten the scars.

He returned, bare feet silent on the rubberized flooring and looking even more like the panther of her imagination. His back no longer bled or caused him pain. He'd become a predator, master of his domain—and her. He carried a large bowl that was angled so she could see it was full of water. When he set it down near her, she caught a sweet, intoxicating aroma. And when he picked a large, blue sponge and began bathing her with it, she sank into the sensations.

A few minutes ago he'd been torturing her. Now he was treating her as if she was precious, valued, valuable.

Valuable, yes.

"You didn't beg me to make it stop." He nodded at her crotch.

"No."

"Why not?"

"I learned. Begging never did me any good."

Frowning, he regarded her. "You're my first *trainee* to say that. The first not to grovel and demean herself."

I don't care about them. I can only be me. "How long—" she ventured. "How long will you keep me here?" *Can you sense that I'm no longer sure I want to leave?*

"Did I give you permission to ask questions?"

Determined not to be silenced again, she shook her head.

"You're learning, just as I'm learning about you." He circled her right breast with the sponge. "And because there are advantages in letting my *subjects* know certain things, I'll tell you that I don't make those decisions. It's better that way because our open-ended association keeps me on my toes and on task. When the powers that be deem you ready for entering your new life, they'll arrange to have you sold."

"You never keep a woman, a slave, for yourself?"

The unwise question earned her a nipple pinch.

"All right. All right!" she groaned as the punishment continued. "I'm sorry. It's just that I understand so little."

"You don't need to understand. You only need to experience." He demonstrated by sending the vibrator into mild movement. Too late she realized he hadn't set aside the control after all but had placed it on the floor next to him. "Experiencing is how the transformation is accomplished." He released her nipple and went back to washing sweat and dirt off her. The vibrator continued its soft, almost soothing hum. "Nearly everything I do and you experience is centered on your cunt, your sexuality. By the time I'm done with you, nothing will matter more than what your pussy feels or is denied. You'll be defined by it. We call it reward and punishment."

"We?"

"Doesn't matter, yet. You're a practitioner of one-night stands. True, you may sleep with a man more than once and don't consider yourself a cheap lay, but when you perceive that a man is getting too close or you start to have feelings for him that go beyond the physical, you back off. Run and hide."

"I don't hide! I'm not afraid—"

Strong fingers around her neck silenced her. She *had* to learn his rules, fast! "Call it what you wish. But from watching the videos on you, I saw fear of commitment. Believe me, I know the emotion."

She told herself that he'd learned how to detect fear from his experience with captured women, but something in his tone suggested a personal component. What could possibly make this strong man fearful? Nothing, she answered. He commanded his world and those who entered it.

But he hadn't always been a man. Once he'd been a child. Helpless and vulnerable. Abused. Alone.

"Videos?" she belatedly thought to ask, then tensed, certain he'd punish her. Instead, he turned his attention to cleaning her hips and legs. Each touch said he had all rights to her body.

Of course he does. He knows me better than I know myself.

He explained that she'd been pre-selected for transportation to the island nearly a year ago based on a number of criteria, but before making the final determination, she'd been monitored extensively. During that time her dating practices, mate choices, sexual preferences, even the way she spent her time alone had been documented.

To her shock, she learned that cameras had been installed in her bedroom. As a result, Zemar had proof that she preferred her collection of sex toys to the real thing. He didn't yet know why, but if he or another of the island's Doms decided it was important, they'd find out. She didn't tell him that it was because she was lonely despite her public protestations to the contrary that she ventured into the dating game. Still, she suspected he knew from her choices, and from his mildly disdainful expressions as he spoke. For although she could have had her choice of wealthy professionals, she'd always chosen men who were her intellectual and career inferiors. She made her selections based on physical attractiveness and the weight of what hung between their legs—and always left long before the men could bring up the possibility of a future together.

"None of them know about your bondage collection, do they?"

"No."

"Why not?"

"It was none of their business."

"Until now you've been content to play with yourself? You haven't ventured into the scene."

An image of her half-hearted attempt at self-bondage the night before she'd been taken—if that was when it was—made her wince. Of course he'd seen that. "It's safer that way."

"Not anymore."

"No. Not anymore."

"It's your curiosity about the lifestyle we embrace here that put you at the top of our *acquire* list. Many women are followed and their behavior documented, but the majority don't survive the selection process. If I were you, I'd take it as a compliment."

The vibrator continued its random, quick movements, forcing her exhausted body back to life. Her breasts and cunt tingled. She kept sucking in her breath. Still, she managed to concentrate on his every word and the nuances behind those crisp, clinical and so-revealing tones. It seemed he was talking more for himself than her, but either way, she needed to understand.

"You fascinate the island's rulers." He rolled her away from him so he could bathe her back. The change of position caused the dildo to press more fully against the sides of her pussy. Had it slipped deeper in her? "They're particularly intrigued by beautiful women who don't allow a man in their lives. Outwardly independent women who are convinced they don't need a male make the best slaves."

How many times was he going to hit her with the word *slave?* No matter how many defenses she erected, he knew how to get around them. Like now. Earlier he'd punished her. Now she felt cherished, safe, and still stimulated. *How do you like being considered a valuable piece of property, Asia?*

"Don't you want to know why women like you make ideal submissives?" He pushed aside the leather harness, spread her ass cheeks and slipped the warm, wet sponge into her crack. She jumped.

"I—you told me not to ask questions."

"So I did." He ran the sponge down from her tailbone, soothing her, touching the tip of the plug. She swore she felt him throughout her vagina. "A great deal of successful research has led the leaders to the conclusion that the journey from arrogance to surrender has a powerful impact on the female psyche, particularly those who tell themselves that their sub-play is just that, harmless entertainment. We suspect the same is true of males, but the focus on Surrender Island is on female subs since our Dom clients are exclusively heterosexual males."

After patting her ass, he placed the leather strap back in her crack and rolled her onto her back again. The dildo shifted, settled, shook. He bent one of her knees, reached down for a length of rope she hadn't noticed, and slowly began wrapping it around her ankle. Trembling but mesmerized, she watched her skin disappear under a half dozen loose loops.

"Everything about breaking down a woman intrigues me."

So matter-of-fact, like it was a foregone conclusion. *As if. Break me down? Not going to happen, not!*

How are you going to stop him? And do you really want to?

She hadn't asked those questions; she was sure of it. What then, the island?

After positioning her free leg next to the bound one, he began wrapping the second ankle with a new length. His no-nonsense approach rendered her immobile. She wasn't afraid so much as she wanted to see what he'd do to her next, what combinations of ecstasy and domination he had in mind.

"But when I've stripped the fight from a woman and taught her the rudiments of living to please a man, I'm ready to start over with a new, raw subject. Ready to take a tamed piece of flesh to auction."

Was that all she was? Flesh for the auction? Somehow she didn't think so.

Another piece of rope appeared in his strong fingers. Still working in his slow and deliberate manner, he hobbled her so there was no more than two or three inches of give between her ankles.

Trapped. Too late to resist.

His. Again his.

"Do you see how easy it is, Asia?" he asked as he helped her sit up. "You've already lost much of your fight."

"No, I haven't! But with that thing inside me, I have almost no control over my body. I have—I have to wait until the timing is right."

"*Almost?*" His chuckle carried no hint of warmth. "I'd say you have zero command of the situation, and I have more than one hundred percent. Turn away from me, slave. Put your hands behind you."

Don't, don't, don't. But because he'd filled her cunt with memories of what had already been done to it, and she'd never met anyone like Zemar the lion or believed one existed, she did as he ordered. She tried not to shudder as he snaked yet more disgusting and confining rope under and over her breasts and then used what was left to anchor her arms above the elbows. If she tried to move her arms, she'd cause the breast ropes to tighten.

His. Helpless.

Not content with this proof of his mastery, he secured her wrists as he had her ankles. He used the breast loops to haul her to her feet, then showed her a roll of black tape. Although she trembled, she stood there while he gagged her with what felt like endless loops of tape that pressed her lips against her teeth and sealed her hair to the back of her neck.

"Now you can concentrate one hundred percent on reaction and connect with yourself. Time to go back inside."

No! I can't take any more!

But she could, she discovered as he dragged her back into the room of shadows. With her legs tied the way they were, she was forced to hop. The vibrations distracted her from the full weight of her anger—if that's what she truly felt.

"Home, sweet home." The door closed of its own accord behind them. "At least what now passes as home for you. You have to go to the bathroom again, right?"

She did, but with leather snugged against her, she'd all but wet herself. Perhaps he didn't care because he hauled her across the room to the small, closed door. That one, too, magically opened, and she saw into the enclosure for the first time. A small, high, barred opening opposite the door let in enough light so she could see they were in a bathroom complete with a luxurious tub and a shower large enough to accommodate two people. The tub and shower included chains hanging from the ceiling and metal rings built into what looked like marble. In contrast, the toilet was utilitarian.

She could have used this yesterday and this morning, but no, he'd forced her to squat on the ground or pee into a bucket.

He ordered her to spread her legs as much as possible and then reached behind her and unfastened the crotch harness and extracted the vibrator.

"Do it," he said. Deliberately not looking at him, she settled herself on the toilet seat and let go. The smell of urine filled the air, but she didn't think she'd gotten any on herself.

"Stand up."

She blushed, and gritted her teeth, but didn't move as he wiped her, remained frozen in place and docile while he reinserted the high tech device and returned the leather to its home against her labia. So easy to command her. So easy.

Under his direction, she hopped back into the large room. He positioned her so she faced the stone wall she'd stared at when she wasn't sleeping or unconscious last night. Then he untied her wrists and breasts, spun her back around, grabbed one wrist and pulled it out so he could secure it to the wall via a metal cuff and a short length of chain. He did the same with her other arm, then stepped back. Her arms were outstretched, her breasts obscenely accessible to him.

What was he seeing? His handiwork, of course, his creative placement of her. But she wondered if he was searching for what lay beneath the surface. She might only be his current assignment, yet he'd mentioned an unexpected strength that set her apart from those who'd come before her. It could only be because he'd become her *everything*, but she needed to believe she mattered to him, that she was more than flesh.

He'd told her what he knew about her pattern of leaving her boyfriends before they could do the same to her, but she couldn't leave Zemar. Instead, she'd remain with him, his to do with as he pleased. And when he'd finished with her, he'd sell her to someone who'd do the same or worse.

Even as she tested the strength of her chains, resignation settled over her. Real life bondage had become her reality, chains and ropes and the ultimate object of her surrender buried inside her. Zemar the lion was responsible. She was his.

Until he was done with her.

She watched, fascinated, as he crouched and deftly untied her ankles, but the relative ease of movement lasted only until he'd snapped a cuff around one ankle and with a series of slaps to the inside of that leg, commanded her to spread herself. He secured the leg in the same way he'd done to her arms, then stood up. Because he'd all but pulled one leg off the ground, she was forced to rest most of her weight on her free foot.

"Time to get rid of this, for now." He reached behind her for the fastening to her crotch harness. He drew it off her, then reached between her legs so he could take hold of the part of the plug that felt as if it had been created to fit her contours. He pulled it, still vibrating, out. Along with relief, she felt a keen sense of loss. "I've got something else to entertain you with, but first I want to be able to hear you."

As he began unwrapping the tape around her head, she admitted he could have brought her inside without binding and gagging her the way he had. The gestures were designed to demonstrate his mastery over her—as if she needed further proof. But no way was she going to grovel. He might control her body, but her mind belonged to her. He couldn't stop her from hating him!

Hate?

Perhaps if she hadn't seen his scars.

If he hadn't caressed and bathed her. Held her.

Another trip to the cupboard had him carrying something that put her in mind of a sleek, oversized fishhook minus the barbs. "No questions about my plans for this?" he asked, then aimed the rounded end at her pussy.

An alarmed squeak escaped her. It took all her self-control and then some, not to try to back away from it. Despite his earlier thorough washing of her, she was instantly drenched in sweat. The straight section of the smooth hook had an eyehole of sorts, and Zemar took care to ensure she saw him thread a length of rope hanging from an overhead pulley through it. His features devoid of emotion, he came at her crotch again.

This time he didn't stop with a threat but separated her folds and guided the object into her. She tightened her belly and tried to lean away, but the stone wall at her back stopped her. She followed the hook's easy journey deep within her. *Housed. Settled.* It didn't look as if it was capable of vibrating, but she'd already learned not to trust appearances.

Once he was satisfied with its placement, Zemar left her with the straight end protruding from her and engaged the pulley. Inch by inch, the rope tightened, securing the hook, impaling her on it. To keep the pressure manageable, she stood on tiptoe. To her relief, he released her tethered leg.

"This is the seat of everything you're going to feel and experience for the rest of your life." He indicated her cunt. "Although I can, and will, address other areas of your body, the granting and refusing of climaxes is the basis of your indoctrination. You've already experienced a series of climaxes you didn't know your body was capable of, but I'm not done."

If not for one thing, she'd call him an unfeeling monster. His loincloth wasn't capable of hiding his erection. She might have forgotten about him as a human being while climaxes lashed her, but the rest of the time she'd known his nearly constant state of arousal. Yes, he was a master in the art of forcing a woman to submit. Yes, he understood her body's needs and limits far better than she possibly could. Yes, he could be a cold-hearted bastard.

But he wasn't immune. If he was at her mercy, she'd taunt and torture and demand that he tell her how it felt to have the tables turned.

Would you? Isn't it the truth that you want this?

10

He'd retrieved a pair of nipple clamps from the cupboard. When he held the first rubber-tipped contraption up to her, she forced herself not to react, in part because awareness of the steel inside her claimed much of her attention. He rubbed the clamp over a nipple. "A good fit, much better than yours. Designed to grip and stay in place. Note the ring at the other end. You know what that's for."

She closed her eyes and breathed deeply. "To hang weights from."

He cupped the underside of her breast and lifted it, cradled. Despite her vow to emotionally distance herself from him, her eyes opened. Was it only her imagination or was he drawing out supporting her breast's weight and learning its feel and warmth?

"There you are," he said. "Didn't leave after all, did you?" He gave the crotch hook a light tug. "No. You're not going anywhere." With a smooth, practiced move, he closed the clamp around her nipple. Instead of immediately releasing her breast, he supported it a little longer while he ran a nail over the underside.

She sucked in air and willed her eyes and mouth not to question his actions. The clamp pinched but wasn't so painful she couldn't bear it. In truth, she found the sensation more stimulating than the small pair she'd ordered on the Internet. How strange it was to have manmade devices taking over her body this way. How erotic. She heard herself pant but couldn't stop.

"Doesn't take long," he mused as he attached the second clamp. "You probably thought you were beyond reacting to any more stimulation today, but the body is an amazing thing." He took hold of the clamps and drew her breasts toward him, watching her reaction. "On there good and tight. Some connect with only the smallest bit of nipple, but these have been designed to wrap around a woman's contours. Keeps them in place. Your owner might decide just to have you pierced."

She wouldn't, couldn't think about that!

"And not just here."

"Why are you doing this? You get off on terrifying your captives? Scaring them so they can't think?"

"You're wrong. I want you thinking." He picked up something from the bed and returned to where he'd left her all but hung out to dry. "But I control the direction and amount of your thoughts." He showed her a couple of weights. Although they fit easily in the palm of one hand, she had no doubt she'd feel them throughout her once they were attached to the nipple clamps.

"Damn it, why must you try to dominate everything about me?" She'd keep him talking, not because she hoped to distract him from what he intended to do, but because if she wanted to survive unbroken, she had to understand the world she'd been thrust into. And him. "Are you afraid of my mind?"

His look made her suspect he'd never been asked that. Not bothering to answer, he attached the first weight. Her breast sagged, sensitive tissues pulled down. She felt the drag throughout her upper body. The message was clear. *Contained. Controlled.* "Your body is waiting for my every move, not sure what I intend to do to it next. And your mind is giving up ownership of your body. Turning it over to me."

You're right. Oh God, you're right.

He fastened the other weight in place so both breasts felt as if gravity had increased. She sensed the change in her groin and knew her juices were soaking the hook. Manmade objects claimed her wrists, breasts, and cunt. How much more of her would he take over before he was done?

Keep going. Please, take me all the way! She wanted to fight, for the sake of her mind, but her body, her nature, wouldn't let her.

"Sexual stimulation comes in endless forms." He stepped back and studied his handwork. "I'm only introducing you to a few of them. Each master has his preferred techniques."

"How—how many Masters are there?"

He shrugged, muscles flexing, chest expanding. "The numbers continue to grow as word of what we have to offer spreads and the ability to identify satisfactory slaves is perfected. In fact, a fast-track system has been implemented, thus the pace I'm putting you through."

Although his admission alarmed her, in some respects she felt as if they were sharing in this *process*. She'd agreed to a cram course to avoid overcrowding. As a result, her education might be incomplete, but she'd understand the basic concepts and be ready for the upper division courses.

But what would those later courses consist of? Beyond the possibility of a pierced labia and rings and maybe jewelry permanently skewered to her breasts, what did her future hold?

She didn't want that! She wanted, what? Surely not more of Zemar.

Please keep going. Take me all the way.

"Pain is a powerful component. Many on both sides of the BDSM lifestyle consider it necessary."

Don't I get a say in this? But she said nothing because he'd do what he wanted. She was the next thing to a deeply hooked fish struggling against an experienced and powerful fisherman's determination to bring her ashore.

This time he didn't go to the hell-cupboard but sauntered over to a wall where a collection of whips hung. He lingered over his selection, holding up several and studying her imprisoned body. He was deliberately drawing out the process probably because the technique had proven to be effective in unhinging the intended recipient. It was working. She didn't know how she could possibly keep him from knowing. If he tested conditions between her legs, he'd find her flooded. Maybe he could smell her.

But she couldn't help it! Being the chosen and helpless recipient of his expertise had turned her on! His mastery turned her on!

Do it to me. Everything you want to. Whatever it is, I'll receive, accept, rejoice. And if you'll let me, I'll demonstrate my gratitude on you.

He returned with a long, slender whip sporting a half dozen thin leather strands. He drew the strands over her belly. They felt like silk, almost. She sucked in a breath as her flesh responded to the gentle caress. "Deceptive, isn't it," he said. "If we both didn't know differently, we'd think I was going to give you a massage."

"What will you prove by wounding me?"

"There'll be no wounds and scarring. That's something I'll never do."

Her mind caught on the cold tension in his last words. Maybe he was making comparisons between what he was about to do to her and what had been done to him. She filled her lungs.

"You know what it's like to be whipped, don't you? I saw your back." She hurried her words. "How can you possibly believe there's anything stimulating about it? I'd never—"

The stinging slap to her hip landed before her mind registered that his hand had moved. Even as she struggled to turn that side away from him, she understood he was determined to silence her. The second lash landed on the opposite hip.

He worked her methodically, arm moving smoothly back and forth, the whip landing alternatively on her right and then left side. Over and over again he struck her, moving up and down, expertly missing the nipple weights that bounced and dragged during her unthinking attempts to escape. Her breast tissue was being pulled down. Instead of being cradled in her sports bra as they were when she ran, they were held in place as surely as her bound arms. At her nipples, the drawing sensation became a sharp sting. He managed to avoid tangling the leather strands around the hook or the rope holding it in place. Held deeply, securely, by the device, she could move only a few precious inches in any direction. Her flesh became fair game. The whip slapped, stung, felt like electric charges.

Again, again, again.

Although it was useless, she kept pulling on the cuffs. It didn't matter that the whip left only the thinnest of marks and never once broke her flesh. She was being subjected to something she'd considered only during the most erotic of fantasies.

She hated the way her muscles jumped and trembled, hated her rapid-fire breathing, hated the way she marched in place and kept trying to swivel her hips away. If only she could remain still, surely he'd give up. But he made her dance.

Made her want.

"Concentrate," he said, his arm working, working, working.

"On what?"

Instead of answering, he focused on her thighs, strip after

strip rudely kissing her. When she tried to close her legs to protect herself there, it felt as if she was trying to fuck the hook. The possibility intrigued her. She could clamp her inner muscles against the intrusion and distract herself from what he was subjecting her to. She'd show him, get off on hard steel!

Building on the possibilities, she imagined that the hook had become his cock. She'd imprisoned him, pulled him to her, and demanded he service her. Because she held the keys to his chains, he obeyed. They were both experts in the sexual arts, he in doing everything within his power to make the experience memorable for her, she in keeping him going.

She'd direct him to repeatedly bring her to the brink of climax, then insist he back off before again presenting his hungry and unsatisfied cock to her so she could draw out the fuck. In her mind his enjoyment meant nothing. She'd insist he be brought to her so he could service her. If he displeased her, she'd keep him awake and trying all night.

Again, she'd demand. *Take me from behind this time. Now flat on your back with me straddling you. No, you're not done; I'm not done. Hands behind you. Now, suck me. Lick me.*

And if he so much as breathed a word of protest, she'd order him strung up so she could beat him.

No! She could never add to his scars!

Unexpected compassion for the prisoner of her fantasy pulled her back into the world he'd created. The whip was now marching down her legs, nearing her calves. She could handle this! Even if he smacked the thin layer of skin over her ankles, at least so far he was sparing her body's most sensual areas. The fire in her belly burned lower, the coals still hot but not being fed anew. She studied the flesh he'd finished with. The marks were already fading. He'd told her the truth. He had no intention of scarring her as he'd been.

"Getting complacent?" The whip began journeying up again,

licking at her thighs. He paused to run a hand over her shoulder blades, and she tried to rest her head on his hand to draw out the disconcerting, almost loving touch.

He withdrew before she could. His eyes darkened. He clenched his jaw. "No. I'm not giving us that. Think of this as foreplay." Higher and higher the whip marched, closing in on her cunt. "And another lesson in your body's pliability and mind's betrayal."

He was right! No matter how much she struggled or tried to take her mind away from what was happening, she remained a slave to his manipulation. This time she kept her legs spread, head back and breasts displayed. She'd gone from constant movement to immobile, shivering anticipation, waiting, waiting.

Why won't you be tender? Don't you know how much I need it?

Her cunt was occupied. But if he heard her silent plea, he'd replace the hook with himself. She hadn't had a cock in her for too long. This time, please, her pussy would house him and not the powerful substitutes he'd subjected her to. She'd feel his flesh on and in hers, their mouths fusing, strong, warm arms holding her, whispered encouragement, sensing his tension in his hard, quick thrusts, climaxing together instead of yet another lonely explosion.

When he stopped striking her, she stared at him in confusion and frustration. Although she hated her weakness, she did what little she could to thrust her pelvis at him, but the hook's rope stopped her.

Don't leave me like this! Please, help me!

He reached for her pussy, causing her to jerk back in an insane effort to keep certain realities from him, but of course he easily ran his fingers over her weeping flesh. "Turned on. No control over your reaction."

"No!"

"Don't lie to me. I know your body better than you do."

Although she couldn't deny the truth of the juices he was removing from her cunt and spreading over her breasts, he didn't know her mind, her thoughts. No matter how completely he transformed her body into what he intended it to become, she wouldn't let him dominate her emotions. Hadn't she learned how to protect her heart from the two men who'd nearly stripped everything from her?

Make me a sub. Give me that dream. Just leave my heart alone. It isn't yours. It'll never be.

She didn't ask what he had in mind when he released the tension on the hook and removed it. She certainly didn't thank him. Although she would have given almost anything to feel him inside her, she refused to beg. Frowning, he studied her for several moments. "What do you want, slave? Say it! You need to be fucked."

"Leave me alone." *Please.*

"Not yet." He slid the whip handle over her slick cunt. She jerked and shuddered. Her whimpers remained buried and safe deep in her throat.

"Think you can win this round, do you?" He sounded, what, uncertain? "Not going to happen, Asia, not going to happen."

He'd been calling her *slave*. Should she read something into his use of her name? She was still contemplating the possibilities when he returned from the cupboard with a spreader bar. He easily cuffed one ankle, forced her to spread her legs, and then cuffed the other ankle. The attached bar kept her legs wide apart. Her pussy waited for his manipulations.

His. No longer hers.

Another trip had him carrying a large vibrator with a tip contoured so it settled over and cupped the clitoris. Like the previous one, this toy lacked an electrical cord. "Damn you."

"Don't tell me you don't want this." Although she struggled to distance herself from him, he easily pressed it against her. "Don't lie to me, Asia. You're thoroughly warmed up and primed for a climax. In fact—" He started the tool moving. "If you were free, you'd stay right here. Beg if need be."

"I don't beg."

Rearing back, he studied her. "I wondered when you'd admit that. Why not?"

"I don't. I don't!"

"What is it, pride?"

"Go to hell."

"Already been there."

Movement kicked up a notch. Her clit responded, and her concentration tunneled down. The skin he'd so expertly sensitized felt unbelievably alive, and the pain and unnatural weighted sensation in her breasts became something else—wonderful. Her head tossed from side to side. Another notch and she pressed against the vibrator. A sharp stab to her right breast brought her attention there. He showed her the clamp he'd just removed. He left the other in place while he massaged circulation back into the newly released nipple.

She hated being at his mercy, and at her body's demands, so she fought both by wrenching her mind off what was taking place. Even as her pussy wept and her ragged breaths echoed off the stone walls, she remembered the two times in her life she'd groveled before men. The first time, she'd been so young, innocent, loving without reservation. His abandonment had nearly destroyed her. Night after night she'd cried herself to sleep, and her grades had suffered. She'd stopped hanging out with her friends and hadn't wanted to do anything with them. She'd avoided looking at herself in the mirror because she'd seen an unworthy, unloved, unlovable child.

And yet, with time, maturity, and her mother's support,

she'd slowly rebuilt her shattered sense of self-worth and as a young woman she'd given her heart to another man. That time she'd given her body as well. The manner and memories of that other abandonment had been different. Only the shameful way she'd reacted had been the same. Once again her heart had been torn apart, her life shattered, ego destroyed. At least she'd refused to give into nighttime tears, and she could study her reflection long enough to put on her makeup and ask herself how she could have been so naïve and why her lover had betrayed her the way he had.

Today's reality slammed back at her. Zemar was removing the second nipple clamp. The rush of blood there burned and ignited, and she silently thanked him while he massaged her throbbing nub. He kept the vibrator against her and increased the movement speed a little as he ministered to her reddened nipple.

He released her breast. "Pay attention. Concentrate."

Vibrations suddenly rocketed throughout her body. The most intense sensation centered around her helpless and hungry clit, but no inch of flesh remained untouched. Everything burned. She felt as if she was being shaken. Because of the wrist restraints and spreader bar, she could barely move. Couldn't make him stop.

"Don't, don't, don't! No, don't! Damn it." She struggled to turn away.

"Feel it, Asia. Experience. Accept. Embrace."

Helpless. Used. "No!"

"Fighting won't do any good. It'll only delay the inevitable, maybe." He pressed, expertly anticipating her jerks and shudders. She tried to back up. The unwieldy bar and strain in her arms stopped her. The vibrator started pulsing. There was no rhythm, only strength and dominance.

"Can't, can't—Stop! Damn you, stop!"

He gripped her chin and forced her to look at him. "You want this. Need it."

"No!"

"Stop lying to yourself."

He released her chin but only to flatten his splayed fingers over her buttocks and shove her toward him. He trapped her against the vibrator.

Pressure. So much pressure. Flaming heat.

"I'm coming, coming!"

"I know it. I feel you."

"Coming." Her clit was on fire. The vibrator clutched her tissues, held her, shook.

No escape. No ending. "Can't! Can't take any more."

"Yes, you can."

Throwing back her head, she wailed. Explosion after explosion hit her. "Enough. No more!"

"This is what you've dreamed of for years."

True, but wave upon wave was too much! She was so incredibly sensitive, nerves overloaded, cunt exhausted but not being allowed rest. "Please, please, please. No more."

"You want me to stop?"

"Yes!"

"What will you do for me?"

"Anything. Anything."

"Wear my brand?"

"Yes!"

"Suck me?"

"Yes." She jerked, then stopped when it felt as if she might dislocate her arms. "Please, please."

Her world had been red-hot flames. Now, suddenly, she could see other colors, gray walls, his dark features and obsidian eyes. She sobbed more than breathed. Drank in as much air as her lungs could hold.

"Coming down?" he asked.

She was because he'd silenced the vibrator, thus handing her pussy relief. "Thank you."

"Gratitude, Asia? Because I was hurting you a moment ago or because you've never gone this far before?"

Air brushed against her drenched labia. Looking down, she watched him remove the vibrator although he held it only a few inches from her cunt. She tried to back-step only to be stopped by her restraints.

"You're not going anywhere so we might as well talk. Reality is damn different from fantasy, isn't it?"

"You think—you think I wanted to be manhandled like that?"

Grabbing her jaw again, he stared into her eyes. "I know you did."

"Damn you to hell."

"I told you, I've already been there. I'm not going back."

You're talking about your scars, aren't you?

"Are you listening, Asia? I want you to admit I just made your fantasy come true."

"How can you say that? You don't—"

"Don't lie and don't play games with either of us. I know your nature maybe better than you do. I'm tapping you into the real you. Do you understand what I'm saying?"

She'd watched bondage videos, listening intently to the women's loud and urgent climaxes while men teased them with all manner of sexual devices. Pressing a battery-run bullet against her clit or trying to find a comfortable position with a rabbit vibrator claiming her both inside and out, she'd worked to imagine she was the one who'd been chained to a wall, the floor, on a bed, in a cage. Many times she'd been able to masturbate herself to climax, but she'd never sounded the way those bondage-loving women did, the way she just had. When she used cuffs or ropes, she was careful to secure them so she could free herself. And when her fantasy was over, she rewound the video, cleaned and put away her toys, took a shower, put on a nightgown, and turned down the furnace.

Zemar had changed everything.

"What do you want from me?"

"For you to be honest with yourself."

She broke eye contact. "I can't."

"Not yet maybe, but it's going to happen. There's a lesson in this. One I believe you'll never forget."

He sounded, what, reluctant? No, surely not.

"You're a fighter. I've never had a woman who battles both me and her innate nature the way you do." His mouth tightened. "The Doms will love that. There's nothing they like more than playing with a slave's defiance." The vibrator dropped to the floor. "But never forget that fighting will either destroy you or get you killed."

"I can't live like this." She indicated her helpless body.

"You don't like it?" He rested his hand over her spent but still dripping pussy.

Your touch, you, not just some impersonal instrument!

"Answer me, Asia." A finger easily slipped into her. "You don't want a man inside you?"

"A cock, yes. Not—not the other."

"Then this—" He indicated the discarded vibrator. "Did nothing for you?"

"You know what I'm talking about!" Arguing with him was bringing her back to life, that and the finger housed in her cunt. If she could, she'd hold him there forever. "Being manipulated, forced—"

"Is a way of life here. And you've always wanted it."

"No." *Why are you lying to him? He's seen you when you thought you were alone.*

"Yes." He punctuated his remark by applying more pressure to a cunt she swore couldn't take any more stimulation. She should be dead down there, but she wasn't. "Asia, the slavery which exists here goes far beyond physical bonds. For the women who pass the selection process, it's because submissiveness is hardwired into their nature. You need to receive as much as the masters need to give. And the sooner you accept what you are, the better it'll be for you."

What did he care about her reactions once he was done with her? "I don't belong here." Her pussy pulsed to life around his finger. Unsure how long she could ignore it, she rushed to speak. "Surely there are endless potential slaves you—you people can choose. Women who trust men and are eager to give up ownership of their bodies."

"You're one of them." Another finger joined the one she already housed, stretching her burnt and bruised tissues.

"No, I'm not!"

His thumb stroked her clit. The wounded nub all but shuddered. "You're a slave to sex. You've been one since the first time you, probably as an adolescent, fantasized about giving up responsibility and control. Many women who want this find partners they trust who are eager to fulfill their dreams, but for reasons I don't yet know, you're afraid to share your nature with a living, breathing man."

"Everyone dreams about sex. They shouldn't—shouldn't be punished for that."

"You call this punishment?" He flicked her clit.

"Yes!"

"Liar." He abraded her clit with a roughened finger pad.

She jumped and shuddered under his watchful eyes but didn't lose herself in the contrast between her skin and his. His touch, the human-to-human contact reached her heart. He became more than her Master, more than a Dom. He'd left the life he'd known because it had failed him. His scars spoke of nightmares. No matter how long ago they'd been inflicted, he hadn't forgotten the details. "You've accused me of lying, but I'm not the only one trying to keep things locked inside. Tell me the truth this time. What are *you* afraid of?"

His eyes narrowed. "Nothing."

"Yes, you are. Despite all the things you've done to me, this is the first time you've touched me as a man touches a woman and let me know you care what goes on inside my mind. I know you want to fuck me. But you haven't. Is it because giving me your cock would make you vulnerable?"

Sucking in a harsh breath, he thrust yet another finger inside her and began stroking her. Her hips rolled from side to side. No matter how much she struggled to stop moving, she couldn't. "Who's vulnerable, Asia?" he demanded, but she sensed uncertainty behind the question. "It sure as hell isn't me."

"Isn't it?" Words became valuable and rare commodities. She had to choose them carefully and focus on them, not on the manipulation she craved. "I—I've seen your cock. It isn't immune. You aren't immune."

She waited for his denial. When it didn't come, she knew she'd won this round. He still controlled and defined the battle, and she'd be a fool if she didn't acknowledge that the ultimate outcome would go to him, but this moment at least belonged to her.

"Why don't—why don't you fuck me?" *Don't pump your fingers in me like that!* "I can't stop—can't stop you from raping me. We both know that."

"I don't rape."

"What do you call what you've been doing? Against my will. Forcing me. Isn't that what rape is about? Isn't it?"

"The island has been sending you its message. Don't tell either of us it hasn't. It embraced you because you're ready to embrace the lifestyle."

"Just because you need it doesn't mean I do."

His fingers stilled but remained in her. "I should have kept you gagged."

"It's too late, *Zemar.*" *You are vulnerable. And human.* "Even if you silence me, it's too late to take back what you've shown me about yourself. Your vulnerability."

"Damn it, you're wrong."

"Then court me, seduce me. Bring us together as a man and a woman, not Dom and captive."

11

He didn't, of course. Instead, he released her from this latest bondage, but not before placing a collar and length of chain around her neck. After freeing her ankles and wrists, he pushed her over to the miserable excuse for a bed and commanded her to sit on it. Then he fastened the chain to the ceiling, leaving her enough room to lie down or walk around the bed if she so chose. Throughout, he didn't speak.

She, too, remained silent both because she hoped he was thinking about what she'd said, and because she was afraid she'd ask him what he planned to do to her next.

He spent most of the rest of the day outside. Because she occasionally glimpsed him through the bars and heard him working, she knew he was engaged in clearing some of the brush around the building. Not that she'd tell him of course, but she loved the way sweat brought his muscles into relief and made his skin glisten. He didn't seem to need to rest, and she imagined him losing himself in the pleasure of a physical task well done. Perhaps he was deliberately wearing himself out.

She imagined that this was their home. While she worked inside on some domestic task, he did the same under the sun. Even as she went about her chores, she looked forward to evening when her man took her, his woman, in his arms.

Of course, that was insane.

As evening slipped through the bars, he came in to give her some water and let her go to the bathroom again, then walked away without a word. Because there weren't any lights in the room, night soon took over. Wrapped in inky blackness, she hugged herself. She hated the dried sweat on her skin, and the ache between her legs was impossible to ignore.

When would he be back? Did he intend to leave her like this all night, belly so empty it was cramping? She was utterly spent, but if she fell asleep, she risked choking herself on the chain.

Surely he wouldn't let that happen to a valuable piece of property.

He undoubtedly had more sexual plans up his sleeve—not that he had a sleeve. The cupboard housed a seemingly endless collection, and as he'd vividly demonstrated, the *tools* were more powerful than anything she'd ever used or imagined. What if he inserted another vibrator and left it on indefinitely? What if he bound her in such a way that she couldn't twitch, pressed some object over and around her clit, brought that object to life, and walked away?

He won't do that.

She told herself she was crazy if she believed he had a shred of humanity, but the thought didn't die. Some of her conviction came from his occasional use of her given name, but she drew deeper meaning from his act of inserting his fingers in her instead of the toys he'd relied on earlier. True, she was collared, but otherwise he'd left her relatively comfortable. And he hadn't stopped her from talking.

But then he'd left her alone in the dark.

Head throbbing, she massaged her temples. The bondage

stories she loved reading were always about sexually insatiable heroines. Even when their Doms or Masters or captors or whatever names they went by were done with them, they craved even more stimulation and resorted to masturbation, but now all her cunt wanted was to be left alone.

Done and done.

Or maybe only he could bring her to life. And not just his fingers and surely not some damn device.

She wanted him, equals fucking.

Unfortunately they weren't equals. He'd been supplied with a great deal of information about her while she knew nothing of him—except that someone had once brutally beaten him.

Surrounded by the bars of her cage, she knelt and stared out. He's coming, she'd been told. Your New master.

Fire licked at her body as she contemplated her future. The auction had gone by so fast that she couldn't remember the details. She recalled being led off the platform and back outside the tent. Her handler, a thin, faceless man, had hauled her what seemed like a long way. Finally he'd pushed her into what looked like a barn. But instead of stalls for animals, she'd seen two rows of cages maybe four feet high. Her handler had removed her cuffs, but a moment later she'd found herself refastened in such a way that chains connected her neck, wrists, and ankles. Showing no emotion, her handler had opened a cage and shoved her inside. The door had clanged shut behind her.

Once she was on her hands and knees, she'd looked at what she could see of the other cages. Each held a woman. One was knitting while another was occupied rearranging her straw floor. All were chained in one way or another. Those who could had their hands between their legs and were loudly masturbating. The others watched them, encouraging.

Her own cunt throbbed. She tried to satisfy herself but the chains kept her hands near her waist. She twisted and tried to press her thighs together, but all she got for her efforts was a wetter, hungrier pussy.

He's coming. Your new Master.

Finally she heard approaching footsteps. Pressing her face against the bars, she stared at the long, naked legs approaching her cage. Heat licked her pussy, and she clamped her thighs together. Her throat felt dry. She wished she could comb her hair and wondered if she had on makeup. Did he like her pussy shaved? What about a tattoo there? Would he prepare her so her ass accommodated him? Maybe he'd want her to wear larger and larger butt plugs until she'd been adequately stretched.

Her cage opened. "Get out here," a man ordered. "Show your gratitude."

Working awkwardly, she managed to crawl through the door. Her restraints gave her enough freedom of movement to stand, but she knew better. Eyes downcast, she slunk closer until she crouched at the man's feet.

"Gratitude, slave."

Delighted to be given permission, she leaned down and began kissing the man's foot. Over and over she pressed her lips against his flesh. And when he gave permission, she bathed him with her tongue. As she did, the pressure in her cunt increased until she couldn't remain still.

"Master, please," she whispered. "May I have permission to come?"

"Not yet, slave. First, my other foot."

She scurried over to it, but before kissing her master's foot, she turned her head to the side so she could brush her loose hair over his instep. He rewarded her by patting the back of her neck.

"That's a good slave. Are you happy?"

"Yes, Master."

"Do you want your chains removed?"

"No, Master."

"Do you want to be beaten?"

"If it pleases you, Master."

He didn't say anything, prompting her to look up for the first time. Zemar's dark eyes stared down at her.

"Please, Master, whatever you want."

"I'm trying to decide what will bring us the greatest pleasure. There's a new whipping post outside. I could string you up to it, invite others to watch, lash you until you come."

"Oh yes, please Master."

Asia had no idea how long she'd been in the dark when she heard the door open. Sitting up, she struggled to shake off the vivid dream and waited for Zemar to turn on the light, but whoever had come in preferred darkness. She smelled onions and garlic and the wonderful tang of something barbecued. Her mouth watered.

"How nice of you to join me," she teased to break the silence. "I've just been sitting here wondering what was on the dinner menu. I like my steak medium rare."

"I know."

Zemar. Of course he did. He probably knew what brand of tampon she used. After a moment she heard what sounded like a tray being set down. Then he snapped his fingers and a thin beading of light between the walls and ceiling came to life. The light wasn't strong enough to read by, and the lingering shadows made her a little uneasy, but it was better than the darkness of night and her thoughts.

He hadn't changed. Hadn't touched his uncivilized hair. His feet made no sound as he closed the distance between them and unhooked the chain attached to her collar. Strong fingers around her elbow brought her to her feet, and she followed him into the bathroom. This time he let her wash her hands and face. She longed for a shower but knew better than to ask.

When she was back on the bed, he placed the tray beside her. He didn't have to tell her to eat. The steak tasted incredible, and she nearly asked if he'd cooked it and the perfectly sautéed onions and garlic resting on the steak. There was also a small red potato and a salad with bleu cheese dressing. Not until she'd wolfed down half of it and drunk most of the lemon flavored iced tea did it register that this was one of her favorite dinners. He stood too close and studied her every bite. "Have you eaten?"

"Yes."

"At wherever it is you live?"

"Yes."

"Did you cook—"

"I order what I want."

Who obeys your orders? Who is eager to fulfill your wishes, a woman? More than one?

"You walked there and back in the dark?"

"Unless they're commanded to do otherwise, the predators leave humans alone."

But an escaped captive or slave would be fair game. Was there no way off the island, no way for a captive to escape her fate?

"They want you tomorrow," he said when she'd swallowed the last bite of steak.

Her heart thumped. "Oh."

"They studied today's videos and want you as you are, raw and wild, not broken."

Suddenly she felt sick. "What—what did you say?"

"I understand their interest—and concerns."

Concerns? About what? She couldn't imagine him giving way to anyone but didn't say so. Instead she asked about the video, and he pointed at random places in the wall. Although she didn't see anything, she understood. "What about when you had me outside? There were cameras out there too, weren't there?"

He nodded.

"You—you don't care." She hated, but couldn't do anything, about the emotion clogging her throat. "It doesn't matter that I'm going to be taken before you've—before you've finished working on me?"

His already night-dark eyes became even more so. "I do my job. Others do theirs."

She supposed she should be grateful because he'd no longer be around with his masterful and knowing ways, but the unknown terrified her.

Only, it wasn't his chains and vibrators she feared. It was the end to what little she'd learned about this remarkable and complex man—and her response to him. She even wanted him to know why she'd never taken her interest in submission beyond solo playacting.

Risking everything, she got to her feet and walked over to where he was leaning against a wall. Except for the collar, she was naked. And except for his loincloth, he was the same. Shaking, she slipped her arms around his waist so her fingertips rested on several of his scars. He tensed. Every inch of his body felt hard and strong and yet she sensed his quickened breathing. "How did this happen?" she asked. *Please tell me before I'm taken away.* "Who did this to you?"

She hadn't expected him to answer, but the rough way he pulled her off him shocked her. He held her as if he expected her to attack him. "It doesn't matter."

"Yes, it does. Zemar, no one has ever done anything that horrible to me, but even before I wound up here, I knew what having no control over my life felt like, and I'm not talking about being fired. The same happened to you when you were beaten. Damn it, I know it!" *And I care.*

"You don't know anything about me."

"Not all I want to, but I've started. Zemar, it matters. You matter. Don't you understand?"

He gripped her upper arms so she could neither touch him nor get away. "Don't go there." It sounded more like a request, maybe even a plea, than an order.

"Why not? Damn it, Zemar, you know all about me. The files or whatever they are. Surely they included everything."

"Not everything, obviously."

"What do you mean?"

"Until now one thing has been universal about the slaves I work with. They've begged." He abruptly wrenched her arms behind her and held her against his rock solid body. Her breasts pressed against him and absorbed his heat and rapid heartbeat. "But even when you want to, even when your sanity depends on it, you don't. Why not?"

She stared up at him. Trying to discover what they had in common was one thing. Opening old wounds before this man who'd already commanded so much of her was quite another. "I should bleed in front of you while you tell me nothing about yourself, the scars?"

His mouth hardened, and his spine stiffened. Although he didn't reach behind himself, she sensed his desire to connect with the marks, maybe attempt to rub them away. "You're the subject, not me. And you wouldn't want me to force the truth out of you."

Looking deep into his eyes, she saw a hint of decency. Between that and his forceful hold, she weakened. "You don't have to because I've decided not to try to hide from the truth. One of us has to be honest."

His mouth twitched. She read, not anger but respect. "It happened a long time ago," she said. "I was a child. At least I was the first time."

"A child."

His soft tone told her that his personal nightmare had its roots in the same place. "Some things should remain relegated to the past, right?" she asked. "It's behind *us*."

Until this, he'd gripped her painfully tight, but now he released her. Before she could decide what, if anything, to do or say, he glanced at her wrists, prompting her to do the same. He'd left the imprints of his fingers on her flesh. Eyes shuttered, he took her hands and began to gently massage away the marks. "Tell me how it began for you." He reached out as if to touch her cheek, then stopped. "Please."

Wondering if her survival might hinge on her response, she shook her head trying to clear it. It would have been easier if not for the heat between them and the dream remnants, with their meaning she could no longer deny. Make-believe about powerful and experienced but faceless dominant men had given way to the real thing—Zemar. "I swore I'd never cry or plead again, never degrade myself by begging a man to love or even care about me. I'd learned it wouldn't do any good. I felt ashamed, abandoned, exposed."

"Like you are now?"

"This is nothing." She indicated her naked body. "You've put my skin and sexuality on display. I refuse to let the same thing happen to my heart."

Certain he'd find a way to throw the words back at her that were now a lie because of the impact he'd left on her heart, she waited. Instead, he lifted her in his arms and carried her to the bed. She'd wrapped her arms around his neck before she realized what she'd done, but it was too late to take back the gesture of trust and surrender.

He deposited her on the bed and settled beside her. His arm around her shoulder sheltered her, and despite the blood singing in her ears, she leaned against him. She'd never known anyone this strong, had never wanted such a powerful flesh-and-blood lover. Health and vitality rippled through him, and she drank from it, from him. *Take from me. Please, if I have something you want or need, I give it freely. No matter what happens, let this connection last for the rest of our lives.*

"You trusted and loved someone, but he betrayed that trust." He brushed her hair off her cheek. "That's what happened, isn't it?"

Don't hold back. Strip your soul as he stripped your body. "I was eight. I didn't understand the meaning of the word 'lies.' Or 'abandonment.' I've never forgotten his lesson."

"His? Your father?"

Take the next step. Hand him complete honesty. "Yes."

"What about your mother?"

"She was there, thank goodness. I slept with her for awhile afterward, holding onto her and she onto me. Our closeness helped me understand that other people had emotions and needs. I, ah, I had her until her death when I was eighteen."

"At least you had her."

You didn't, did you?

"Eight." His gaze said he was trying to see her at that age. "I never know about a captive's childhood."

"Maybe—maybe you should tell whoever tracks potential sex subjects to include the early years and not just let the island make the decisions." His arm was still around her, his strength and energy keeping her going. She couldn't distinguish the line between the terrible need to let him see into her soul and physical craving. Maybe there wasn't one and everything had blurred together. "My childhood molded me, just as it impacts everyone, you included."

He laid her down, her back resting on the mattress with her breasts, belly, pelvis within easy reach. She couldn't and didn't want to move. And when he stretched out beside her and propped himself up on an elbow, she didn't hide from his searching gaze.

"Your father walked out of your life?" He again brushed back her hair.

"I tell people that he divorced my mother and me. I—I begged him not to leave, but he pushed me away and slammed the door. It—that was the day he told my mother he'd found someone else. I—maybe I thought he would take me with him. He used to call me his princess. Every day when he came home from work, I'd run outside so he could hug me and carry me inside. I remember telling everyone that I was going to marry him."

"You never heard from him again?"

In a controlled voice she told him about her father coming back a week after the separation so he could take her to see where he was living. She'd sat in the back seat because a tall woman with short hair was seated next to him, and although he'd reached around to briefly squeeze her hand, she hadn't liked his new cologne or haircut. When her father told her that Carol was going to have his baby and he expected her to call her Mom, she'd refused. Although Carol had said to give her time to get used to things, her father had called her a stubborn brat. When he dropped her off back home after showing her Carol's immaculate second floor apartment with his clothes now in the closet, she'd clung to him and begged him to live with her and Mommy again. He'd shaken her off, picked her up, and deposited her on the doorstep. Heartbroken, she'd dropped to her knees and clung to his legs until he kicked her away.

He'd returned a few days later for the rest of his belongings, and she'd again wrapped her arms around him, groveling. Because of her tears, she couldn't see his expression, but the way he'd peeled her off him and stomped away left no doubt that the man she loved most in life had no use for her. He was going to divorce Mommy and marry Carol instead of waiting for her to grow up. And he was going to have a new child so he didn't need her at all.

"I called him every day for the first month or so." *You're really telling him this, aren't you? The first person since Mom.* "I kept asking when I'd see him again. He'd say he wasn't sure and then hang up. He did drop by with a birthday present a few weeks after I stopped calling—and to tell me that he and Carol were moving across the country. I didn't see him again until I was eleven. They had a daughter."

"Bastard."

Talking had exhausted her, either that or everything she'd been through since she'd been spirited away from her world had finally caught up to her. Whichever it was, she clenched her chattering teeth and stared at the ceiling.

"And the second time?"

"The second time what?"

"That your heart was broken, and you realized begging wouldn't change anything."

Oh God, she had said that too, hadn't she? "I don't want to talk about it."

Smiling faintly, he cocked his head. "I could make you."

"Fine. String me up by my thumbs. That'll do the job."

She felt him jerk. "Don't even say that."

What's going on inside you? I touched a button, didn't I? "Can you blame me? I have a pretty good idea what you're capable of."

"Torture isn't what Surrender Island is about. If it were, I wouldn't be here."

"Why are you?"

Abruptly, he sat up and turned away from her. She shouldn't have been surprised. She hadn't really expected him to answer. Not giving herself time to question the wisdom of her action, she ran her fingers over his marred back. He stiffened, then she sensed an internal battle as he relaxed. Her sensitized fingers traced countless scars. Despite the disfigured flesh, she continued her exploration. The hard ridges were as much a part of him as his sculpted muscles. Wondering at the hell he'd been forced to endure, she let tears fall for the first time in years.

"When my father walked out of my life, I felt as if my heart had been ripped apart." *I give you honesty so, maybe, you'll do the same.* "I don't know what I would have done if I hadn't had my mother. Although she too was hurting, she put my needs first. She held me when I cried, and when I asked her why my daddy stopped loving me, she said it had nothing to do with my worthiness as a human being and everything to do with his own selfishness and failings. Eventually I believed her."

She'd been careful to apply enough pressure to his back so that she didn't tickle him, so she couldn't blame her touch when he stood and walked over to the front door. "Please come back," she whispered.

He did, his magnificent body closing the distance between them. Her own hummed. She'd never felt so restless or on edge. "What are you afraid of?" she asked again.

"Afraid?"

"You're right. That isn't the right word." Holding out her hands, she waited until he placed his large, strong ones in them. The contact seemed like a miracle. "Leery. Wary. You've kept a huge part of yourself locked away." Although she wanted him back on the bed beside her, she stood so she could press her breasts and belly against him. His cock felt like a barrier between them until she shifted so she sheltered it with her body. Still only half believing what she was doing, she clung to him.

"You've seen every part of me." So much was changing. Could she go from being his prisoner to, maybe, his equal? "Touched everything." She pushed her pelvis at him and moved from side to side, applying friction to his hidden cock. "Why won't you let me do the same to you?"

"You know." He'd been standing there, his arms at his side,

rigid as if he didn't trust her. Now he pressed his hands over her buttocks and applied enough pressure that she couldn't back away. It didn't matter because she had no intention of letting this moment get away. He was responding!

"No, I don't. And don't tell me it's because it's part of some damn technique you've perfected as a Dom. When's the last time you let a woman past your barriers? Do you ever share your dreams, your thoughts, with anyone?"

The shudder that passed through him said more than a million words could, and she again wept inwardly for what he'd been forced to become. Something terrible had been done to him back when he'd had a child's trust. As a result, he'd closed himself off and isolated himself. She understood. "Do you have dreams?" she ventured.

"Yes." *Yes. But I don't know how to share them.*

"So do I." She pressed her lips to his chest. "I've had a couple recently that have been incredibly revealing. But right now the only one that matters is wanting to fuck you."

Taking hold of her arms, he pushed her away so he could stare down into her eyes. "You want—"

"To fuck. Have sex. Make love. Please."

12

Don't mess it up. Whatever you do, don't do anything to make him bolt. The thought that she could cause this domineering man to flee should have been laughable, but as she ran her hands through his tangled and overgrown hair, she sensed his fragility. His body was powerful, magnificently honed for a physical life, but beneath the surface beat a vulnerable heart.

Trusting her instinct, she drew him near the bed. With trembling fingers, she reached for the cord holding his loincloth in place but didn't try to remove it. Whatever sturdy material the cloth was made from provided maximum protection, moving when he did, always keeping his cock covered. The way it bulged when he was aroused, which seemed to be most of the time, left her with no doubt of his size. Yes, she'd gotten a glimpse of the real thing, but she'd never been given the opportunity to study what taut skin and swollen veins said about him as a male.

He'd deliberately kept himself covered while insisting she remain nude as a powerful message about the difference between them. If she exposed him, it would change a great deal about their relationship. But that move, if it ever came, would have to be initiated by him.

"Everyone has flaws." She sat with him standing close enough for their legs to touch. "The physical ones are obvious. It's the emotional that cause the most trouble."

"And are the hardest to identify."

If she wanted him to reveal more, she'd have to move cautiously. Still, she could rest her head against his hard belly, couldn't she? "I can't imagine what it would be like to be perfect." She chuckled. "To have become an adult without tears or heartache—someone like that couldn't possibly be mature. If we don't make mistakes or learn from our mistakes . . . My mother used to say she wanted to get old enough that she'd have made her allotment of mistakes for one lifetime. But she died too young."

"What about your father?"

Let's talk about you, not me. "I assume he's alive. I don't care enough to find out."

He rested his hands on the top of her head. When she felt hot tears behind her closed lids, she couldn't say whether they were for her or him. "I could if you want me to."

He'd do that? But he was taking her somewhere to be sold tomorrow. Suddenly sick at the thought, she forced her emotions to go no further than this moment. "I don't." *You're what's important, not me.* "Zemar, what about your parents? Are they alive?"

"I don't know."

"You've never tried to—"

"After what they put me through, I want nothing to do with them."

"I understand," she whispered, although she didn't. His barriers were so strong, the protective layers he'd built around himself maybe impenetrable. But tonight there was nothing except the two of them and this unexpected closeness. She kissed the base of his rib cage. He caught his breath. "Will you tell me one thing?"

"Maybe."

"What did you do before you—before you came here? It *was* willingly on your part, wasn't it?"

"To a large extent, yes." He ran a hand under her chin and lifted her head so she was looking at him. A shiver ran through her. "I didn't fit where I was. Fishing off Alaska kept me away from cities and that was good. But it's dangerous work."

"I know." She imagined him standing on the deck of a violently rocking boat, endless storms battering his body, driving wind and rain abusing his flesh. "I mean, I read that deep sea fishing there is the most dangerous job in the world. Why were you doing that?"

"Good money."

Not enough reason. Maybe you were hiding from yourself. Trying to stay alive kept you too busy for anything else.

"One day I was thrown overboard during a storm. I knew I was drowning. I had only one regret, that in many respects I was still the child I once was. I wanted to feel power, to be the one in control."

"And—and that's when you wound up here?"

He nodded, and the line of his mouth told her he'd said as much as he would, or could. Wanting to let him know it was all right, she repositioned herself so she could run her tongue over a nipple. She touched silk stretched over steel. He'd recently taken a shower but whatever he'd used hadn't cleansed his flesh of his essence. He tasted alive, male. When she closed her mouth around his nub, he grabbed hold of her hair but didn't pull her off him. Loving the mastery implied in the act, feeling the impact deep in her groin, she bathed first one nipple and then the other. A muscle in his chest quivered. She took the nub in her teeth. Another shudder accompanied his quick breath. Then she walked her fingers over his rib cage, learning what she could about his lean, muscled strength, trying to imagine what it had felt like to be alone and freezing in the middle of the ocean. If he'd died—

If it hadn't been for the growing heat between her legs, she might have been content to devote everything to his needs, but his manipulation of her body had triggered a primitive reaction she couldn't, and didn't want to, ignore. Needing his touch, she moved his hands from her hair to her shoulders, then returned her mouth to his chest. Strange how someone so strong could remind her of satin.

As she again took a nub between her teeth and lightly nipped him, she felt his fingers at her throat. He slid the collar back and forth. Instead of being reminded of her slavery, she reveled in the sensual feel of metal against her flesh.

Then he ran a finger under the collar and all she felt was him.

This time when she reached for the loincloth, she didn't hold back from reaching under the fabric. She touched the sleek, velvet flesh that encased the core of Zemar's strength. She'd known he was well hung but to actually have her hands on him caused her heart to race and her cheeks to heat. As yet incapable of making the contact any more intimate, she ran her knuckles over him. They grazed his balls and traveled his length, circling the underside of his head, journeying over it, finally reaching the tip. A drop of moisture waited for her. She captured it, reluctantly withdrew her hand, and licked her finger. She tasted heat. Was it possible? His sperm, the essence of life, actually rested on her tongue? Then she looked up into smoldering eyes.

"I thought I knew what I was going to do if you gave me the opportunity," she whispered. Saltiness reached the back of her throat. "But I don't know my boundaries, what you'll let me do, when you'll make me stop."

"There's no stopping tonight."

His simple words filled her with life and promise. They only had this single night, but like her, he wanted it to mean every-thing. To last forever. Her world closed down, and there was no morning. Her slavery belonged to another time, to a woman who cared about more than giving herself to this incredible man.

Is it really the island or even my submissive nature and your dominance? Maybe it's me, you, us.

He settled his hands around her waist and guided her onto the middle of the bed. Then, caressed and revealed by the muted light, he removed his single piece of clothing and dropped it to the floor. He stood over her, huge and proud. Ready. Hungry. Starving, she spread her legs and reached for him. When he climbed onto the bed and knelt beside her, his weight pulled her toward him. She might have rolled onto her side if not for his hand pressing on her thigh.

Touch me everywhere. Please, let every inch of my flesh get to know you.

Smiling faintly, he gripped her thigh and studied her sex. Unashamed, she waited. *This is me, the private, vulnerable, hungry essence beneath the surface. I give it to you, freely, joy-fully.* His gaze heated her even more. Before, her core had been his to do to as he chose. Now she offered herself as a gift.

She ran her fingers up his legs, drawing out the journey from knees to thighs to hips. Her fingertips traveled up and over his pelvic bone, ventured closer and closer to his cock. Instead of denying her access, he turned his attention to her pelvis.

I accept your gift, his dark gaze seemed to be saying. *I un-derstand the true meaning behind this exploration.*

At times she barely felt his touch. Then, a heartbeat later, he'd press a thumb or finger against her, igniting her in always new, exciting ways. She brushed his cock. Over and over again she made contact but carefully avoided any kind of a pattern. His intense eyes watched her every movement. She sensed his wariness. No wonder. After who knew how long he'd spent manipulating and conditioning women, he'd forgotten—if he'd ever known—that sometimes there were no ulterior motives. Sometimes two people simply wanted to fuck.

Fuck. Sex. Make love?

Dizzy with a need she couldn't articulate or contain, she scooted around until she'd positioned her legs on either side of him. She kept her hands on him, learning, gifting. Eager to deepen the contact, she increased the pressure on his legs. They now fit securely between her knees. She reached up and tried to pull him down over her. She didn't care that she'd assumed the missionary position because even now, even in this, he was her lord and master.

Stroking his neck, shoulders, and arms by turn, she returned his gaze. It bothered her that she couldn't read his mood. When he stretched out over her, she felt a momentary panic, then squelched it. *Live in the moment. Keep it everything.* His cock brushed her mons, sparking a volcanic response deep inside. Spurred by heat and energy, she bent her legs and arched her pelvis toward him, calling him home.

My gift to you, to us.

He slid in so easily, so fully that the penetration was complete before she'd comprehended the journey. He loomed over her and trapped her between his body and the mattress. She smelled only him, felt nothing but him. Her cunt had expanded to accommodate his size, and she felt his balls pressing against her flesh. Sudden panic snaked through her. Then she felt his muscles relax and believed he'd read her fear. Wrapping her arms around his neck, she looked up at him.

The strange lighting kept his features in the dark, but maybe it was better that way. She could concentrate on the union between them and the mutual gifts of their bodies.

Speak to me without words. Sense my honesty, my trust.

He pushed in even deeper. She felt his strength build. It flowed over her, weakening her tendons and muscles. *You're everything, my everything.* But she didn't want it to be take and surrender between them, not this time, this first—no, she would not think "only"—time, so she locked herself in place. *I'm strong. Strong.* Her cunt felt alive. He filled her and more. She couldn't distinguish between them. His body, his cock, became part of her, finding nerve endings and switching on yet more circuits. Hot and strong and weak all at the same time, she ceased to exist as a separate person. It didn't matter. This moment was everything.

With every thrust he absorbed more and more of her. Her cunt, and her soul, became his, and she gave them willingly. She embraced his cock and heartbeat in ways she'd never comprehended, felt only their shared heat, his relentless driving, her pelvis and hips and belly reaching up to him. When strength deserted her arms, she flung them out and transferred everything into their union.

Her thighs trembled, and her bowed back ached, and her feet threatened to slide on the bed, but she held herself in place. He drove down on her, his grunts as strident as hers.

Find me. Find me. I want to sing and shout for you, for both of us.

"Now, now, now!" she cried.

"Now what?"

Don't know. Don't care. She locked herself in place, held her own as his cock pummeled her. It was if the air had been sucked out of the room, causing her to gasp. She smelled his sweat and hers. She tasted him, tasted herself, bit the inside of her mouth, didn't care.

"Now!"

"What?" He strained against her, his body rigid.

"Coming! God, coming!"

"Wait—for me."

Somehow she did. Somehow she held the force at bay. His cock retreated slightly, impaled her again. Repeated. Held.

"Now!" He loomed over her, his sweaty chest sliding over her breasts. "Now!"

"Coming!" She struggled to repeat the word but only screamed. Screamed and screamed. He plowed into her and lifted her buttocks off the bed.

Slowly, she started to come down, but after grinding his elbows into the bed, he thrust and thrust. She clung to him, gripped his powerful ass with aching, trembling fingers. Then he exploded inside her. His come filled her and drowned her. *Thank you. Thank you.*

His sweat-drenched body settled over her, and even as his cock retreated, she kept herself loose and open for him. He rested on top of her. They panted as one.

It's all right. Everything is all right. For this moment.

He rocked back a little but not enough to break the contact. "It wasn't supposed to be like this," he muttered.

"I know."

"It won't happen after tonight."

"I know."

Instead of getting off her, he pressed his lips against hers, pushed his tongue into her mouth, tasted and explored, and as he did, his cock again swelled. He folded her legs tight against her belly and caressed her breasts. "I can't get enough of them."

"I can't get enough of you touching them." *Tell me how I'm going to get through the rest of my life without this, without you?*

The words clogged in her throat. She held him with one hand on an elbow and the other around his neck. His cock continued to expand. He easily pushed deep inside her slick, hot passage. "Yes," she whimpered.

Unlike the first time, now his strokes felt long and slow. He caressed tissue that should be numb, kept her on the edge, not allowing her to fall into her climax even though she whimpered and strained.

"I love feeling your need." His breath feathered against her ear.

"I can't—I have no control . . ."

Neither do I.

She'd heard his thoughts. She had no doubt of that. But her muscles trembled, and she became heat, and she couldn't concentrate.

He slid his hands under her buttocks. The instant his cock ran along the front of her vaginal wall, she came.

And kept coming.

She didn't know how many times they fucked that night or how many times she'd climaxed.

Later when she rose on unsteady legs and started toward the bathroom, he stopped her with a hand on her thigh. "You told me about your father, but when was the last time you asked a man for something?"

"I was eighteen."

"Still a girl. What happened?"

After everything they'd shared, she felt no need to hold back anything. "My mother had been dead for six months, but I was having a terrible time dealing with the loss. There was this man. At least to me, back then, someone who had graduated from college was a man. His mother and mine had been friends, so I'd known him for a long time. We started seeing each other shortly after the funeral. I needed—I needed to feel as if I belonged to someone, wasn't alone. Then I got pregnant."

He drew her down and held her against his strong body.

"I had this fantasy that we'd get married and raise our child together. Create a family."

"Did you love him?"

"I thought I did." Her throat felt tight, but she knew she wouldn't cry. Those tears had been spent years ago. "He didn't say much the night I told him, but the next day he called to say he'd just gotten his first job, had student loans to pay off, wanted to do things with his life that didn't include children or a wife. He wanted me to have an abortion."

"Did you?"

"No. That tiny life inside me was precious. Having him say what he did hurt almost as much as losing my mother had. I—I did something I'm not proud of. Something I've spent years trying to forget."

"Tell me, please."

Please. "I went to his place. When he opened the door, I got down on my knees and begged him not to abandon me and our child. I told him how scared I was of being alone. That I'd rather die than lose him. That I'd do whatever he wanted to make it work between us. It—it became like it had been with my father all over again. He tried to push me away and I wrapped my arms around his legs and begged some more. I don't know. Maybe he became my father in my mind." Still appalled by how she'd demeaned herself, she nevertheless met Zemar's gaze. "He kicked me off him and said I was making a fool of myself and he was disgusted." She briefly closed her eyes. "He was right, you know."

"You were desperate."

"Yes. But pleading with him wasn't going to change him. He was who he was."

"A selfish bastard."

"And honest."

Zemar frowned, then nodded. "You went home then?"

"I was in no condition to be driving, but yes, I went home. A week later I miscarried. I left him a message telling him, but he never got in touch."

"Miscarried. I'm so sorry."

"At the time I thought I'd die. Losing her—I was already convinced I was going to have a girl—nearly destroyed me. But

I healed, finally. Learned how to insulate my heart. I've never allowed myself to hurt like that again."

"I understand."

"Because of your back?"

"Because I was so damn wrong to believe my parents understood the meaning of the word love."

13

Early morning sunlight touched Asia's eyes. She started to turn away from it, then stretched. Last night slipped into her mind. She clung to the memory of touches, words, bodies sharing. Beside her Zemar slept.

Her full bladder wakened her even more, and she sat up. The promise of a shower should have sent her into the bathroom. Instead, she leaned over him so she could run her lips over his marred back.

These scars are part of you, part of what I want to learn about you.

She was still kissing him when the door to her prison opened. Two men clad entirely in gray stepped in. Jumping to her feet, she started back-pedaling. The taller one reached her first, grabbing her tangled hair and forcing her to her knees.

"Guess who?" the other one said. Out of the corner of her eye, she saw Zemar surge upright.

"This is your morning wake-up call," the man holding her down said. "From what we saw last night, we didn't think you'd be up at dawn."

"Damn it, don't hurt her," Zemar ordered.

"Don't worry. We know how to handle the merchandise. Go back to sleep. We'll take it from here." Not waiting for Zemar to answer, he used his hold on her hair to haul her to her feet and into the bathroom. The shorter man also squeezed into the small space and positioned himself so she could no longer see Zemar.

The taller man turned on the cold water faucet and shoved her into the shower. She gasped and tried to get away, but his firm grip kept her in place. Shivering, she had no choice but to stand under the chilling spray with her head bent uncomfortably toward the man holding her. The other reached in and used a rough, soapy sponge to thoroughly scrub her. He got soap in her eyes and mouth, distracting her a little from his intimate invasion of her body. No matter how she struggled to get away, he washed her throat, breasts, back, belly, arms, and legs. He left her inner thighs and labia until last and lingered over the task. When she tried to back away, he dug his fingers into her hip and all but buried the sponge in her cunt.

Ashamed and on the brink of tears, she stopped fighting.

The water was still running when they yanked her back into the larger room where they pushed her face-first against the nearest wall. The taller man swiped at her with a towel, paying particular attention to her breasts and between her legs. They cuffed her hands behind her and rammed a ball gag in her mouth before releasing her.

Barely trusting her legs, she turned around. Zemar was leaning against the wall opposite the bed, still naked, his features unreadable.

"You know why we're doing it this way," one of the men said to Zemar. "The video."

"Yeah," he said without expression. "I stepped over the line."

"We didn't have to see much of what went on here last night.

You've lost objectivity with this one." He jerked his head at her. "Crap, I've never seen so much fucking in one night in my life. Didn't know it was possible. I don't suppose you'd have much use for her for a few days anyway. She as hot as she looked?"

"Listen to me. You hurt her and I'll kill you."

"Like I'm going to damage the merchandise?"

"Did you hear me?"

"Yeah."

"Good. Now get the hell out of here."

"We intend to," he said as the other man pushed her toward the door.

She started to send Zemar a pleading look, then forced herself not to acknowledge his existence. If he truly cared about her, if he had any concern for her fate, he'd stop those men. But he was a Dom with a job to complete. Last night had been an aberration, brief insanity on both their parts.

The men shoved her into a vehicle that resembled a golf cart. Instead of having space for golf clubs, however, it had been constructed with what she thought of as a roll bar. They released her wrists only to refasten them to the overhead bar. Arms outstretched and her ankles anchored to the bar's base, she was forced to stand during the ride. The vehicle didn't have wheels. Instead, it hovered a few inches over the path as it sped through the jungle. At least the trip was smooth, saving her from having to fight to keep her balance. What she wasn't saved from was a profound helplessness. By the time she'd finally gathered her senses enough to look over her shoulder, the prison and Zemar were out of sight.

Her captors obviously didn't care whether she heard them talking, probably because they considered her less than human. The taller one who seemed to be in charge was pissed at, and confused by, Zemar's break from regulations and maintained Zemar would need to undergo retraining before being entrusted with another initiate. The other, who kept reaching back to fondle her breasts and reach between her legs, was inclined to cut Zemar a measure of slack. He understood how a trainer could lose control and fuck a slave in training.

After cursing his companion, the man in charge pointed out that a rare combination of domination and self-restraint was necessary if a trainer was going to remain in control of both the situation and himself. Fucking a newly captured woman was against the rules. Everything was about forced orgasms, bondage, making the female feel like an object instead of a human being.

Zemar knew better.

"Damn straight he did," the other man remarked as the vehicle stopped moving. "But if you think they're going to slap his wrist you're crazy. With his reputation and seniority, the leaders will probably turn the video into a training tool. Brainwashing 101. Ain't that right, slave? Got you all confused." He punctuated his remark by again trying to insert a finger in her. Fortunately, they'd left her with enough freedom of movement that she wrenched to the side. Still, what if he'd been right? Zemar had deliberately made her think he cared?

Numb, she had to give herself a mental shake before she could take in her surroundings. She couldn't call where the two men had taken her a city. Enclosed by tall wooden fencing that put her in mind of a frontier fort, its size was more in keeping with a village. From what little she could tell as she and her handlers approached, it looked as if the fencing was designed to be added onto as the population grew. As soon as they passed through the massive, solid gate, it closed behind them.

They were now in a large courtyard of sorts with brightly colored seating arrangements set up in the middle of a circular drive. The seating was full of men, most of them ominously sporting black loincloths. The way they conducted themselves left no doubt that these were men of power and position. The arrangements consisted of comfortable and sturdy seats at graduated heights so everyone had a clear view of whatever went on in the drive.

There was enough room between each seat that a trio of naked women, with golden chains dangling from their pierced nipples, were able to circulate, carrying drinks and food-filled trays. All three gave off an unmistakable air of subservience. They kept their eyes downcast, and when a man snapped his fingers, they stopped and allowed him to fondle them.

As if that wasn't enough, each man had at least one woman with him. Most knelt before their Masters, although two stood with their hands behind them and their legs widespread, ready to perform tasks she didn't want to think about. The majority were naked although several wore what looked like chastity belts. All had on collars with chains. None of the women resisted, but their owners kept a tight grip on the chains—in what seemed to be a matter of one-upmanship. The more tightly a man constricted his slave's movements, the more she resembled a beaten animal, the more superior the man's demeanor.

"Quite a display, don't you think?" the man who'd just tried to shove his fingers inside her asked. "Gives you an idea what to expect."

As if proving the point, a Master suddenly grabbed his slave's breast and hauled her closer. Asia shuddered at the thought of naked knees scraping along the cement risers. Despite her obvious discomfort, the woman struggled to comply. The man slapped her face and shoved her head toward his crotch. Trembling, the woman lifted his elaborately decorated loincloth and took his enormous cock into her mouth.

The vehicle she'd been bound to started moving again. This time it bumped over the rocky surface, causing her to nearly lose her balance. If she hadn't been tethered, she would have. As it was, she rocked back and forth, her breasts swaying. Noticing that a number of the men were looking behind her, she glanced in that direction. Another vehicle had pulled into line. It too held a naked, bound, and gagged woman. This one had long white-blond hair and pale blue eyes. Her breasts were enormous—obviously surgically enhanced. Like the women she'd seen in the stadium, this one looked both resigned and excited.

She was still trying to comprehend the moods when a sound alerted her to the arrival of a third display vehicle. This one held two women. One was so fair that Asia wondered if her skin ever saw the sun, while the other was African American. They'd been displayed in such a way that the contrast between them was heightened. Bound so their backs were to each other with rope wrapped around their waists and their buttocks touching, they appeared as halves of a whole. A human yin and yang. The fairer one had a wide-eyed, startled look, while the other seemed to be all but licking her lips behind her gag. Her generous hips exaggerated the vehicle's movements.

Almost as one, the male audience leaned forward. Some applauded while others crudely teased in loud voices about which of them was man enough to master both slaves at once. Although Asia shuddered at the thought of the women's fate, at least she was no longer the lone center of attention.

Once she'd been paraded in front of her potential buyers, her driver positioned her so everyone had an unobstructed view of her. The other vehicles parked nearby, the one holding the two in the middle.

On display.

A tall, distinguished-looking man, dressed entirely in black complete with a cape and mask, stepped in front of the vehicles. He held a small microphone in one hand. In the other was a long, thin whip.

"We have quite a selection here today, gentlemen," he began and the crowd fell silent. Even the groveling women turned their attention to the new captives. A few shivered, probably remembering when they'd been the ones up for sale. Several glared, maybe upset because their standing with their masters was in jeopardy. "We'd hoped to have a larger lot ready for your purchase and amusement, but we can't always have a bumper crop, can we? These two"—he indicated the mismatched pair—"are a true treat and will be sold together. This one"—his whip flicked over the other woman's large boobs—"spent more time in training than we'd hoped because her resistance to her new life took longer than anticipated to break down. Rest assured. Despite her impressive and expensive mammary glands, her surgery didn't result in lessened responsiveness there."

The whip snaked out, expertly landing on both nipples. Shrieking behind her gag, the woman fought her bonds. Several slavers applauded. "She's inordinately protective of her assets, an attitude her new owner can either use to his advantage or beat out of her. She's multi-orgasmic and has been trained to take cock up her ass. She doesn't like it."

That resulted in more applause and several obscene remarks about how much fun forcing her to submit would be. The woman's eyes became even wider. She shot Asia a pleading look.

"And then"—the auctioneer spun toward Asia—"we have an unknown quantity. This one was assigned to Zemar."

Nods and approving muttering followed his announcement.

"I need say no more, do I, gentlemen? She's been handled by the best. The decision was made to terminate the training early. Rest assured, there's nothing defective about the merchandise. The island chose her according to the proven criteria and standards, and she is highly sexed." A flick of the wrist landed the whip between Asia's legs. Grunting, she struggled to close them.

"What happened?" a man called out. "She bite off Zemar's balls?"

"Hell no," another retorted. "More likely Zemar got her so worn out he couldn't do anything more with her. That it, slave?

Getting speared by his instruments 'bout killed you? Nothing left of you 'cept an empty shell?"

"What's the truth?" a third demanded. "There anything left of her?"

"Ah, you want proof that the merchandise is as advertised, do you? Nothing is simpler." With that, the auctioneer held aloft the whip base. His gesture resulted in lewd laughter from the men accompanied by demands that he use it for the demonstration.

Horrified, Asia jerked and twisted in a desperate but futile attempt to escape. She sobbed into her gag when the hooded man stepped onto the platform where she'd been tethered. Although she thrashed from side to side, the bastard clamped his hand over her buttocks with such strength that pain slammed into her. She didn't recover to resist until it was too late. The smooth, warm whip handle slid into her defenseless opening. Gasping into the gag, she rose onto her toes but couldn't free herself from the horrible invasion.

"Give it to her!"

"Start her twisting."

"Off with the gag. We want to hear her scream."

The auctioneer manipulated the makeshift dildo so it spun inside her. Even as she lifted herself as high as she could, she looked down at herself. The man's hand hid what he was doing from her view, but she didn't need to see to know. If that wasn't bad enough, he grabbed hold of a breast and cruelly kneaded it.

This wasn't happening. It wasn't! And yet, she was responding. Not being able to move, exposed, and violated, mirrored her most powerful fantasies. In the past, her imaginary tormentors had been featureless. Now, however, she saw *his* face—Zemar.

Zemar was doing this to her! He knew her limits and desires, dreams and the depth and breadth of her sexuality. Although being fucked by the whip base came close to being painful, the delicate balance between agony and pleasure mesmerized her. Heat and sexual electricity ran through her, and although she hated her weakness, she began trying to fuck the dildo. Lost, she closed her eyes. Her head lolled to the side, and she ceased to live anywhere but in her cunt.

Do me, Zemar! Please, turn me into a slut! Force me, force me to come for you.

Sudden shouts and curses pulled her back into the real world. Opening her eyes, she spotted a tall, powerful figure striding toward her.

Zemar jumped onto the platform and struck the auctioneer so violently that the man fell off, slamming his head on the ground. Ignoring him, Zemar yanked at the straps holding her gag in place. Only then did he pull the improvised dildo out of her. His fingers lingered at her opening, and she had no doubt that he could feel her juices. If her reaction disgusted him—

"She's not for sale," Zemar announced as the auctioneer struggled to sit up. "Not today and not ever."

"Why not?" someone demanded. "You keeping her for yourself?"

He didn't answer.

14

The door closed behind Zemar. Although the room he'd carried her into intrigued her, Asia didn't take her eyes off the man. The air smelled of a curious mixture of spring mornings and sex, adding to her agitation. Because he'd released her chains, she absently massaged her wrists. Her mouth ached from what had been shoved into it, but that was nothing compared to the sensations still pounding in her pussy.

"I should have come earlier." He gestured toward the comfortable looking recliner to her right, indicating he wanted her to sit. She complied because she didn't trust her legs to hold her. Because it was Zemar, she'd do whatever he asked. "But there were things I needed to do first."

"I was going to be sold." She couldn't keep the disbelief out of her voice. "As if I were some animal. If you hadn't shown up—" She shuddered. "It was worse than I expected. And yet the idea excited me. After all those years of dreaming about being part of the lifestyle, it felt right."

Nodding, he positioned himself in front of her. Although her awareness of her nudity threatened to command what little ability she had to concentrate, she rested her hands on the padded armrest and studied his dusky features. He seemed even larger and more imposing than when he'd kept her bound and helpless. "Was there anything you didn't like or understand?" Despite his seemingly casual question, his gaze was intense.

"The way the slaves were forced to act, the chains."

"You believe they're forced?"

"I don't know what else to call it. One woman—her Master made her give him head in front of everyone."

"And if you touched her cunt, you'd have discovered she was all but flooding herself."

Just as I did when the auctioneer mechanically fucked me.

"The island is a world unto itself, Asia. Fantasy and fulfillment. No boundaries."

Although she kept her attention locked on him, she allowed more memories of the past few minutes to surface. She'd been scared because she hadn't been able to move and didn't know what was going to happen to her. At the same time, having years of sexual dreams become reality had been an undeniable turn-on. She'd even enjoyed the crude things the masters had said and being the center of attention—even now she wished she could see how bidding was going.

"This was your fantasy," he prodded. "Something the island identified and tapped into. On the day you lost your job, you made it clear you wanted someone else to take over ownership of your body, someone who understood your secret thoughts and desires. Your deepest needs."

He leaned over and rested his hands on her arm rest. Now she smelled only him, was aware only of him. He became *everything.* "You understand that's why you were chosen to be brought here, don't you? Because you belong on Surrender Island."

Her heart raced. "But you—you said it yourself that I didn't act like any other prisoner you've worked with."

"That doesn't mean you don't want the lifestyle." Not taking his gaze off her, he moved to her side and ran a hand between her legs. She started to clamp her thighs together, then, sighing, relaxed. "You crave this." He stroked her, and she felt her response throughout her loose-as-melted-butter-body. When he transferred his hand to her mouth, she shamelessly licked her juices from his fingers. "You're alone in the world, Asia. Just like me."

"I—I have friends."

"Who will go on with their lives just as you will carve out a new one here."

She thought about sitting up. She just couldn't convince her muscles to make the effort, not with his hands now on her shoulder holding her in place—holding her ready for him.

"That's why I was slow getting to the auction site," he said. "There were things I had to take care of."

"What things?"

"Arranging to have my other slaves sold."

"Your—your other . . ."

Although she tried to straighten, he refused to let her. *I'm yours. Yours.*

"I have two right now, beautiful but simple and highly sexed creatures, who care only about themselves."

Jealousy washed over her. Mindful of his position of power on the island, she struggled to contain it.

Watching her intently, he slid a hand to her throat and closed his powerful fingers around it. "I'm going to collar you. Only I will be able to remove it. It'll stand as partial proof of my ownership of you." Both hands moved to her breasts, covering and flattening them under his palms. "And I may have you pierced here."

Hot currents arced through her.

"Slender rings but not so delicate that they're useless, because I want to be able to easily control you." Sudden, hard pressure on her nipples drove his message home. "Silver or gold links attached to the rings will keep you wherever I want you, however I want you."

As his words fed her imagination, the current took up residence in her pussy. Trembling and excited, she lifted her pelvis toward him. Ignoring her blatant plea, he used his grip on her nipples to bring her to her feet. Instead of releasing her, he forced her onto her toes. Her arms hung useless at her side as she fought the discomfort and her legs threatened to collapse.

"This is my place. I have another, larger one in the jungle, but when I come to the village, I stay here. I bring my slaves so I can participate in the lifestyle and entertainment. I intend to present you, to demonstrate your submissive nature. When I do, you will conduct yourself as a slave, do you understand?"

A slave. His slave. "Yes," she whispered. It took all her self control not to touch his cock. "I understand, Master."

"You don't fully yet." His fingers continued to cut off the circulation in her nipples. "But you will by the time I'm done training you. You want that, don't you?"

Not trusting herself to speak, she nodded. He *rewarded* her by spreading her legs. As she widened her stance, hot juices trailed down the insides of her legs.

"I smell you. If you'd been able to go into the stands today, you'd smell sex on the slaves. If you looked into their eyes, you'd see a submissiveness that goes into their souls."

"I know, Master." *I truly do, now.*

"They live for this." After releasing her nipples, he began his assault on her sex by sliding his fingers over her mons but quickly reached deeper. She felt his fingertips gliding over her slick and hungry opening and started to lift her pelvis toward him. "Have I given you permission to move?" he demanded and pinched her labia.

"No, Master. I—I am sorry."

"Pain will bring you pleasure." He demonstrated with another pinch, which she fought by imagining his fingers, his cock, inside her. "And when I take you naked and restrained to a banquet and command you to kneel at my feet and eat out of my hand, you will love your treatment, won't you?"

Images of what he'd just described made her face heat. An even greater heat hugged her cunt. "Yes, Master."

He flattened his hand over her pussy and pushed, bringing her back to her toes. "Even if you could leave the island, you wouldn't, would you?"

"No, Master."

"Because I'm offering you the life you've long, secretly wanted."

"No, Master. At least that's not all of it."

He released her and stepped back so he could regard her, but because he hadn't given her permission to close her legs, she remained open to him. "Not all?"

Risking his displeasure, she lifted her head so he could see into her eyes. "It isn't just being mastered that I want. I used to imagine it was, that being forced to obey, to have everything revolve around the granting or denial of sexual satisfaction would be enough, but it isn't."

"What else do you want?"

"You, Master. Only you."

"Why?"

"May—do I have permission to touch you?"

A short nod supplied her with the answer. Ignoring his straining cock, she stepped behind him and ran her mouth over his scars. When he shuddered, she brought her tongue into play and slowly, gently bathed the old wounds. Someday, hopefully, he would tell her everything, but just as she was learning to trust him, she'd have to earn the same from him.

Several scars extended to his buttocks. With trembling fingers, she untied his loincloth and let it drop to the ground. She wouldn't always be able to do this; she understood his ability and right to control every aspect of their relationship. But he needed this acknowledgement of his past and the resultant emotional scars. Kneeling, she tongue-bathed his marred buttocks. And moment by moment he relaxed.

"No woman has ever done that."

Not slave, woman. Understanding what the distinction said about the depths of their relationship, she lovingly traced the scars with her fingertips. "Maybe you didn't let them?"

"They didn't care. Their journey, the change from freedom to slavery, sexual satisfaction—that's all that mattered."

"They saw you as a Dom, a master, not a human being, a man."

"Yes."

"I'm not them, Master."

"I know," he said and turned around.

Still on her knees, she looked up at her lord, her lover, her future. Her life.

Not waiting for permission, she lifted his cock and guided it toward her mouth. Inch by slow inch, she brought him into the moist cave of her mouth.

Now his hands were at his sides and hers on his flanks. Her fingers stroked the silken flesh over muscles made of steel and she comprehended, deeply and completely, how strong and powerful her Master was. Her tongue, teeth, throat caressed and teased. Maybe she should have told him she'd never done this before but she suspected he already knew.

For a long time, she tested and rewarded, loved and worshipped. As she did, she learned his taste, his width and length, his capacity for self-control. And she learned that putting his pleasure ahead of her own became everything. Even as her pussy trembled and wept, even as her nipples tightened and her cheeks burned and her blood raced, only he mattered.

And when he began thrusting at her, she took and gave. In her mind, her mouth became her pussy, and she brought him to the brink of climax and beyond. Held his come in her mouth before letting it slip down her throat.

And as she did, she came. Long, strong.

Finally he stood before her, his cock soft and resting. He kept her on her knees with a hand on her head.

"You belong to me." He sounded both masterful and in awe.

"I know, Master."

"And I belong to you."

I know.

The Mask

1

"What's wrong with the rope? Damn it, we don't have all day."

Although she was buck naked, Ferren Cooper planted herself in front of Richard Witson. Ignoring the cameraman and two robe-draped women standing to the side of the set, she glared at Richard. "First, I don't need you yammering at me about time management. I'm a pro."

"A pro who's being a pain in the ass this morning."

Grinning, Ferren wiggled her rear at the middle-aged man. Then she turned serious. "Every porn site on the Net uses red rope. You want Cages to be unique, right?"

"We are unique. For one, we put up with spoiled bitches like you."

"And I'm worth every penny. Look, you wouldn't have hired me if you didn't trust my judgement. I know what I'm talking about."

Richard stared at her over the top of his glasses. "We hired you after you came begging for a job."

It had hardly been like that. Cages hadn't been the first porn business to try to lure her away from Leather 'n Chains. When she'd started out in the business, she'd done whatever Leather 'n Chains owner Philip Blackwell told her to, and as a result had learned an incredible amount about what it took to be a valuable commodity in a cutthroat industry. Unfortunately, among the things she'd learned was that beneath his suave exterior, Philip was a slimeball who treated his models, especially the women, like pieces of merchandise. She even had a couple of whip scars as proof of what he was capable of.

At least he no longer pulled his shit on her. She'd jumped ship and signed on the line with Cages when they'd promised her steady work, health insurance, creative input, and most importantly, respect.

Once she'd been assured of a steady paycheck, she'd blown the whistle on Philip via the underground network. Her mother had pressed her to sign an abuse complaint, but she hadn't wanted the exposure for either herself or her mother.

"Read my contract, Richard." Feeling no embarrassment, she folded her arms under her generous and natural breasts—breasts which had a lot to do with why she was in such demand. "I have as much say as you do on how things are handled, and I'm telling you, red rope strung all over my body is going to make it look like a cheap Christmas tree decorated by morons. Leather's sexier, black leather with large, shiny buckles."

Richard, who went by the title of creative director, took her in from the top of her long, pale-blond hair (not her own color) to her new pink toenail polish. She had no doubt he was contemplating how the leather would look against her all-over tan. Spectacular.

"All right, damn it. You win. This time."

Fifteen minutes later she was all but encased in leather. One strap that turned out to be stiffer and more abrasive than she'd hoped secured her wrists behind her back while another cinched her elbows so close they nearly touched. The same arrangement kept her ankles and knees together. Straps above and below her breasts pushed them out, providing the finishing touch. As always when she was tied up, a hot calm seeped over her. She was no longer responsible for anything. Nothing mattered except responding to her body's carnal messages, living as a sexual creature. At the moment she was lying on her back on a rubberized mat pretending to be terrified as she stared at a closed door in a set resembling a holding cell.

What would her former classmates think if she went to a reunion and pulled out photographs demonstrating what she did for a living? How would she explain to those who'd thought of her as quiet and conservative, a brain with an early-to-ripen body?

My mom told me to do what I love and success will follow. And I love just about everything to do with sex.

Like they'd understand that?

The tall, skinny cameraman pushed in for a close-up of her face followed by a slow pan down her helpless body. She writhed about, moaning in fear to add to the effect. At least the college acting classes she'd taken had paid off. If she hadn't dropped out, she'd have signed up for more for the heck of it.

Work. Get into the scene.

In her mind she was no longer on a set being bathed in bright lights with a camera lens all but checking out her ear hairs. Instead, she'd been captured by pirates and was aboard their ship while it steamed toward some secret island where she'd be secured next to ill-gotten treasures. The pirates might fight over her, but in the end, she'd become the prize of the biggest, most virile of the bunch. Hopefully her captor had heard of a toothbrush, and the island came with soap and deodorant. Otherwise, her time as his sex toy would be a miserable experience.

Fantasy. Think fantasy.

Unfortunately, she'd been drawing on the same daydream or a variation thereof since getting into the business, and images of cowering helplessly at the feet of some powerful man no longer turned her on. These days getting her sex to cream took more and more stimulation, as did conjuring up enthusiasm for showing up for work. Climaxing on cue was hardly a cakewalk.

Concentrate. Earn your keep.

What if *her* pirate had a hook instead of a hand, a smooth, shiny, clean hook with a nicely rounded end which he slowly slid into her defenseless pussy?

The door to the set opened. In walked a man dressed in black complete with a black hood which obscured everything except his eyes. She'd known she'd be working with C.J. so there was no surprise about her *captor's* identity. As riggers went, C.J. was a master at getting women's bodies to respond. Thanks to him and his expertly applied vibrators, she'd climax several times before this session was over and not have to do 90% of the work making it happen.

It didn't get any better, right?

Do you understand, old man? You might not give a damn about your daughter, but countless men jack off watching me. Guess I'm not a throwaway after all.

Falling into her role, she sobbed and tried to wriggle away. Of course the bonds kept her from accomplishing that. Still she kept up the pretense of being terrified.

"Save your strength, slut." C.J. knew his lines all right. His forceful tone added to the role playing. "You belong to me today." He stood over her, his left hand wrapped around a light-weight whip. "And if you don't do what I say, I might never let you go."

Suddenly something she couldn't put a name to pulled her attention off C.J. Hopefully the camera wasn't on her face, but even if it was, no way could she hide the unexpected pull on her senses.

Male, her nerves shouted. *Down and dirty male. Sex appeal to the max.*

Outsiders were hardly ever allowed on a set, but the man lounging against a four by four that was sometimes used to string bondage models up to, was a stranger. Intriguing and yet frightening.

He wore a white dress shirt open at the throat, faded jeans that rode his lean hips and muscled thighs as if they'd been made for him, tennis shoes but no socks. Enough of his arms showed so that she had no doubt he worked out regularly. His flat belly said he watched what he ate and respected his body. He was tall, at least two inches past six feet, a day overdue for a shave and at least a month on the downhill side of needing a haircut. His eyes, like his hair, were black. Piercing. Probing. Rolling over every inch of her. He stared openly, not with the air of a man who was being turned on—although the bulge in his jeans was too large for an at-rest cock—but as if he needed to take his measure of her.

Needed?

What are you looking for?

She'd been stared at by more men than she could count, to say nothing of the nameless tens of thousands of porn site members who paid to watch her bondage videos. One more shouldn't make a difference.

But it did.

Warm fingers slipped between her legs and aimed unerringly for her pussy. "Look at that," C.J. said. "You're so wet you're going to drown me."

Any other time she'd be tempted to remind C.J. that she knew how to get her body to respond—it was after all part of the job requirement—but he was right. Today she wasn't just damp. There was a flood. How had that happened?

Like you don't know?

Even with C.J. trying to spread her legs despite the restraints, she couldn't keep her mind or eyes off the newcomer. Was it just his hard and knowing gaze, the thin slash of his mouth and slightly askew nose, his undeniably hunky body, the arrogant bulge? Or did her subconscious sense something about him that the rest of her didn't?

Assaulted by thoughts of those strong hands roaming over her, she shivered, shuddered.

"Got your attention, have I?" C.J. said. "I would hope to hell so."

But C.J., the script, the rolling camera, the leather holding her prisoner, had nothing to do with her reaction. Only the big man with the black, deep eyes did.

You're what I expected, they said. *What I was looking for.*

2

Moonlight glistened off the tree-surrounded lake. Hidden owls hooted. Their cries blended with the ageless call of frogs. She sat on the edge of the small boat dock, bare legs dangling over the edge. She thought she was naked but couldn't be sure.

He was coming. His boots thudded faintly on the weathered boards, and his weight caused the dock to rock gently.

Standing on suddenly weak legs, she turned toward him. Eyes dark as midnight returned her stare. He was dressed as he'd been before—white shirt, molded-on jeans.

"You have been waiting for me," he said.

"Yes."

"Knowing I would come."

"Yes."

"Do you know who I am?"

She waited until he'd come closer, until only a few feet separated him. She felt him on her skin and in her pussy. Although they were at his side, his hands seemed to stroke her breasts.

"You are my destiny."

"And your Master."

* * *

Something brushed against Ferren's consciousness and pulled her out of her dream. Even as she tried to make sense of what had awakened her, she ached to return to that fantasy lake with the all-too-real man.

She lived alone in a modern condo complete with security guards and a front door that unlocked only for those who knew the code. She had nothing to fear in her quiet and richly appointed bedroom—nothing except for the occasional middle of the night question about what she was going to do with her life once she could no longer pay her bills with her body.

Was the dark man from today's shoot still waiting in her dreams? If only she could sink back into sleep.

She rolled from her stomach to her side and bent her knees. With no sense of embarrassment, she slipped her hand between her legs and touched her labia. One of the benefits of sleeping naked meant she had ready access to herself. If only she wasn't alone in the silk-sheeted bed. If only today's stranger had joined her.

There. Her dream. Just out of reach.

Willing her mind to slide off to that place where reality never overwhelmed, she tried to recall what the owls and frogs had sounded like and what the man's presence had felt like. He'd been speaking to her about—

Something, or someone, tore the sheet off her. She grabbed for the fabric. Instead, she encountered a solid frame. A scream boiled up in her throat, but before it broke free, something was shoved into her mouth.

A ball gag!

As whoever had inserted the rubber ball went about fastening the straps around her head, other hands clamped down on her wrists and held her in place. Once the gag was secure, the strangers—she thought there were three of them—slammed her onto her belly and wrenched her arms behind her. No matter how she thrashed, they effortlessly cinched broad leather strips around her wrists, elbows, ankles, and knees.

Just like yesterday's shoot!

Sweat slickened her skin and stuck her to the bottom sheet. She prayed they'd stop once they'd secured her, but even as she whipped her head from side to side, she spotted the faint outline of cloth descending toward her eyes.

No!

Too-strong fingers clamped down on the sides of her head and held her immobile as someone else blindfolded her. Only then did her captors release her. Despite the blindfold, she knew someone had turned on a light.

"Shit. No wonder he wanted her. What a piece."

"You're sure we need to get her to the island tonight? Can't we take her somewhere and have our fun?"

"Is a little poke and go worth losing your nuts over? Don't be an idiot. It's time to get the package out of here."

He wanted? Island?

"This explains why we're getting paid so well. He knew we'd be tempted."

"Shit. Jack off on your own time. Or better yet, watch some of her videos." She sensed someone leaning close, felt hot hands squeeze her breasts. "Surprise, surprise, slave. From now on you won't be playing at being a bondage slut. Starting tonight, it's the real thing."

Daddy! I need you. For the first time in my life, I need you.

"Shoulders back. Let's show those tits."

Rough hands gripped her nipples and pulled Ferren toward the speaker. The blindfold prevented her from seeing who had hold of her this time, and she had no idea where she was. Her bare feet were on what felt like packed earth, and she heard the mutter of voices, mostly male. Today, fortunately, she wore only handcuffs, but she was still naked—as she'd been since being abducted four days ago.

The endless hours had been a nightmare. Her work often called for her to act as if she'd been kidnapped, and she'd gotten pretty good at displaying her body to advantage while pretending to resist. The real thing terrified her.

When this was over—she refused to say *if*—she'd storm into her mother's office and demand action. It would serve these bastards right to have a hard-nosed attorney from the D.A.'s office take them on

"You're third up. In the meantime, I'm your handler. Just a little more staging and you'll be ready."

"For what? Please—"

Her plea earned her a slap on her ass.

"No questions. How many times do you have to be told? On Surrender Island, you're a piece of meat, a submissive. Get that little fact in your head, and you'll have the ride of your life. Fight and you'll rob yourself of a hell of a lot of fun."

She'd been told that several times while huddled in the cell she'd been locked in nearly full-time since the boat journey to the place her *handlers* called Surrender Island. The ride hadn't taken that long, and she didn't think it had taken them more than an hour to drive her to where the boat waited. But there *was* no island in this part of the state. Someone—she couldn't keep the various men who'd come in and out of her life since her kidnapping straight—had laughed while he explained that Surrender Island didn't exist on any map. Instead they insisted it was a product of vivid imaginations and sexual energy—like that made any kind of sense.

At least she hadn't been alone in what had to have been a prison. The other cells were occupied by equally naked, confused, and scared women. They'd talked when they were alone, and from what she'd learned, she realized they had certain things in common. They were all young and attractive with a fair amount of sexual experience and little inhibition. Except for her, their natures were submissive. Most had only dreamed of giving up control and being mastered but several had experimented with bondage.

When she'd told her fellow prisoners that she was a bondage model/actress, they'd pressed her for more information. They'd quickly lost interest when she explained that she'd chosen that career for reasons that included more than getting paid to have orgasms. With her well-proportioned body and casually sexy posture, she could have been a fashion model—if she'd been willing to exist on one meal a week.

Instead, she'd opted for the porn industry because it paid incredibly well and sometimes under the table. She set her own hours, got to act, and now that she'd severed her relationship with the disreputable Philip, she had creative input. Feedback from the membership about her suggestions left no doubt that they loved the elaborate sets, model interviews, and having stories incorporated into the shoots. The orgasms were a great bonus, but if she'd been treated like a piece of meat, she'd be in some typing pool.

Or in college getting that degree she'd turned her back on.

"You're being sold today," her handler explained, pulling her back to reality. "Got that? Sold. Paid for. No more free room and board. From now on, you're going to be a man's property. Do what he wants, and you won't have many complaints. Play the bitch card and he'll make you wish you were dead."

She already wished she was—or she would if not for the unwanted heat coiling through her. She was used to parading around with nothing on and wearing restraints. What could be exciting about—about being sold? No, she couldn't possibly want this. Surely what she felt was fear greater than any she'd ever experienced.

What do you think of your daughter now, Dad? Oh that's right. You never think of me.

From where she was, she could barely make out what the man she took to be an auctioneer was saying. He spoke so rapidly that his words ran together. Obviously he enjoyed his work. A breeze occasionally brushed her, and she felt the sun's heat. She supposed she should be grateful for being outside after so many hours in the cell. Maybe she would be if she could see.

Mom? Are you looking for me? You always encouraged me to grab life by the balls, but you never thought it would turn out like this, did you? What about Richard? He has to wonder what happened to me. And my friends must be concerned.

But she'd all but fallen off the face of the earth. How could anyone find her if the island didn't exist?

The auctioneer stopped doing his thing. Enthusiastic clapping started, then stopped. He started talking again. Because she didn't dare take a step, she had to stand close to her handler. By the way he kept playing with her breasts and buttocks, she had no doubt that he'd rather be mounting her than standing here.

What if he bought her? What would life under his—or any man's rule be like?

No! Damn it, no!

More applause cut short her thoughts. Her handler slipped something around her throat. She felt leather and heard something click into place. After forcing her to lean forward, he untied her blindfold. Before her eyes could adjust to the sudden light, he snapped a chain onto the collar and started walking, tugging her behind him.

He was leading her toward a raised platform with lounge chairs surrounding it. The chairs were all occupied by men who stared at her as she stumbled up the wooden stairs. Her handler turned the leash over to the auctioneer, a bull of a man with tattooed arms who put her in mind of a professional wrestler. Hating her cowardice, she shrank from him. She'd never felt more naked.

He yanked her close and pulled up on the leash, forcing her onto her toes. She tugged uselessly on her cuffs.

"We have a treat here, gentlemen. Item number three so embraces BDSM that she makes her living at it. She's a porn star specializing in what we all know and love. However, she's also frustrated because she hasn't found a *real* man to give her what she craves."

Looping an arm around her, he turned her to the side and rammed his hand between her legs. He ran his fingers over her labia.

"See." He held up glistening fingers. "Our natural little slut is already good to go. All she lacks is the right stud to show her the way to total surrender. To put her in her place. Because she hasn't been able to find that man on the *outside*, a certain someone arranged to have her brought here. He doesn't have the time to personally tend to her, to break down her inhibitions. Still, he's committed to fulfilling her dreams. Gentlemen, which of you is going to get the honor of working her? Of showing her what a true Dom is about? Think about it. Once her training is over, you're going to have a trophy sub, one who'll earn her keep producing videos for our industry if that's what you want her to do. And who'll follow you around like a bitch in heat. I don't need to tell you it's a rare opportunity for her lucky owner."

Ferren was shaking so she could barely concentrate on what the auctioneer said. Much as she longed to run, she knew better than to try to fight the collar and leash. *Sold. Someone is going to buy me.*

Despite her disbelief, she managed to take note of those staring up at her. There were about twenty men, but they weren't the only ones in the audience. Each was accompanied by a woman— naked and collared females who crouched at the men's feet. A few had their heads between their master's legs and were sucking their cocks but most knelt passively, anxious eyes on those who held their leashes.

Help me! Someone help me. I don't want—

The auctioneer hauled her to a post and deftly fastened her leash to it via a ring near the top. Pressure on her neck forced her onto her toes. Still, she willed herself to look over her shoulder.

One of those men would soon own her—or at least he'd think he did. But he'd be wrong. She'd never belong to another human being. Never!

"Put our sweet slut out of her sexual misery," the auctioneer boomed. "Get her started on the road to surrender."

Loud laughter accompanied the comment. The auctioneer grabbed her buttocks and forced her around until the potential bidders had a clear view of her breasts, belly, buttocks, legs. By grinding a fist into the small of her back, he forced her to thrust her pelvis forward. "She's a prize, gentlemen. Raw and wild and spoiled according to her mentor but full of promise. And here's a real plus. Those are her own tits." He pinched both nipples, forcing her to cry out. "Who wants to open with ten grand?"

A human being might spend ten thousand dollars on her? Tears burned, blurring her vision. Still, something in the audience caught her attention. No. Not something. Someone.

Black eyes stared back at her and forced her to return to the day when she'd insisted on being restrained with leather straps instead of red rope.

Oh God, the man who'd watched her the day before she'd been kidnapped!

As the bidding went from ten to twelve thousand, she noted that he alone didn't have a naked woman at his command. He sat straight and still, taking in the action while keeping his hot gaze on her. She couldn't read anything in his expression and couldn't guess his mood. Because of where he sat, she didn't know whether the sight of her strung up like some newly captured wild animal had aroused him.

Tension seemed to have taken up permanent residence inside her since she'd been spirited away from her apartment but looking at him added yet another layer.

Only, what she now felt wasn't fear.

She was being turned on!

By his eyes.

3

As she was being led down the stairs, Ferren's legs nearly gave out. She'd just been bought for twenty-one thousand dollars by the black-eyed man!

"Don't blow it," her handler warned. Although he held onto her leash, he also gripped her elbow, steadying her. "One thing you gotta get through your skull. You have no rights on this island, nothing except the right to be what you were designed to be, a sub and a sex slave."

No! I'm not! This is a mistake, a terrible—

As if reading her mind, he swatted her backside. When they reached level ground, he released her elbow, slung her leash over his shoulder, and turned his back on her, forcing her to shuffle after him. Dampness still clung to her legs, but the unwanted excitement she'd felt earlier had died. What had come over her? She'd never gone into heat because of the way some arrogant bastard filled his jeans. So he had remarkable eyes. Big deal!

Her handler led her into something resembling a corral complete with posts driven into the ground at random distances. Two women were already inside with their arms lashed behind them and gagged with rope strands that forced their lips apart. Their ankles were chained so close together they could barely move, and their leashes had been snapped onto the posts.

Hating this man, she nevertheless didn't fight as he hauled her to one of the posts. Even if she got free, where would she go? What could she do with her hands cuffed behind her? He secured her to the post and pulled a length of rope out of his pocket. She started to twist away, then stopped. No matter how much she fought, he'd eventually win. The rope he forced between her teeth tasted like old burlap but at least it didn't have any rough edges. Feeling the ankle restraints close around her flesh unnerved her more than the gag did because they were metal and required a key to release.

"Your Master will come for you when he's good and ready. In the meantime, think about how you're going to show him you intend to behave."

Behave? Like a chained-up dog? Never!

Master? I have a Master?

The sun beat down on her, and the top of her head was being burned. If only she could sit down, but the leash and collar kept her in place. Another five women—slaves—had joined her and the other two. She'd made fragile friendships with all of them while they'd waited in their prison cells, but now everyone was gagged; there was no talking.

Someone gasped. Turning as best she could in the direction the woman was staring, she saw that a number of men were coming toward them, making a show of opening the corral gate, chatting and laughing as they approached. She strained to make out her *owner*, but there was so much to concentrate on and comprehend.

A sudden presence caused her to spin to the right. At least

she tried to. Unfortunately, the leg hobbles got in the way, and she stumbled. A solid male body kept her from falling. Sun-warm, powerful arms briefly embraced and then straightened her. He released her.

"I'm taking you to my cabin," the dark eyed man who'd paid for her announced. His voice raked over her flesh and seeped into her veins. "Then we'll begin."

Begin what?

He must not give a damn about her because he didn't so much as look at her. Instead, he spoke to her handler. "I've got my Jeep, but she's going to walk. Get her ready, starting with something to drink."

"What about her papers? The bill of sale."

His broad shoulders under yet another white shirt shrugged. "Bring them when they're ready. I want to leave."

"Yes, sir. You don't need anything else?"

"No." Spinning toward her, he gripped her shoulders so tight she winced. "We're doing it my way, got it. From now on, I control the script. I can and will change it whenever I want, as I see fit. And when I'm done with you, you're going to bow down and thank me."

Never!

"I can guess what you're thinking. That you have a damn good idea what's coming and can hardly wait. But it's not going to be that easy. This is *my* movie. I'm director, producer, and male lead. Or should I say the villain."

At that he released her shoulders but only so he could close his hands over her breasts. He cupped them in his rough paws and kneaded sensitive flesh. Her nipples hardened while the rest of her felt weak. She dropped her gaze in a desperate attempt not to let him know what she was feeling. He twisted her nubs until she squeaked behind the gag.

Help me. Someone please help me.

Dad? Damn you for abandoning me.

Thank goodness the black-eyed man—she couldn't bring herself to think of him as her Master—hadn't heard her plea. If he had, he'd believe she was a heartbeat away from terror. Although she was undeniably off balance and alarmed, right now at least terror wasn't complicating things. She suppose she could credit the countless times she'd let herself be restrained.

Either that or this dominating male had hypnotized her.

"I own you." His fingers tightened. "You've been bought and paid for. And here that's all that matters."

Ferren couldn't say how much time had passed since her Master had made his proclamation until now. After releasing her breasts, he'd stood back and watched, saying nothing, while her handler prepared her for travel.

The shorter man had produced a length of soft cotton rope. After looping it twice around her waist, he'd drawn the remaining length between her legs and fastened it to the rope at the small of her back. She'd fought when he tightened the crotch rope, but her struggles hadn't done her any good. Even when she stood still, the cotton pressed against her pussy lips, constantly reminding her of the erotic confinement.

A lesson learned. All those sessions with a crotch rope in front of a camera had been make-believe. This wasn't.

Although she had no use of her hands, her handler further restricted movement by lashing her arms together above the elbow. She'd been tied like this countless times as part of her job, but before she'd always known she could, and would, protest if the position proved painful. Now, no one would listen to her. No one cared.

Weak. Helpless. At Master's mercy.

Although the collar remained around her neck, at least the leash had been removed. She might be more grateful if the man who treated her like a side of beef hadn't fastened one end of yet another rope to where the crotch and waist ropes joined.

Now whenever someone tugged on the loose end, she'd feel the strain in her crotch.

Her once again hot and oozing crotch.

At a nod from her handler, her owner pushed away from the railing he'd been leaning against and slowly, appraisingly approached. He checked the positioning and tension of her various ropes, spending the most time making sure she could breathe freely despite the rope gag.

"Good job."

"It should be. I've been doing this long enough. You're new to Surrender, aren't you? I haven't seen you before."

"I only recently learned about it—and what it offers a man like me." Grabbing the just-created crotch leash, he tugged, forcing her to stumble toward him. He kept the pressure up until her shoulder pressed against his side.

"Like they say, money can buy everything."

Her handler's words echoed through her, distracting her from what her new Master had in mind. Another, rougher tug on the leash had her hurrying after him. He walked with his back to her, the rope over his shoulder as if he was leading a docile cow. Instead of taking her somewhere to be branded or milked or turned into steaks, he led her to a blood-red open Jeep. The vehicle fit the man, rugged and durable, strong.

To her horror, he tied her leash to the rear bumper. *Oh shit*, she thought. He was going to force her to run after the vehicle!

He climbed in behind the wheel. The Jeep roared to life. He glanced back at her. "This rig is my pride and joy. I'm not letting some slave ride in it." He shifted into first. "Time for you to learn what it is to be a piece of property."

At first, the Jeep barely moved, but it soon picked up speed, forcing her to walk at a brisk pace. As they left the compound that had been her world since her abduction, her stomach clenched. Much as she'd hated it, it had become a known quantity. Now there was only the encroaching jungle. And her owner.

A longtime jogger—job security depended on a fit, and sensual body—she had no trouble matching the pace he set. Once she'd become as accustomed as possible to the tension in her arms and between her legs, she started taking in her world. This was hardly a deserted or desert island. Instead, it was alive with vegetation, birds, insects. She imagined it was home to a variety of wildlife, hopefully none of them meat-eating. Except for the lack of stifling humidity, it reminded her of parts of Florida which she'd visited a number of times because she enjoyed travel. The Jeep was traveling down a single-lane road made of packed sand surrounded by trees and other rich growth.

She'd been dropped into the middle of Tarzan's jungle!

Was the man hauling her into his world a modern-day Tarzan?

A wave of electric heat sparked in her pussy and spread out to encompass her. As a child she'd dreamed of joining Tarzan in his well-constructed tree house. She'd been unclear about what they'd do—at that age sex wasn't even on her radar scope—but she imagined she'd have monkeys and apes for companions. She'd dine on delicious fruit, travel from place to place by clinging to Tarzan's back as he swung from sturdy vines. He'd bring her endless wildflowers and they'd bathe under waterfalls while iridescent fish swam around their feet. She'd ride on the backs of elephants and weave brilliant feathers into her hair.

Reality was far different.

Reality was spelled out in ropes and handcuffs and a primitive response to the strands that trapped and stimulated her sex.

Or, if she was being honest, the dark man who'd become her world was responsible for her heat and energy.

The sound of another vehicle jerked her out of her thoughts. Her heart leaped. Could help be coming her way?

Her owner—how she hated the word—pulled over to the

side of the road and stopped. Cheeks flushed, breath coming fast, she positioned herself as close to the road as possible. *Please! Please see me. Stop this insanity!*

Except for its smaller size, the other vehicle bore a strong resemblance to a military vehicle. The windows were down, rap music blaring. A man who appeared to be in his forties was behind the wheel. When he drew alongside, he stopped and leaned out the window. She couldn't hear what he and her owner were saying but didn't need to because before long the newcomer pointed at her and nodded in approval. After staring at her for a few seconds, he gave her owner a thumbs-up sign. Then he started moving again.

As he passed, she glanced in the back seat. Two bound and blindfolded women leaned against each other as if seeking comfort.

4

Mayer White pulled up in front of the cabin that had been re-
served for him and killed the engine. After getting out, he
walked back to where the woman waited. He knew her name.
Hell, it had been drummed into him. But if he was going to
play this the way his employer wanted, he needed to think of
her as a piece of property, a subject, a slave. To play his role and
earn the money he needed more than he wanted to think about.

It wouldn't be easy.

He told himself things would be different if pride and self-
respect didn't dance in her eyes. If he'd been someone other
than who he was, he might not have understood what he was
looking at, but years spent turning himself into a man who bore
no resemblance to the frightened and lonely boy he'd once
been had taught him to recognize the emotions.

And it wasn't just her defiance despite being all but hog-tied
that had him against the proverbial wall. The broad was a
looker, a fox. Sensual didn't say near enough. Neither did sexy.
She oozed everything that was female though her pores. The
way she moved carved deep and unwanted inroads in him.

It had to be the situation. Sure as hell he wasn't attracted to more than what she meant to him moneywise. If he cared about her, he'd have called his employer a sick bastard and refused to pull off that damn stunt with the Jeep and lead rope. But not getting close to her meant he'd be able to follow the meticulously thought out script he'd been given.

When he untied the leash from the Jeep and tugged on it, she backed away. Interesting. He'd thought she'd already be deep into the scene, maybe even dropping to her knees so she could rub her cheek against his cock as he'd seen happen in Internet sites devoted to BDSM. But for a deep down submissive—which he'd been assured she was—she was doing a hell of a good job of resisting.

Fine. He could play the game too. Despite the effort.

Because he'd watched a mind-numbing amount of bondage films in preparation for this gig, he knew what was expected of him. Just the same, mauling a woman he hadn't so much as introduced himself to felt, what, wrong?

Patience. Patience, White. This is the only time you have to do something like this. Once you've collected your paycheck, you become your own boss. Never forget that, your own boss. Besides, she wants it. Might as well enjoy yourself.

Even if I can't look myself in the mirror?

The screened-in front porch with its comfortable wicker furniture and slowly rotating ceiling fan was his favorite part of the one bedroom cabin, but he didn't give his *slave* time to study it. Maybe he would once he'd given her the ordered lessons in confinement.

Because locking doors on Surrender Island wasn't necessary unless there was someone another someone wanted to keep inside, he simply turned the knob and hauled her into the dark interior. He'd closed the blinds over the two living room windows before leaving today so his slave's new home would remain a mystery to her until he decided to change things.

Not yet. First he needed to wrap her in the world that was Surrender Island.

She held back, prompting him to grab her hair and haul her to his side. The instant he did, he cursed. Damn! He felt like a randy sixteen year old around this particular lush body. Hiding his reaction from her and his cock in his pants wasn't going to be easy.

The trek through the jungle had caused her to sweat. Her damp flesh and earthy scent gnawed at him. Her slight tremor was no doubt a response to her circumstances.

Response?

Shit, yes.

Teeth clenched, he shoved her onto the couch. No reason to put off getting down to cases. When he'd started watching those damnable bondage videos his employer had sent, he'd gotten such a hard-on that he'd had to jack off. But after awhile, he'd stopped lusting over naked and nubile female bodies—sensory overload?—and started concentrating on tricks and technique. He'd finally gotten to the point where the whole scene bored him. After all, what was so damn exciting about watching play-acting women on the boob tube?

The problem today was his slave wasn't play-acting and she wasn't on TV. She was a living, breathing woman, naked and sexy as hell.

And he wasn't about to forget that she wanted what he was going to do to her.

His eyes were adjusting to the gloom, making it possible for him to again study his prize. Because he'd shoved her hard enough to knock her off balance, she was leaning back, her spine supported by the back of the couch. She was trying, less than successfully, to keep her knees together.

She loves it, needs it. And once she has a true Dom and truly understands what it is to be a Sub, it'll show in every scene she does. Then she'll really be able to make some major money doing what she loved.

A harsh chuckle boiled up in his throat. She wasn't the only one motivated by money. He'd held out for an obscene salary before agreeing to come to Surrender Island and *buy* the broad. Under other circumstances, they might spend time discussing what they intended to do with their respective windfalls.

Weary of his thoughts, he stalked toward the naked woman. She tried to shrink away, but he easily grabbed her knees and pressed down, separating her legs at the same time. If his cock had been any larger, it would have struck his chin.

When she stopped struggling and stared up at him through chocolate eyes that had mesmerized him from the first time he'd seen them, he slid a hand under the crotch rope at her belly and pulled. Mumbling into her gag, she lifted her ass off the couch.

Her pale hair clung to her throat and challenged him to caress it. The contrast between the nearly transparent strands and her dark eyes and deep all-over tan was nothing short of spectacular.

Still gripping the rope, he ran his other hand along her trapped labia. She'd soaked both it and herself.

"You love it, don't you?" He worked the rope to the side of her, found her opening, and rested his thumb against it. "Fight all you want, slave. Curse and try to kick. This tells the truth."

She shook her head repeatedly, eyes never leaving his. Two of his foster mothers had told him that he had the devil's eyes because they were so dark. He wondered if she would say the same thing. Wondered if he'd ever ask her.

"They say dreams sometimes come true. But then the same thing can be said about nightmares. Which is this, slave? A dream or a nightmare?"

Her thighs trembled from the effort of keeping the crotch rope from digging into her. Reluctantly leaving her sex, he caressed her thigh with his wet fingers. As he did, his cock all but poked a hole in his jeans. "You're strong. In great shape.

Unfortunately for you, I have no intention of letting you take advantage of those firm muscles. And if you kick or otherwise fight me, I'll punish you." He jerked up on the rope, forcing her to arch even more. "This is lesson number one. Who knows how many there'll be, or how many you'll beg me for."

Eyes burning holes in him, she thrashed her head from side to side.

"Now, now, is that any way to show your gratitude? You need some lessons in subservience."

Releasing her thigh, he reached for her throat intending to remind her of her collar. Just then his cell phone rang. They both jumped.

"Don't move," he warned. He glanced at the readout. "And don't bother trying to yell for help because this particular caller approves of what's happening—and is going to happen."

"What do you want?" he barked when he picked up the receiver.

"I told you to call me," the man on the other end said.

"I was going to."

"When?"

"When I'm not occupied."

"Do you have her?"

"Oh yes, she's bought and paid for. Hospitality's a little thin here, but she'll get used to it."

"What has she said?"

Something in the man's tone caught Meyer's attention. He didn't sound curious so much as concerned. "As you ordered, she's gagged. We haven't had a conversation."

"Don't let her speak."

"Don't tell me what to do."

"As long as I'm paying you, I'll say whatever I damn well please. You know what you're supposed to do, right?"

"Yeah, I know." Funny, in the past the conversation had been about how much Ferren Cooper longed to bury herself in the BDSM lifestyle. What was this crap about being ordered to jump to his employer's tune?

"You better. I picked you because you're a bastard. You don't care about anyone."

Was that true? He'd been called a bastard enough times and knew how to seal himself off from emotion, but looking into Ferren's too big, frightened eyes, he wasn't sure he'd succeed this time.

Or whether he wanted to.

"What did you call for? I have work to do."

"I want to make sure you'll be filming everything. And e-mailing the footage to me."

"You're a sick bastard."

"I might be a bastard, just like you. Maybe I am sick; I don't give a damn. But first and foremost, I'm rich. Rich enough to pay for what I want—and give you the stake you need. Don't ever forget that."

I won't, damn it.

Philip Blackwell listened to the sound of the slamming receiver, then leaned back in his leather recliner and stared at the mirrors on his office ceiling. Broads were used to bedroom mirrors. Hell, most of the ones he brought here spent as much time staring at their reflections as they did humping him—at least they did until he decided to show them the errors of their way.

They eventually learned, all of them. By the time he was done with them, they no longer whined about working conditions and salary or the extracurricular activities he insisted they participate in when he entertained his wealthy clients and business associates. A few learned the hard way, and two never had gotten it through their thick skulls.

And then there was Ferren Cooper. The bitch had done more than quit on him and go to work for his number one competitor. She'd shot off her mouth. As a consequence, getting his hands on fresh meat had become damn near impossible. He'd cursed her and threatened to get her fired. That's when the bomb had hit. She'd told him who her mother was.

When he'd dumped that piece of information on his lawyer, the slicker had damn near quit. He would have if Leather 'n Chains hadn't been his highest paying client. After making sure no one was listening, his lawyer had offered up a simple, and fascinating option. Despite her boast, Ferren Cooper was probably an embarrassment to her legal eagle of a mother. If she made good on her threat to blab to the press and the press learned she was a *sick* bitch who truly and completely got off on whips and chains and groveling before anything with a penis, no one would take her seriously. Not even her mother.

Great idea! The idea of the century.

By the time the patsy he'd hired to work Ferren was done with her—and had the pictures to counter anything she said against him—she'd be laughed out of town.

Unless he decided on option number two.

Smiling faintly—smiling was rare for him—he stood and walked over to his well-supplied bar.

White might have played macho rebel with him a few minutes ago, but he'd had him investigated. He knew the man's weak points. Number one, he was a loner who didn't give a damn about anyone.

5

"So far you've gotten off easy."

Ferren licked her lips, working feeling back into her mouth now that she was no longer gagged. She wore ankle restraints and her owner had fastened a slender chain to her collar. The other end was secured to a wall ring, restricting her movement to a five-foot radius. Thankfully her arms were no longer behind her. He'd positioned them so they were at her belly and connected to the damnable crotch rope. She didn't need to have it spelled out; he intended to keep her awareness of her sexuality on high.

She wasn't about to tell him that just looking at his solid form with those densely muscled thighs and powerful shoulders was enough.

"Easy?" She kept her voice low. No point in antagonizing him.

"At the moment we're only playing half the game."

She had no idea what he was talking about, but had no doubt that he'd explain when he wanted to. Now that he'd opened the blinds, the cabin's exterior surprised her. She'd expected to be taken to some primitive structure complete with bugs and sagging bed—if there was one. Instead, whoever had designed this place hadn't had to cut corners. The furnishings in the living room, which was the only room she'd been in, were top quality, the cream carpet plush. There were a few landscape pictures on the walls but otherwise no personal touches. Under other circumstances, she would have loved the two large windows with their expansive views of the tropical vegetation. She had no doubt that she'd be unable to break the glass.

From the four-poster bed she'd spotted through a door leading to what she guessed was the bedroom to the support post in the middle of the main room, the place was designed with restraint in mind. Metal rings had been placed at random in the walls, ceiling, even in the floor. One corner of the room was taken up with a cage no more than four feet high.

Another corner held a desk and chair with a state-of-the-art laptop. There was also a video camera setup that rivaled what Cages had. She knew enough about such operations to realize the camera functioned both as a hand-held and fastened to a tripod that allowed the camera to rotate and pick up different angles. There was also a big screen TV. If this was indeed an island, TV service and Internet access must come via satellite.

Two closed doors briefly held her attention. She hoped they led to a bathroom and a kitchen.

The man had handled her as if she was little more than a dog he intended to keep chained, his touches quick, efficient, impersonal. Watching him insert a disk in the DVD player, she tried to determine something, anything about him. Tall, dark, and broad shouldered, he indeed was in admirable physical shape, his movements smooth, almost fluid.

Insanely she wondered if he carried that effortlessness into fucking. She couldn't imagine he didn't know the impact he had on women, and yet there was nothing overtly sexual about the way he handled himself—and he hadn't forced himself on her, yet. Naturally sexy pretty much said it.

Seeing him walk toward one of the closed doors reinforced her opinion of a man who wore his sensuality as if he'd been born to it. He disappeared, leaving her alone. Before she could wrap her mind around the concept of being by herself, he returned carrying a water bottle. He held it to her lips. Gratitude nearly forced out a 'thank you', but the reality of her dependency on him kept her silent. Still, she felt humbled by his kindness. When she'd finished drinking, he ran the back of his hand over her cheek. The unexpected touch weakened and warmed her. She might have tried to kiss him if he hadn't spun away and picked up the remote.

"Watch."

The TV sprang to life, and there she was. Because there'd been so many, she wasn't sure which shot this one had been. She recognized the dungeon set as one used on Leather 'n Chains. The damn place had always been either too hot or cold and the air stale. In this particular scene, she was on her knees before some man with a ridiculous number of tattoos and one of the biggest cocks she'd ever seen. Naked except for the clips on her breasts, she stared up at the man as he slowly circled her. Despite her position, she was rather proud of the way she'd thrown herself into the shoot. She hadn't been hired for her acting ability, but she definitely looked both apprehensive and excited.

The tattooed rigger stopped behind her and grabbed her hair, jerking her head back. She made a feeble attempt to free herself, but he easily looped a rope around her upper arms and secured her. After making sure the restraints weren't going to loosen, the rigger pushed her onto her belly.

Now she remembered! Damn Philip Blackwell. As they were setting up the shoot, she'd told him in no-nonsense terms that having her weight on her boobs while wearing clips would hurt like hell. But had he listened? Of course not. Instead he'd interrupted to point out, as he'd done before, that because of competition from other porno sites, he had to keep things edgy. If she didn't like the working conditions, she could walk. He'd deduct space rent, rigger, cameraman, and lighting technician's salary from her paycheck. Then he'd sue her for breach of contract and give her address and phone number to members who expressed their outrage at not getting footage they'd paid for. Knowing he wasn't bluffing, she'd given in.

Her owner had sat down in the recliner. Although her legs ached from the long walk, she stayed on her feet while she split her attention between the bondage scene and the man who'd taken over her world.

"Think you can back talk me, do you, you slut." The tattooed rigger pressed against her back, keeping her in place. "Putting me down in front of my boss. I'll show you."

That speech had been part of the script. Her role had called for her cursing him, but because she hadn't been comfortable with the profanity Philip insisted on, she'd done more grunting and groaning than anything else. The rigger had slapped her buttocks a number of times, turning it red.

Afterward, she'd confronted Philip, reminding him that her contract called for no marks. So walk, Philip had taunted in his usual way. It wasn't like he couldn't replace her with any number of broads, all of them better looking whose climaxes were so wild that the site's membership flooded the inbox with approving e-mail.

How she'd hated working for Philip! No matter that she'd earned every penny and judging by membership feedback was Leather 'n Chains' most popular model. Philip always pushed the limits. The sick creep got off on pain and extreme bondage. He wanted his models scared and compliant.

Scared and compliant.

Was that her now?

Instead of looking at the man who said he owned her, she stared at the TV screen. The rigger had placed a rope around an ankle so he could bend her knee back, keeping it that way by securing her ankle to her wrists. He moved out of camera range. The lens zoomed in for a close-up of her exposed pussy. Although she managed to wriggle off her belly, easing the pain in her breasts, she had been enough of a professional to keep her pussy within view.

The rigger returned, a bullet with a remote control in his hand. "You're had it too much your way, Zena. Yelling at me when you don't get what you want. Well, you're going to get to come all right, over and over again."

The dialogue was corny, the thinnest thread of a plot dangled around scenes of sexual submission and punishment. Although she knew the membership got off on simulated and sometimes not simulated whippings, she'd never been comfortable with that scene and had crossed it out of her contract with Philip—not that he'd paid any attention.

Damn it, she was an intelligent and independent woman who loved sex—the good parts like climaxing until she darn near passed out. She didn't get any satisfaction from whips. True, those sessions were invariably followed up with vibrators and hand jobs that led to nerve-humming climaxes. But being subjected to pain for the benefit of money—paying perverts had left her with ever increasing feelings of self-disgust.

As her image on the TV squirmed to get away, she glanced at her owner. He was sitting back in his chair, intently studying the scene, his features sober.

Not turned on, sober.

"You'll be begging me to let you go before this is over," the rigger announced as he positioned himself between her legs. He placed a hand over her cunt and separated her lips. Holding up the bullet for the camera, he pasted on a phony smile. "Open up, bitch. I've got a present for you."

Much as she hated having to watch as the rigger slipped the bullet in and secured it via a crotch rope, she had to understand why her owner was showing her this. By the time this scene had been shot, she'd made the decision to shove her resignation in Philip's face. As a result, she'd thought she'd be able to disassociate herself from this particular sexual manipulation—right up to when the rigger had kicked the vibrations into high gear.

Damn Philip! She'd told him plain and clear that she didn't want to lose control because some silver bullet forced her to press down on her pinched breasts! She'd been willing to have her excitement filmed, but she'd made it clear that pain wasn't her thing.

Had Philip listened? Of course not. Unknown to her, he'd instructed the rigger to give her a ride to end all rides. As a result, by the time he'd finally pulled the bullet out of her, she'd climaxed at least three times one time after another, loudly. The scene had ended with the rigger removing the nipple clamps to reveal her red and abraded flesh.

Now, to her disbelief, she was staring at what had happened once she'd recovered.

"Damn you!" she'd yelled with tears of pain in her eyes. "That's not what we agreed on."

"Sorry," Philip said from out of camera range. "Guess I misunderstood."

"The hell you did. Get these ropes off me. I've had it! Had it."

"You became a bitch when you didn't get your way, didn't you," her owner said, tearing her attention off the TV.

Unnerved by his use of the past tense, she studied him.

"Why were you a porn star?" he asked.

Were? "None of your business."

"Everything about you is now my business—as is your body."

She shuddered and fought the need to close her eyes so she could regain her courage. "Why are you doing this to me?"

"You'll learn, eventually."

"I have money put away, more than you—you paid for me.
I'll give—"

"I'm not interested. And whether you're willing to admit it
now, neither are you." As he stood and walked toward her, another shiver raced through her. Despite her best effort to stand
her ground, she tried to back away. "Don't, Ferren." He
grabbed the crotch rope.

"What do you want? What kind of sick game—"

"This isn't a game. Not any longer."

She hated him! Absolutely hated him! And yet something
about him touched her human to human. Maybe it was the
loneliness in his eyes—a restless seeking she sometimes spotted
when she looked at her own reflection. "What do you mean,
not any longer? What has it been up until now?"

For a heartbeat she believed the question had caught him off
balance. Then he dragged her next to him, and his heat reached
her through his shirt. After years of playing at bondage and
BDSM, acting had become reality. This big man with his too-
dark eyes and powerful physique was indeed her universe.

"What—what are you going to do to me?"

"Whatever I want."

"Hurt me?"

He didn't answer.

"Rape me?"

More silence.

"Kill me?"

"No."

Ordering himself not to think, Mayer took in his surroundings. On the heels of her nervous questions and his short answers, he'd silenced her by gagging her with a wooden dowel
held in place with leather straps. Philip had assured him that

she got off on not being able to communicate, but her eyes and body language were telling him something different.

The first time he'd been locked up, at thirteen, his moods had ricocheted between fury and fear. After a while, he'd learned to submerge those needs behind a hard-ass exterior. His gut-level guess was she was doing the same thing, looking for the balance between having her world turned on end and her deep-rooted need to be helpless and controlled.

Who the hell are you kidding? What rational human being wants to be a slave?

Damn it, Mayer, just because you don't understand people like this doesn't mean they don't exist.

Leaving her to watch silently, he checked the settings on the video camera. He was uncomfortable with having what was about to happen be recorded on film because there was always the chance it would wind up in the wrong hands. If it did, he could kiss his about-to-be-realized career good-bye. But if he didn't do this one last thing as a hired gun of sorts, the future he'd long dreamed of and needed for his sanity and self-respect would never happen.

Hell, she wasn't the only one who was trapped.

Returning to her, he removed the crotch rope. She sighed behind the gag but whether in relief or disappointment he couldn't tell. When he unlocked the ankle restraints, she stood her ground, reminding him of a stray dog that keeps going by sheer will. As a ward of the juvenile justice system, he'd mucked out cages for the county's animal control facility. At first he'd hated the job, particularly having to wear coveralls that identified him as a criminal. But after a while he'd become immune to the smell of shit and urine and had tapped into the vibes coming from lost and abandoned dogs. Some of them had relentlessly attacked their cages but most became resigned to their lot in life—and had demonstrated a beautiful capacity for affection.

In time his request to exercise the *inmates* had been granted, and he'd taken countless mutts for countless walks. He'd talk to them and tune into to what they had to say in return. And although he never told anyone, he'd fallen in love with many of them. He held them when they trembled, rejoiced when some were reunited with their families or adopted, cried hidden tears when he led others to where they were put to sleep.

Don't go there. Damn it, don't go there. Just do your job. Get paid and go on with your life.

6

The video camera was running.

The rubber dildo was large but not the biggest she'd ever seen. Maybe she should take comfort from that fact, but under the circumstances, she couldn't. Knowing it also functioned as a vibrator made it more imposing, but what truly unnerved her was the question of how her owner intended to use it on her.

Why hadn't she asked him his name? She needed to make him human, somehow.

Because she knew she wouldn't win this battle, she hadn't fought when he positioned her over the dildo which was at a right angle to the floor and secured her ankles to two floor rings that kept her legs apart. The dildo pointed at her crotch.

Once he set her up the way he wanted and secured her over the black rubber, he stepped back, studying her. She stood with her legs immobilized, arms behind her, naked and sweating, silenced. Her hair fell forward, and she tossed her head back, nearly losing her balance. Effectively warned not to move, she straightened and stared back at him.

What did he see? A naked and helpless woman, yes, but was there more to it than that?

Why was he doing this? She would have understood being raped or forced to give him head, but what did he hope to get out of manhandling her this way? Maybe he was a disgusting pervert, but something she took to be instinct told her it wasn't that. With his healthy body, he wouldn't have any trouble getting a woman to jump into his bed. Why would he want to do *this* when he could easily get the real thing?

Who are you? What's driving you? And why do I feel like a newborn?

"What about what happened in the clip made you so angry?" He remained several feet away, his well-honed body speaking to her despite the distance. "You got to come. You love coming, right?"

She refused to acknowledge the question.

"I'll get my answer. And so will you. By the time we're done, your body will have told both of us the truth."

Don't do this. Please, don't do this!

"No little bullet this time. And you have no say in what happens—nothing to do except experience."

Please, no.

Although she drew blood from biting on her lower lip, she couldn't still her tremors. Stepping close, he clamped his hands over her hips. "Anticipation? Excitement?"

She violently shook her head.

"Fear then?"

A nod.

"I'm not going to hurt you." Taking hold of her chin, he forced her to return his hard stare. "You will *not* be hurt. Trust me."

Trust?

The continued pressure on her hip made her wonder if he

was trying to force her to stop shaking. "You want this. Think about that and nothing else. This is what you crave."

Something sparked between them, a connection she hadn't expected, told herself she didn't want, and didn't know what to do with.

But trying to understand would have to wait because he released her and turned his attention to the length of rubber aimed at her pussy.

He started guiding it toward her. Looking down as best she could, she tried to stand on her toes, but he'd cinched her ankles so she couldn't. The hard and unrelenting object brushed her labia, then retreated. She sucked in a breath.

Start the joining. Take me where I've never been—walk each step with me.

Reaching between her legs, he separated her labial lips and repeatedly stroked her. She'd expected his touch to be harsh, even painful. But although his fingers were callused, he understood the meaning of the word gentle.

Ripped from her world, bound and naked, forcefully silenced, she was desperate for any hint of kindness or humanity.

Those things existed in this stranger's hands.

At any time he could make a lie of what his touch had demonstrated, but she'd take this moment. This simple act of kindness.

Her mind hummed. She drew comparisons between what she was experiencing and what it felt like to be falling asleep. The world slipped away. She connected with herself, with her body. It spoke to her of primitive pleasures and wild cravings. In her fantasy, he hadn't forced himself on her after all. Instead, she'd willingly turned herself over to him because he knew what she needed far better than she did.

Her legs felt hot and both weak and strong. Any second she'd collapse. At the same time, she half believed she could stand like this forever, her sex exposed to him, his rough, wet fingers gliding over her most intimate places. He touched her clit with a quick, furtive contact, then returned to caress her hot and swollen labia. The need for more grew stronger, stronger. Surrendering to the powerful, pulsing craving, she flexed her knees and lowered herself a few precious inches, begging him with her body to penetrate her. To grant her that elusive and vital thing called relief.

Dropping to his knees, he did something to the artificial dick. Once again it touched and then pressed against her. Knowing there was no escape, she tried to open her stance so the object could slide into her, but he refused to grant her request. Again she looked down at herself—or rather at the top of her captor's head. Damn it! This was her body, not his! How dare he try to manipulate her. If not for her bonds, she could have kicked him where no man wanted to be kicked.

But she'd been robbed of that exquisite experience.

His hand returned to her hot and ready flesh, and he again exposed her opening. At the same time he lifted and manipulated the dildo so it slowly, relentlessly penetrated.

No, damn you, no!

Thank God. Finally.

It pushed up and in, claiming more and more of her, filling her in ways both new and familiar. She again tried to stand on her toes and held her body in a straight, trembling line.

Millimeter by millimeter the object claimed her. Took over. Her cunt expanded to accept the invasion and then tried to close down around what it didn't understand but craved. The unyielding toy continued to bury itself in her warm, wet cave, sliding home, filling her.

"Hmm, Hmm," she moaned behind her gag. Although she should keep her attention on her captor, she closed her eyes and experienced, simply experienced.

The dildo claimed her. Owned her. With every involuntary

tremor, the invasion felt new and exciting. She could do nothing to escape it. It pressed on countless nerve endings, relentlessly taunting her to ignore it. The hard, dark rubber had become part of her and she part of it. It was in and on and around her—perhaps forever.

No escape.

Sweat beaded on her temple and forehead. She began to sweat under her breasts, and although she hated doing so, she struggled to press her thighs together so she could feel even more.

All right. So she was prisoner to a piece of rubber. She'd weather the sensation, somehow, ignore her hungry clit, somehow. As she did during lengthy shoots, she'd distract herself from primitive responses by taking her mind somewhere else.

Mind? Oh yes, she did have one—somewhere.

Had she made plans for the weekend? A long bike ride followed by a stop at her favorite coffee shop would be nice. She wanted to talk to her financial advisor about shifting more of her money to tax-free investments. Her condo was overdue for a thorough cleaning, and she'd been thinking about buying a couple of new houseplants. Wasn't there an upcoming pottery show? She could pick up some hand-painted pots to—

A touch, butterfly fingers low on her belly.

"Don't try it. You're not going away."

Eyes wide open now, she once again looked down. He held something she couldn't see in his free hand. Damn. She already had more than enough to concentrate on thank you very much.

"I'm probably not telling you something you don't already know, but there's a particular massager I've been assured will turn every woman into putty. That's what's going to happen to you today. I'm melting you down."

Alarmed, she tried to see what he was talking about, but he kept whatever he had out of view. He pressed on her belly, forcing her against the dildo. Although she knew he wouldn't heed her, she violently shook her head.

"So far I've been easy on you, but I signed on the bottom line. I know what I'm suppose to do."

What are you talking about?

"Step two. Introducing movement."

He held up the object. She gasped, thoughts sinking down until she was aware of nothing except what the large, red vibrator was capable of. It wasn't enough that the head was curved to fit securely around a woman's pussy. Strong electrical current, not batteries, controlled it. Still pressing his fingers against her belly, he aimed the high tech tool at her crotch.

No! No!

It touched, nestled, cupped, trapping her sex under it. She clenched her teeth and held her breath.

"Not yet. First things first. I'm getting tired of being on my knees. I'd rather step back and watch the show. Fortunately, keeping this latest toy in place is going to be easy. I'm sure that pleases you."

She waited for him to chuckle at his sick joke. Instead, he picked something up off the floor. *No! Not tape.*

Helpless to stop him, she could only stand and shake as he taped the vibrator to the pole keeping the dildo inside her. All too soon the newest object was securely nestled against tissues already in overload.

No, no, no! Her head whipped from side to side, making her dizzy.

"Yes," he said as if reading her mind. "Yes because this is part of the program."

She heard a faint click. The vibrator began moving. Sensation sparked through her, igniting her pussy, thighs, pelvis, belly, even her breasts. Frightened, she continued shaking her head. Even when her vision blurred, she couldn't make herself stop.

"That's low speed. I'll be back."

Back?

He couldn't leave. He couldn't. She'd been rendered absolutely and completely helpless. As long as the ropes on her wrists and ankles remained in place, she was a slave to the two foreign objects. Only he, the man responsible, could save her.

But he was gone.

The vibrations weren't stronger than what she'd gotten from her collection of sex toys or experienced at work. But she couldn't do anything except ride the sensation and that made all the difference. No matter how stressful her day had been, no matter how many questions she'd asked herself about what she intended to do with the rest of her life and why she did what she did for a living, those issues fled when she masturbated.

Her body had been conditioned to respond to stimulus—maybe it had been born to do so. Whichever it was, she quickly and totally surrendered to relentless movement against sensitive tissues. Shit, she loved it. A whole body massage given by naked body builders couldn't possibly do more for her libido—more to melt all resistance.

All right. She'd enjoy. Live in the moment. Entertain the fantasy that this was what she wanted.

He returned, footsteps nearly silent, her nerves recording his presence. With an effort, she dragged her attention off what was happening to her.

"Still in the here and now, are you?" he asked. "Probably because you've experienced this before." He tapped the vibrator for emphasis. "Done it to yourself. The thing is, I have it on good authority that there are bridges you refuse to cross—until now."

Any thought she had of trying to convey the question to him fled when he kicked the vibrations up to the next level. She strained upward, twisting her body as much as she could. Movement assaulted her. It wouldn't stop. She couldn't do anything to make it end!

Mewling behind her gag, she pleaded with her eyes for him to shut things off. It was too much! Thunderclaps of movement tearing her apart, forcing themselves deep inside her, taking over. She'd never felt anything quite like this, never allowed her body to be worked this hard. Philip used to try, but she'd be damned if she'd allow the heavy-duty ammunition to be used on her. She could get off without it, thank you. Let other models take it up to that level. No way would she allow herself to be manipulated like that, countless climaxes ripped from her.

Her legs started burning. She was nearly on tiptoe, the ropes around her ankles cutting into her skin, calves threatening to cramp, body hunched forward as if trying to protect herself.

"No, no, no." Although muffled, her words were clear.

"I'm not listening to you, slave." He stepped forward and placed his hand on the control button. "Deep down you crave this. Fight it or surrender, it's going to happen."

Not thinking, she tried to lean back and would have lost her balance if he hadn't grabbed her shoulder.

"Watch it. Think about what you're doing because you're about to feel third gear."

He was still holding her when he again hit the switch. Electrical shocks coursed through her. Her belly became drenched in sweat. She opened her mouth to scream, then bit down on the gag. If any part of her remained untouched by the nearly violent shaking, she was unaware. Although it put her balance at risk, she kept staring down at the dark knob pressing against her. The distinction between mons and clit evaporated, leaving her to wonder if they'd become one.

Every inch of her had become unbelievably, terrifyingly sensitive! Something akin to a monster's hand gripped her cunt and relentlessly shook it. Although she fought her restraints, she couldn't say whether she really wanted to be free.

She'd turned into a sex machine—was been turned into one. Nothing remained of the woman she'd always been. Her bones, flesh, veins, and mostly nerves had been stolen—not by the red toy but by the man in charge of it.

Fire. Fire everywhere. Bolts of lightning and thunderclaps. Nerves misfiring over and over again until she felt as if she was being torn apart.

She hated this! Loved it!

The dildo turned slick with her fluids. Her cunt clenched, clung to the intruder, danced with it. But much as she loved the manmade cock, she hated and feared the vibrator. Too strong! Too powerful.

Ignoring her shoulders' protest, she struggled to bring her hands in front so she could push the vibrator off her. She spotted her clenching and unclenching fingers out of the corner of her eye, but no matter how she strained, her arms remained tied behind her.

Helpless!

Up and down now, up and down. Calves tightening and loosening relentlessly although whether because she was trying to free herself or fuck the dildo she couldn't say. She lost herself in her rhythm and embraced the marriage of flesh and manmade cock.

Her belly caught fire. Her pelvis all but screamed. Her pussy flowed.

"Coming!" she screamed into her gag. "I'm coming!"

Her owner gripped a breast and twisted. At the same time, he pressed down on her mons, increasing the contact with the vibrator.

Coming. Weak. Strong. Dying and coming to life. Flying apart. Explosion!

Her climax seemed to go on forever. It stripped her of everything except the strength needed to keep her feet under her. She no longer tried to reach the invaders, no longer worked at fucking the dildo or escaping the vibrator. Instead, she stood on quivering legs and came over and over again.

Slowly, so slowly, her body began taking breaths. Exhaustion flowed through her, and she wanted to cry out her pleasure. Only a primitive need for dignity kept the cries locked inside.

Coming down. Regaining sanity.

She repeated her mantra until her head pounded. Weary and satisfied beyond belief, she focused on her hot and wet pussy. Climaxing with a lover had meant feeling his cock wither inside her, and when she played with herself, she removed her toys after she'd come. But the monster that ruled her body remained. She was a prisoner of the thing inside her. Even more disconcerting, the vibrator continued to attack at full force.

Weary hunger started lapping. No matter how she fought to distract herself, her tissues danced to the twin tunes. Something foreign had taken up residence in her cunt and insisted she acknowledge its presence. She would have if the vibrator hadn't demanded so much of her attention. It shook and shivered, causing her to do the same.

Flames started licking her pussy lips, her bud.

"Stop! Stop!"

"You're saying something? Speak up."

Damn you to hell! Fury rolled through her, silencing her. She would not beg.

Something fed her flames. She couldn't say and didn't care what it was, probably a combination of what he'd imposed on her. She couldn't free her mind of him. He'd secured her wrists, short-tied her ankles, silenced her.

Given her a drink and touched her cheek.

And now he was leaning against a wall watching her. Watching her shiver and sweat and silently scream to his tune.

Hate you, hate you, hate you, want you dead.

But if his heart stopped, she might remain like this forever.

At his mercy. Her body obeying his commands. Loving and hating the hard, fast rhythms surrounding her clit, cunt sucking on his dildo, climbing the mountain again.

She couldn't—couldn't survive another earth-slamming climax.

When the explosion hit again, she sagged and shuddered and somehow stood her ground. She was dying, being torn apart. Being born. Crying silent and exhausted tears.

7

Mayer deliberately didn't look at Ferren as he carried her to the bed. Holding her put him in mind of a rag doll, not that he'd ever held one. He suspected she lingered somewhere between unconsciousness and awareness.

He supposed he could ask her how many times she'd climaxed, but what the hell did it matter? Enough, maybe enough to satisfy the bastard who'd sent him on this devil's mission.

He'd e-mailed the damnable footage and pulled back the covers before releasing her from bondage. Then he'd guided her into the bathroom and helped her sit on the toilet. The act was intimate, something people who deeply trusted each other did—at least it should have been. He'd thought she might insist on walking into the bedroom under her own power once she understood his intention, but she'd all but collapsed when she tried to stand and hadn't protested as he settled her against his chest.

Now she lay on her side, eyes nearly closed, hands tucked between her knees, breathing deep and a little too fast. He wanted to say something so he could take his measure of her but couldn't think of anything. Most of the women he'd dated had criticized his lack of interest in carrying on conversations. The truth was, he didn't want to let down his guard.

His fingers ached with the desire to stroke this woman's cheeks and throat.

So how do you feel about me now that I've shown you what it really means to be helpless?

If Philip was right and this was what she wanted, she'd thank him. Hopefully pull herself together enough that she'd take pity on him and his painful cock.

In your dreams, you bastard.

He'd just pulled the sheet over her naked body when his cell phone rang. He stepped into the main room but didn't close the door before answering because he wanted to keep an eye on her.

"Why the hell didn't you beat her?" Philip demanded by way of hello.

"My call. I decided she didn't need it." *And I've never done that to a human being.*

"Damn it, you know the script! You want to get paid—more than you've made so far this year I add—you'll do it my way."

"You got the reaction you were after."

"Why the hell did you stop as soon as you did?"

"Soon? She couldn't take any more."

Ferren lifted her head and stared at him through the hair plastered to her cheeks.

"You don't know what she can take. I do."

Is it that it or are you all about getting your kicks? "You aren't looking at her. I am. She's wrung out."

"Shows what little you know about a sub. The rougher it gets, the more they like it. Cage her for the night. In the morning, I want you to take her outside and take digital shots of her in a *natural setting*. Send them to me right away."

"What do pictures have to do with what you're paying me for?"

. "None of your damn business. Just do it."

Don't push me, you bastard.

"I've arranged for a delivery tomorrow. Use it on her."

"What is it?" .

"None of your damn business, for now. Let's just say it'll help get her where she needs to be."

"And if I say no?"

"You won't."

"Is that a threat?"

"Depends on if I decide you need one. Look, if you don't have the stomach for this, there's any number of Doms on the island I can turn to."

Then why didn't you?

Ferren remembered bits and pieces of what her owner had said, but although the conversation had been about her and thus essential, she'd lacked the concentration necessary to pull things together.

He'd let her sleep for awhile before telling her to take a shower. He'd kept the glass door open so he could watch, but although his flared nostrils and the way he occasionally touched his straining cock left no doubt of her nudity's impact on him, he hadn't forced himself on her. Once she'd gotten rid of the accumulated sweat and cooled her heated flesh under a tepid rinse, he'd ordered her back to the bed and had chained her foot to the floor. He'd left for several minutes and returned with milk and several granola bars. She'd all but wolfed down the bars, even eyeing his as he ate at a slower pace.

She'd spent the evening perched on the bed while he was in the living room. From the faint clicking sounds, she concluded he was working on the laptop. He might be sending and responding to e-mails, but he took so long at it that she didn't think everything had to do with her.

What kind of life did he have when he wasn't on Surrender Island doing any and everything he wanted to her? Was there a heart beneath that hard chest, a soul? Not that she cared. Not that she wanted to learn anything about him.

Finally he'd returned, released her ankle, and ordered her into the bathroom. Although he hadn't given permission, she'd taken the time to brush her teeth, then had stood in the doorway looking at him, unable to take a step.

"Come here."

Arms wrapped around her middle, she'd complied. Drumbeats seemed to accompany each step. Maybe condemned prisoners felt this way. And maybe this emotional overload came from another source, one she refused to acknowledge.

At the moment, she wore no restraints. If one didn't look beneath the surface, he or she might believe the cabin was occupied by lovers and energy defined them. But she told herself that what she felt had nothing to do with sexual equality.

Nothing to do with wanting his body.

Instead of raping her or forcing more bondage on her, he pushed her into the cage in the corner. Forced onto her hands and knees, she managed not to cry or beg when he locked the door. He turned out the light. A few moments later a bedspring squeaked.

Trapped. Imprisoned.

Terror crawled up her throat; she forced it down. Reaching around, she found a small pillow and a blanket. He might have reduced her to animal status, but he hadn't gone all the way—yet.

He'd become her world. His extended no further than this cabin. There was only this space—each other.

The need for the oblivion of sleep nibbled at her, but she refused to give in. Her world had been turned on end and altered in ways she'd never imagined. Close as she and her mother were, they often went days without speaking, especially when her mother was working on a complex case or she'd packed a few suitcases and was indulging her wanderlust nature. Her coworkers might wonder why she hadn't shown up for work, but she didn't think any of them would jump to the conclusion that something terrible had happened. She didn't have what she could call a best friend, someone she truly cared about and cared about her.

She was alone. At the mercy of a man she'd never understand.

One who had taken over responsibility for her existence.

Instead of another wave of fear, relief washed over her. As long as she wore his ropes and chains, ate when he said she could, got fucked when he dictated, she didn't have to plan her future. He made those decisions.

Although she'd have sworn that all sexual response had been wrenched from her, her body heated degree by slow degrees. The stranger's hands were masterful. He knew how to work the toys he used on her. Even more unsettling was her reaction to his presence, when a touch became nothing more than a touch. Remembering the way he'd cradled her as he carried her to the bed, she rested her hands over her cunt. Her flesh was tender there but not painful, tired but not stripped.

If he opened the cage door and beckoned, she would crawl to him. Like an animal conditioned to respond to a food treat, she'd obey his every command. She imagined herself turning her back to him, lowering her head, and presenting her dripping pussy.

Fuck me, please. Let me feel you. Your cock.

No! What could she be thinking? Only a few days ago she'd been a modern woman in charge of her life. She wasn't about to turn her back on everything she'd worked to achieve. She wasn't!

And yet, his touch . . .

The sun felt wonderful on her shoulders. Being outside had brought her back to life. If she could turn, she'd let the rays caress her breasts and belly, maybe even give her a sunburn. But her owner had positioned her so she couldn't control anything. Not only had he pulled her arms over her head, securing them to a tree branch, but he'd tied her ankles to a spreader bar so her legs were widely splayed.

He wore no shirt this morning, and his shorts revealed too damn much of his solid thighs. When he turned in a certain direction, sunlight danced over the dark hairs there. His leather sandals added to the image of a man vacationing on a tropical island.

She debated screaming, but would that do any good? This island had been designed or created or something for one purpose—to live up to its name.

"What are you going to do?" She couldn't keep nervousness out of her voice—or was it a simple matter of nerves? Gratitude had flooded her when he'd opened her cage and let her out earlier. She'd thanked him when he let her use the toilet and wash her face. The same words had passed her lips when he pointed to the kitchen where a bowl of cereal and a banana waited. How could she not be reminded of how his power and control encompassed her? How could she not want to please him?

She too easily imagined how she looked now, a helpless, well-formed woman waiting for whatever her owner wanted to do to her. Strung up and helpless, perhaps he saw her as his present to himself. He'd tucked several items into his shorts' pockets.

"What are you going to do?" she repeated.

"Take you down. Lead you to surrender. Take pictures of your progress."

"I don't want to go there."

He studied her, his gaze slowly and thoroughly gliding over every inch of exposed flesh. "It's going to happen. Here where you can see but not embrace the wilderness. Where everything except you is free."

No negotiation. No way out. Why hadn't she fought him this morning? But she'd been savoring the banana when he grabbed her wrists and bound them together. After that it had been a simple matter for him to haul her here.

Still studying her in his dark and intense way, he reached into his left pocket. Out came yet another gag. This one consisted of a wooden dowel with metal rings at each end. Leather strips dangled from the rings.

He stepped closer, stopped, took another step.

"Do it!" she all but screamed. "Get it over with."

Instead, he continued his slow and measured approach. *Mine*, his eyes seemed to say. *Mine.*

I know.

His heat touched her before he did. When he reached for her breast, she didn't try to evade him, and when he closed his fingers around a nub, she remained still. A sigh escaped. Off balance, she arched toward him. His glance said he hadn't expected that; neither had she.

He rubbed first the dowel and then the metal over her breast, his fingers containing and controlling. Another sigh rolled out of her.

"Beautiful. You're a beautiful woman."

"Thank you."

Her word seemed to pull him out of whatever shadow he'd stepped into. Muttering something she didn't understand, he slapped her breast. Then he stepped behind her and grabbed her hair, forcing her head back. She could have clenched her teeth but didn't because in the end he would win anyway. The dowel slipped in, stretching her lips and again silencing her. She flinched as he fastened the leather behind her. Like so much of what had happened since he'd walked into her world, the gag would remain part of her until he felt like removing it.

"It's time for you to think about the difference between your surroundings and what's happened to you. To distinguish between the two. It is a perfect day for being outside, isn't it?"

Not sure whether he wanted a response, she nevertheless nodded. Her work called for her to spend a great deal of time inside. Maybe as a consequence, she loved seeing new territory, bike riding, hiking, anything that kept her out from under roofs.

"Who would want to be in a cage on a day like this?" He again reached into a pocket, this time pulling out silver nipple clamps. "I could keep you chained to the living room floor looking outside, but it has been decided that you need a taste of freedom."

Freedom? Is he joking?

"The kind of freedom that comes from being close to nature." He indicated the tree he'd tied her to, the dirt and rocks, a couple of birds flying overhead. Her heart went with the birds. "Giving you a taste of what the sun and wind feels like. As a sub, your Dom will dictate when and whether you'll be allowed to be outside. Please him, do what he requires, and you'll be rewarded—sometimes."

She couldn't concentrate on what he was saying when she felt so helpless. Working within the porn industry meant she had contractual rights. This was different. For one, she had no say in what use those clamps would be put to.

"Lose yourself in the sensation." He cradled a breast and

lifted it. "Take what you feel deep inside yourself and make it part of you."

Unnerved, she tried to pull away. But her arms remained secured overhead, and she could barely shuffle, thanks to the spreader bar.

"Maybe fighting's instinctual. No matter what a person's inclination, survival mode kicks in." He glanced at the digital camera he'd placed on a nearby rock, shook his head, and unceremoniously closed the clip over her nipple. Pressure slammed into her, causing her to suck in a sharp breath. She'd worn things like this before and understood the sensations. But in the past she'd first given approval.

Looking down at the tenacious clamp, she tried to shake it off. Pain spread through her breast, stopping her.

"It's not going anywhere for a while."

A while. Fear gnawed at her. Knowing how vital it was not to panic, she ordered herself to take this one second at a time, to live in the present, to give him what he wanted so he'd be finished. Wondering if she truly could do what she needed to, she willed herself not to flinch as he took hold of her other breast. If anything the second clip hurt more than the first. Yet she sensed the familiar change within herself.

She'd refused to give a name to what she felt while filming a bondage scene. If she didn't acknowledge a certain response, then she wouldn't have to own up to it. But her breasts no longer belonged to her. This nameless man who'd bought her could do whatever he wanted with them. Even more unsettling, she'd climax as many times as he dictated. She'd become his puppet, dancing at the end of his strings—or ropes in this case. He controlled her access to daylight, to a warm breeze.

Surrender. The end to responsibility. A life defined by sex. His possession.

He picked up the camera and took a number of shots while

circling her. She hated the thought of anyone seeing the pictures. As for the man responsible for what she looked like—what did she feel for him?

The question distracted her from the pressure on her nipples and made her slow to realize that he hadn't emptied his pockets after all. Once more he reached in and showed her a slender silver chain. *Damn! Damn!*

Trying not to shake, she waited as he attached the chain first to the end of one clamp and then the other. The chain dangled between her breasts, adding to the image of a thoroughly captured woman. After taking a few more pictures, he put down the digital. Then he took hold of the chain and pulled, drawing her breasts toward him. The clamps remained securely in place.

"It's easy to control you this way. Maybe you'd like to wear them full time."

She shook her head.

"What are you saying? That you don't like this?" He reached between her legs and ran his fingers over her. The touch went way beyond a matter of flesh against flesh. Of course his still holding the chain had something to do with her reaction, but that wasn't all. His fingertip pressing against her entrance served as another inescapable reminder that he'd wrenched ownership of her body from her and taken it for himself. How could she fight a man who weighed nearly double what she did, who had paid money for her flesh, whose arsenal included ropes, chains, dildos, and vibrators? Who knew how to use those things.

Who understood how she'd respond.

"You're wet," he announced unnecessarily. "Don't tell me you don't like being restrained and played with when the proof is running out of you."

I can't help it!

"You want this. Don't ever lose sight of that simple fact. Deep down you want and need to be handled like this."

No! I don't. And even if you're right, I'm never going to admit that you know more about me than I do.

"You had it pretty good yesterday." He gave the chain another tug and slipped a finger in her. To her horror, her cunt invited him in, pussy muscles closing around him, heat and juice welcoming. "You're not getting off so easy today."

He no longer sounded as remote as he had a few minutes ago. Maybe handling her was getting to him.

But what difference did it make? He still called all the shots.

As if proving her point, he pushed up and in, skewering her on his finger. She rose onto her toes, leg muscles straining because the spreader bar had her off balance. Maybe yesterday's sexual barrage had conditioned her to need more, and maybe it was all about real helplessness after years of playacting.

Did it matter?

He pulled out, leaving her empty. Although she hated herself, she tried to push her pelvis at him. A quick jerk on the chain brought her up short, and she waited, docile and tamed. After a moment, he released the chain. But before she could make sense of what he'd done, he pressed the heel of his hand against her mons, forcing her to lean away.

"It all falls apart for you when I touch you down there, doesn't it? Instinct comes into play. Your defenses die."

Her head started pounding. If only he'd let her talk!

No! She had nothing to say to him.

"Right here." His hand slid lower, around her mons, stopping when he reached her clit. "It all begins and ends here, doesn't it?"

She tried to twist away, but he snagged a clamp and used it to hold her in place. "They say a man's cock rules him, and speaking from personal experience, that's pretty damn true. But women aren't any different, are they?"

He stroked her clit, the touches alternating between whisper soft and hard and possessive. Unable to stop herself, she again struggled to back away.

"You aren't going anywhere. The thing I don't understand is why you keep trying."

Because I'm scared of you. And of myself. When you do these things, I feel as if I'm looking into a cave and finding myself in there—chained to the walls, begging you to fuck me.

"Where were you?" He punctuated his question by grabbing her around the waist, lifting her off the ground, and turning her away. She couldn't see him, couldn't anticipate!

A few seconds later, she heard the digital start clicking again. "I have my orders. I agreed to this. Maybe I shouldn't be telling you this, but what the hell." With his free hand, he stroked her shoulders, making her half believe he was taking pity on her straining muscles. "I've done a lot of things I was told not to. What's he going to do, shoot me?"

His disembodied voice behind her made her wonder if he existed only in her mind—except for the large and capable hand on her shoulder. "I know what it is to be helpless," he said softly. "I swore it never would happen again. It made an impact I've never forgotten." He slipped the small camera into a pocket and placed both hands on her shoulders. He ranged lower, finger walking down her spine, exploring her waist, reaching around to touch her rib cage. He didn't touch the clamps or chain. Still, the anticipation kept her on edge.

"I used to dream about being the one in charge, an adult, no longer a child."

Smooth fingernails lightly raked the skin over her pelvis, causing her to shudder and her breathing to quicken. Still she struggled to make sense of what he was saying.

"Then I grew up and learned adulthood isn't all its cracked up to be. Nine. I'd like to be nine years old with a bike and an allowance."

What should she take from the revelation? If only she could think beyond his fingers dancing over her. If only she didn't need more from him.

More?

What would fucking him be like? Her body would easily mold itself to his. All it would take was to crush her breasts against his chest and she'd want to spend the night with him— as his equal.

Equal?

The word slapped at her, forcing her back to reality. He was dressed in clothes of his own choice while she hadn't worn anything except restraints since she'd been brought to the island. He had full control of her body while she couldn't so much as touch him. She had no use of her limbs and couldn't speak. Couldn't bring him to the same sexual level he'd forced on her. Maybe he thought of her as less than human, an object he'd committed to conditioning for the future someone else had chosen for her.

So many unknowns.

He grabbed her hair and pulled her head back, forcing her to look at him. "I warned you. Don't leave me." She tried to shake her head which earned her another jerk. "I zoned out enough times. I know what it's like."

This time she didn't make the mistake of trying to move. Instead, she spoke to him with her eyes, asking him to allow her to communicate. She thought he understood but couldn't be sure. At least he released the tension on her hair so she could straighten. She looked up at her tethered wrists. At the cloud-dusted sky.

"Do they hurt?"

Surprised he would ask, she twisted so she could look at him. If she indicated yes, would he free her? The greater question was, did she want back the use of her arms? Even with the fear and uncertainty, some primitive part of her longed to experience his control—his touch, his mastery.

"Do your arms hurt?"

Before she could begin to form a response, the cell phone clipped to his waist rang. He cursed but punched send after the third ring.

"Yeah?" he said.

The response was muted.

"Don't give me orders. And for the record, I don't believe that shit you told me yesterday about my being dispensable."

More mumbling accompanied by unmistakable anger on her owner's part.

"I know that, damn it. But there are lines I don't cross over, get it. Things I will not do. I thought you understood that."

He opened his mouth to say more, but the caller interrupted with loud, angry words.

"That's not going to happen," her owner interjected. "Don't even ask. Either you let me do this my way or I'm walking. I don't—"

Another outburst cut him off. His free hand formed a fist, but he waited out the other man.

"Oh yeah. I hear you. Loud and clear." With that, he terminated the call.

When he turned his attention back on her, his eyes put her in mind of an unlit cave. He glanced at the camera poking out of his pocket, then dismissed it. Stepping closer, he ran his knuckles over her side. The touch was so light, so intimate. Gentle.

"You're a beautiful woman. Your looks are at odds with what you do." He stroked her other side, and she shivered. "It's a hard business. It conditions people to think of their bodies as merchandise."

For the first time in so long she couldn't remember when it had last happened, she was ashamed. All her no-nonsense defenses of her career fled. *I don't know how it happened,* she wanted to tell him. *I love sex. I'm a halfway decent actress. The money is great and having a hand in the creativity is a kick. But when I was growing up, I never thought I'd end up like this.*

But because he'd rendered her silent, she could only fight tears and struggle to stay in place while he walked his fingertips over her ribs and belly.

"So soft. Soft. Complex."

8

At the knock, Mayer spun around. Because he'd fastened Ferren's three-foot-long neck chain to a wall ring, he didn't have to keep an eye on her. Or maybe the truth was, he'd secured her so he no longer had to risk his sanity by remaining close. Before stepping to the door, he slipped into the bedroom and came out holding his pistol. Her eyes widened, making him wonder if he should tell her it was a tool of the trade for the business he was going into.

The knock wasn't repeated. He strained to listen, then relaxed when he heard a vehicle driving away. Opening the door, he discovered a small package. The return address left no doubt of the sender. Cursing, he slammed the door and faced his naked captive. He hadn't tied her arms or gagged her, but she hadn't said anything.

He placed the package on the desk holding his laptop.

"It's from Philip, isn't it?" she said.

"What?"

"He's behind this. He has to be." She rubbed her eyes. "No one else would want to do this to me."

Unwilling to lie or evade, he nodded. *What do you think of that, you bastard? She fingered you.*

She indicated the package. "It's something to use on me, isn't it?"

Ignoring her and the trepidation in her eyes, he dug into the wrapping. The last thing he needed was the damnable Philip trying to pull any more of his strings. Ferren fascinated him. He wanted to get to know the woman beneath the layers, try to understand what had brought her to this place in her life. And maybe tell her about his own journey.

The box held a total of six leather straps with buckles. In addition, he uncovered a large silver bullet powered by electrical current. The note attached to the bullet read: *give the bitch the ride she deserves.*

"No." Ferren's voice was small but determined. "No."

She hadn't read the note of course, but he'd made no effort to hide the straps or bullet. About to drop the damnable note, he noticed an image bleeding through from the opposite side. Turning the paper over, he instantly understood what Philip intended for him to do. His stomach clenched. At the same time, memories of the way her body embraced sex flooded him. He could make her sing and cry. And when the song and crying was done, she'd crawl to him and—

He's got you, you bastard. Don't you get it? He saw the holes in you and is exploiting them.

An envelope bearing his name was in the box. Dropping the bondage tools, he lifted the flap. A standard size piece of paper had been folded so it fit in the envelope. Inside the paper was a check made out to him. A check for ten thousand, two hundred, and fifty dollars.

Call this a bonus, Philip had scrawled on the paper. *Or maybe a bribe. If my sources are right, this is exactly the sum you need to lease your office for the first year. Its yours if I get the pictures I trust you took outside and a certain video feed by tonight. Otherwise, I'll put a stop payment on the check. Let the accompanying photo guide your imagination. One more thing. I want to hear everything she says.*

From where she all but hugged the wall, Ferren studied the man's expression, instantly recognizing his quick flash of anger. Then as he studied what she took to be a check, he turned contemplative.

"What did he say?" She hated the trepidation in her voice. "What—what does he want you to do?"

"Shut up."

"And what? Stand here and take it?"

A sound that reminded her of a dog growling rolled out of him. His steps were slow but determined, effortlessly closing the distance between them. Then he abruptly changed directions. Unable to move more than a few feet from the wall ring, she watched as he took the video camera into the bedroom. She couldn't feel her legs. If she didn't concentrate, she'd collapse.

When he returned, he pulled on the chain attached to her collar, forcing her to bend close to the ring. She planted her hands against the wall to brace herself. After refastening the chain so she had only a few inches of play, he collected the straps from the desk and moved behind her.

"Hands back."

"No!"

Grabbing both wrists, he forced them behind her. She fell forward so her forehead rested against the wall. Unable to straighten, she barely struggled while he wrapped and cinched the leather around her wrists. He tightened another strap around her waist and elbows so she couldn't so much as lift her hands off her buttocks. He completed his handiwork via the third strap which secured her upper arms and pushed against the swell of her breasts. Only then did he release the neck chain. The leather was softer than what she'd worn her last day at Cages. Or was it? maybe his applying the restrictions made all the difference.

He led her into the bedroom and turned her so she faced the tripod and camera. Because of the way the lens was angled, she could see herself, a nude and disheveled woman with her upper body wrapped in black leather. A straight jacket couldn't have held her more securely.

"That what you want?" he said, obviously speaking for Philip's benefit. "All right so far?"

Grabbing her elbows, he pushed her toward the bed and threw her face down on it. She managed to turn her head so she could breathe but didn't fight when he strapped her ankles together. After all, what could she accomplish without use of her arms?

Besides—besides, although she hated admitting it, anticipation gripped her. This man hadn't hurt her. Almost everything he'd done had been aimed at exploiting and exploring her sexuality. It wasn't as if she wanted a real relationship with him.

Surely not!

If he hadn't straddled her legs, she might have been able to turn over. As it was, she could only wait for his next move—not that she couldn't anticipate it. He began by kneading her buttocks, loosening her resolve and weakening her muscles. Slowly, maddeningly, he spread her ass cheeks. His thumb glided over her anus, and she let out a puppylike squeal. Ignoring her squirming, he worked his way to her cunt, thumb barely grazing her labia but creating a hot flood. It dribbled out and slid down her. She imagined her juices soaking the coverlet.

Gathering some of her offering, he bathed her inner buttocks until she nearly cried out her embarrassment and excitement. Finally done, he ran a finger inside her and let it rest there, not moving and yet sending out countless messages. She clamped her muscles around it, but he could easily escape if he wanted.

"Ready, aren't you." He pushed in a little farther, then withdrew.

Mewling, she struggled to look back at him. She caught a glimpse of the invasive and all-recording camera but didn't care. The strain in her shoulders made her fall back against the mattress. His finger rested at her entrance.

"One more thing," he said. "Not the same as a dildo, but it's going to stay put."

It?

The answer came when he ran the smooth, rounded bullet over her buttocks. Obviously in no more of a hurry than he'd been when he'd been kneading her, he took care to imprint every inch of her ass. She'd had dozens of bullets inserted—or had done it herself—but no way could she draw on those experiences for comparisons.

After what felt like a lifetime of teasing, he removed his finger from her labia. This time she barely lifted her head before giving up. He shifted so he now knelt near her thighs. With one hand, he separated her thighs. With the other, he brought the bullet to her cunt. She might have fought. Should have. Instead, like the dumb hungry animal she'd become, she waited.

Panted.

The bullet briefly pressed against her labia but then found entrance. It went in easily, its way lubricated by her liquid hunger. It took almost no effort on his part to push the object all the way in., but instead of stopping there, he placed his finger against the base and shoved even deeper. As he held it fully inside her, she arched her back.

"What does it feel like?" he demanded. "He's going to want to know."

"Go to hell, Phillip!"

"You hear that, Philip? She knows its you."

Withdrawing his finger, he pressed against the sides of her hips, probably to assure himself that the insertion was complete.

It was.

She'd forgotten about the other two straps, but he soon reminded her of their purpose. He secured her knees with one. The other now held her thighs together—and kept the bullet firmly in place. Even if she thrashed about, she had no doubt she wouldn't be able to dislodge it.

How long would it remain there?

Damn you, Philip! Damn you to hell.

The mattress rose. Unnerved and disoriented, she again tried to lift her shoulders so she could take in her surroundings. She watched as he plugged in the bullet. Instead of turning it on, he undressed starting with his sandals. Hearing his shorts zipper and watching them fall to the floor was unnerving, but he was hardly the first naked man she'd ever seen.

Then, standing where she could easily observe, he shucked his hip-caressing briefs. Of course she'd already noted his erection, but the sight of his swollen and dark cock made her dig her toes into the coverlet.

"What are you doing?" She couldn't tear her gaze from his cock.

"What I've wanted to since the moment I saw you." He ran his hand over his chest, stopping at his waist.

If he was trying to both frighten and excite her, he was doing a damn good job of it. Perhaps she should take comfort from the fact that he had no hidden weapon on him, but she couldn't move. That alone definitely gave him the upper edge. Then there was the object he'd rammed inside her.

Spinning away, he faced the camera. "I'm conducting a little experiment here." He spoke deliberately. "If she's truly what you say she is, she's going to respond in certain ways guaranteed to turn me into a happy camper. And if you've been feeding me a raft of shit, we're going to find out."

He turned back toward her. "Ready to get the experiment started?"

"I didn't ask for this."

"Maybe not in so many words, but sometimes body language says it all. So far we've been dancing around the edges. However, the man paying the bills wants you prepared for your new life. It's time to stop playing."

"Playing? Is that what you call it?"

"Don't you?"

"Why are you doing this?"

His eyes narrowed. "Because I just accepted a bribe."

At least he hadn't said he got off on pulling her into hell. "You want money? I have a lot in savings and investments. I'll match whatever he gave you."

Something in his eyes told her he hadn't expected that. "And miss the experience of a lifetime?"

"I don't want this. Damn it, I don't!"

"You're lying. At least someone is. And today's about me getting to the truth." He fondled her cunt.

A powerful sense of defeat washed through her. How could she have been so stupid not to realize he was doing this for reasons beyond money? Cages thrived because it fed the fantasies of countless men and women. In their real lives, they might have no opportunity for, or personal desire for, bondage and submission. But they dreamed their secret dreams and wanted to see them played out on their computers or TVs.

This strong and complex man had been given the job of his dreams. And she'd pay the price.

"I hope you go to hell." Lowering her face to the coverlet, she continued in a muffled tone. "Go on. Have your fun. But I want you to remember one thing. You aren't going to change who and what I am."

His feet brushed the carpet. Then he grabbed her hair and forced her head up. "Who are you? Other than a woman who earns a living getting sexually worked over, who are you?"

I don't know! I keep looking for the answer, but I haven't found it.

"Answer me!"

"It's a living. A damn good living."

"One you walk away from at 5 P.M. Only now that has changed." He glared down at her, dark eyes challenging and yet guarded.

"Go to hell."

"I've already been there. I climbed out, and I'm not going back." With that, he released her hair. Once again her face sank into fabric, his last words swirling around her. She didn't know anything about him, not his name, where he came from, or why Philip had selected him for this *job*. What did he need the money for and most important, what, ultimately, did he and Philip intend to do with her?

Reality slammed into her and weakened her muscles. This wasn't a game, a well-choreographed scene, part of her career. If he wanted, he could take her anywhere and do anything he wanted with her. He could even point his pistol at her head and fire.

Sick and scared, she tried to roll onto her hip, but without use of her hands, she couldn't. *Rest a moment. Think. Plan. Then do what?*

The various straps dug into her flesh. He hadn't tightened them to the point that they were painful, but her muscles could handle being in one position only for so long. As for the bullet—

Almost on cue, it surged to life.

For the first few seconds, she waited for her nerves to react. The messages they sent were disorganized and confusing. They'd gone from resting to being under attack and didn't know how to respond.

The bullet beat rapidly, endlessly against her pussy walls. Heat built, alerting her to the instrument's dual functions. Just like that, her body reached overdrive, primitive and hungry. She wanted to curl around the overpowered sex toy and play with it, experience everything it had to offer. Become the toy's toy.

"Ah, ah."

The man placed a hand on her buttocks. Could he feel the vibrations? She both wanted to lean into his surprisingly comforting touch and hit him as hard as she could.

Slowly, relentlessly, the vibrations increased. She tingled, not just in her pussy but seemingly everywhere. She hated and loved her confinement, loved her growing reaction, feared it.

"Oh shit."

He slapped her ass. It stung but barely distracted her. The inner power grew. The need to move and work with the foreign strength pounded at her. She'd already reached that place where little mattered except reaching the peak. But if she gave in this quickly, he and Philip would have won without a battle having been fought.

She had little, only pride and strength.

If her owner was manipulating the bullet, she couldn't tell with her face turned just enough to allow her to draw breath. Still, she needed to know if he was responsible for the shift from a steady vibration to quick assaults followed by almost a second of rest. Over and over again, the toy attacked her too-sensitive walls. Then, just when she despaired of being remaining on top of the wave, the toy went still.

She waited. Anticipated. Feared.

It surged back to life, snarled, relaxed again. Now the pauses lasted longer and longer. At the same time, the vibrations built, shaking her almost as a dog shakes a stuffed animal. In her mind, she became that helpless cloth creature being yanked back and forth. From the top of her head to her toes, there was only one thing—the inner explosions.

"Ah, ah!"

"Ride it, Ferren! See it through to the end."

How dare he tell her what to do? And how dare he go on slapping her ass? Loathing him and the straps he'd applied, frightened and hot, she squirmed. The coverlet twisted under her. It felt as if it were trying to strangle her. She managed a rocking, rolling motion that turned her body wavelike. At the same time, she struggled to twist from side to side. Anything to distract herself from the tireless beast.

"Shit! Oh shit! Oh, God, oh shit."

Sweat poured off her. She clenched her teeth and risked breaking them in a frenzied attempt to hold back the building, burning climax. It became a tidal wave, a raging storm, tornado and hurricane.

She couldn't escape. Could barely move.

"No, no! Ah, no!"

She tasted blood. Had she bit her tongue? Her lower body caught fire. Muscles screamed and fought exhaustion.

No climax! No giving into this damnable toy! I'm not your plaything. I'm not.

The thunderclap hit.

Sobbing, maybe shrieking, she gave up all pretense. Her thighs tensed and then trembled. Her cunt cramped and closed down around the bullet as if trying to squash it. Ignoring her pitiful attempts, the toy continued its relentless dance. As her climax rolled on, the vibrations shifted once again. They pulsed, fierce electrical shots that slammed her inner walls.

"Stop it! Please, stop it!"

Horrified by her helpless tone, she clenched her teeth. No begging, none!

The pulsing continued.

Gurgling sounds welled up in her throat and flowed out. Her grunts reminded her of an angry pig, but she couldn't stop them.

Her climax rose and kept rising, lashing her into near unconsciousness. She was being ruled by a ridiculously small man-made object that cared nothing about human limitations. Always before she'd had a safe word, not that she'd had to use it at Cages because they understood that once her climax began, she insisted on riding it to its natural end.

Because she'd trained herself to come on cue, she needed only mild stimulation. Once the spasms started, her reaction would provide any porn site member with his money's worth.

She'd never understood other models who raved about non-stop forced climaxes.

Now, finally, she did.

She fought the bed, fought herself, fought what she couldn't escape. The bullet became even warmer, stilled for a brief period—she couldn't track time—then screamed back to life. She screamed back.

"Can't! Can't! Oh, God I can't—damn it! Make it stop."

"You don't like this?"

She wrenched herself onto her side. Because she couldn't bend her knees to balance herself, she flopped back down. Her breasts were drenched and nearly as hot as her weeping pussy. "Stop it!"

Grabbing her straining upper arms, he hauled her onto her back. The wire leading from the bullet pressed into her thigh. The assault slowed and nearly stopped as if the toy had worn itself out. But unlike a cock, this *thing* would never need to rest.

She tried to bring the man into focus, but sweat had dripped into her eyes. Either that or she was crying.

Beg. Plead with him. Make him understand you can't take any more.

He shoved his hand between her smashed together thighs and reached up. The bullet gave off a mild buzzing. She could handle this gentle movement, could start to find her way back from insanity.

Trembling, she waited for him to speak, to *do*. His mouth opened, but nothing came out. She wanted to crawl into a heated pool and fall asleep while lulled by gentle waves. She needed a shower, a massage, a stiff drink, a cigarette even though she didn't smoke.

Done, movement banking down even more, dying. Fine. He'd won. Had his fun. At least the game was over.

The bullet rumbled back to life. This time there was no measured build-up. Instead, the beast stormed her over-stimulated pussy.

Terrified, she strained to sit up. When that failed, she struggled to bend her legs. If she could somehow get to her feet, maybe she could outrun her climax.

Instead, she remained imprisoned on the bed while the bullet worked its cruel magic inside her flowing, short-circuiting cunt. Again it pounded against her walls. Again heat spread out from her pussy to fever her.

And once again she climaxed.

9

Certain what was happening to Ferren, Mayer rested his hand on her entrance, but much as he wanted to experience at least some of what she was, she was moving around too much.

Men and women's bodies were different in ways that hadn't occurred to him back when he'd begun noting the intriguing differences. Where men shot their loads and then had to rest and regroup before winding up for another run, given the right stimulation, women could climax almost nonstop.

But that begged the question of how much they could take. Studying her frantic slithering, he came to a not too brilliant conclusion: not much.

Despite what he'd told her, he didn't know why he'd stripped—at least he hadn't gone looking for an explanation. Now, seeing his hard-as-hell cock, he knew exactly what he wanted to do with it. However, she was hardly in any condition to want to fuck him, and he didn't rape.

"Arr! Wmp."

Even jerking as if blessed with super muscles, she sounded

exhausted. What he could see of her pussy was bright red, and her abundant juices glistened. She was sweat-washed, eyes rolling back in her head, legs straining and toes sticking straight out.

"Haar!"

Concern for her heart sent him diving for the plug. The moment he yanked it out, the high whining died. He was both excited and shocked by how helplessly vulnerable she looked. *Fuck you, Philip. I'm not playing this your way.*

Still, what man didn't fantasize about having his own sex slave? As long as everything remained within the realm of make believe, imaging having ultimate control over a nubile woman's body was a killer turn-on. At least it had been until he'd seen the real thing. Filled with self-disgust, he approached. She gave no indication she was aware of him. If it wasn't for her rapid and ragged breathing and the way her legs jerked, he'd have thought she'd passed out.

Was she crying?

Not giving a damn what the camera picked up, he sat on the side of the bed and released her legs. Then he pulled out the drenched bullet and threw it onto the carpet. Instead of granting her a bit of modesty, he studied what he'd exposed. Her labia were swollen and red, her clit large and hard. Much as he wanted to touch and, yes, soothe her there, he knew better. After the way he'd treated her, she'd kick him in the balls.

Speaking of balls, his felt as if they were trying to crawl into his throat. So, he acknowledged, despite his concern and self-disgust, what was primitive about him didn't give a damn about anything except fucking.

"Thank you."

Her voice sounded as if she'd been screaming for hours. Surely she wanted something to drink. But she'd have to wait because he wasn't ready to leave her.

"That's not going to happen again."

"You—you mean it?"

Again mentally telling Philip to go to hell, he nodded. Then he helped her sit up so he could attack the buckles holding her arms. The marks left by the straps served as testament to how much she'd fought. When he removed the last piece of leather, she struggled to sit up. Although he wanted to help, he didn't. If conditions were reversed, the last thing he'd want was to be touched.

Positioning herself so she sat cross-legged before him, she rubbed her wrists. Her head sagged forward, and her angel hair curtained her face. Her position left her pussy exposed, and he had to clench his fists to keep from touching her there. The relentlessly watching camera recorded.

"Where did you get the gun?"

"What?"

"The gun. Why are you carrying one?"

"I might need it in my job."

Her head came up, revealing wounded and yet determined eyes. "What do you do?"

"It doesn't matter."

She started to slide away, then stopped and looked down at herself. After studying her brutalized pussy, she lightly ran her fingers over herself there. Maybe the series of forced climaxes had robbed her of all modesty; maybe her career had put an end to that years ago. He wished he could believe she felt comfortable around him, but that would be a damn lie.

"Does it hurt?"

"Hurt?" Her nostrils flared. "It's too late to care about that, isn't it?"

"Yeah, it is."

"Then why—never mind. I feel as if I could sleep for a week, but no, it doesn't hurt." She actually grinned, briefly. "Tell me. If I tried to leave right now, would you stop me?"

He didn't know. That was the hell of it. "Are you going to try?"

With one hand still on her sex, she massaged a thigh. "I don't think I can walk. Please tell me about this job of yours. You know everything about me."

"Hardly everything."

"Enough." She glanced around the room, then focused on the discarded bullet. "So small. So powerful. Damn it, this is the first we've talked, really talked. I need to make it count."

So do I.

"What do you do when you aren't being a Dom?"

He winced. "I'm about to open my private detective business."

"Oh. Oh." Her eyes swam with questions. "What's your name?"

She didn't know that basic thing about him, did she? "Mayer. Mayer White."

When she nodded, her hair stroked her throat. "Did you tell me because I'm never going to get off Surrender Island? I won't ever be able to report to authorities that you captured me?"

"I didn't capture. I bought."

She straightened, showing a strength he thought had been stripped from her. He'd been in countless rooms with countless women, but he'd never been on this journey. It frightened him, yet he wasn't ready to walk away.

"No you didn't. The bastard who is paying you provided the money for that charade didn't he, which technically means I belong to him. Why do you want to be a private detective?"

Because I need to be my own boss and its about time I got my act together. Because I've finally found something I'm good at.

"You need a shower."

A quick grin again transformed her features. She reminded him of a young girl facing a room full of birthday presents. He slid off the bed, took her ankles, and drew her toward him. Much as he wanted to believe she'd relaxed, he sensed her tension. Given everything that had gone on between them, he sure as hell didn't blame her. Neither could he say how the rest of their time together would play out, but at the moment he didn't care.

Whether she wanted a solo shower or not was beyond the question. They were going in together. She leaned away as best she could while he adjusted the water, then tolerated his hand on her shoulder as he guided her in. The stall was standard issue which meant they had to stand side by side, not that he minded. Showering with a woman had always touched him as a particularly domestic event, something married couples did. Although he'd allowed a number of women to soap him and had done the same in return, the confined space always left him on edge. Today, however, his nerves came from another source.

Close. So close. Naked body touching naked body. Their relationship defined by sex. And bondage.

Giving himself a mental shake, he watched as she faced the water and lowered her head to wet her hair. It streamed down like a waterfall, hiding her features. More water beaded on the back of her neck and shoulders. She looked so damn small.

Not debating the consequences, he ran his knuckles over her back. She tensed but didn't try to move away. The small bones of her spine fascinated him. Her choice of careers demanded extraordinary flexibility. Seeing and touching proof of her skeletal structure left him in awe.

A washcloth was draped over the top of the door. After wetting and soaping it, he began lightly scrubbing her back. He didn't want her asking why he was doing this because he didn't have the damn answer. She pushed her hair out of her eyes, then stood with her hands at her sides, body slightly hunched over, long toes curling against the tile. Soapy water gathered on her buttocks. He washed her there, squeezing the washcloth and watching the suds run down the back of her thighs.

She stood motionless while he washed her arms and legs. Although she sucked in her breath, she let him turn her toward him and watched as he circled her breasts with the cloth. It belatedly occurred to him that neither of them had spoken.

His erection held, water running off both sides.

When he reached her belly, she held out her hand but, not about to relinquish his cloth, he slid his hands between her thighs. After a moment, she widened her stance. Back now arched and fingers lightly clenched, she studied his every move as he brought the cloth near her core.

His vision blurred, and dizziness made him lightheaded. Shaking his head, he went back to work. Pressing his palm over her belly, he gently backed her against the wall. Holding her there, he returned his attention to the V between her legs. At first she continued to scrutinize his effort, but soon her head sagged back so the tile supported it. Her lowered lids made her look sleepy. Because she was trembling, he knew she felt something far different.

The bullet Philip had insisted on had been hard and unforgiving, relentlessly assaulting her. In contrast, he kept his strokes with the washcloth light and teasing in a kind of tactile apology. She didn't need repeated cleaning, but she sighed and moved her pelvis every time he touched her pussy so he stayed with his task. Fighting his own sexual needs had given him a headache. She'd have to be deaf not to notice his labored breathing. And she wasn't blind.

He expected her to resist his attempts to touch her sex, but if she was afraid, she hid her fear beneath her simmering excitement. After treating her like an animal being taught a lesson, he needed to give her something else—something of himself.

As for where things might end and what the consequences might be—

10

So much water had run over the washcloth that most of the soap had gone down the drain. Finding a still-soapy corner, he worked it inside her, taking things slow and easy. Instead of protesting, she widened her stance. Her arms dangled. She continued to let the wall support her. Her eyes closed. She sighed.

Another wave of lightheadedness nearly caused him to lose his balance. He braced a hand against the wall and continued.

What the hell are you doing?

I don't know. Damn it, I don't know.

The water was deliciously warm. Because she occasionally stuck out her tongue and took some into her mouth, Ferren was no longer thirsty. Existing somewhere between lethargy and excitement was disconcerting, and if she stayed in here much longer, her skin would start to wrinkle but Lordy did what Mayer was doing feel good.

Mayer. He had a name. And a life beyond what had brought them together.

He's the enemy. If he keeps this up, you'll lose yourself.

But he was using a soft cloth to cleanse her of memories of

what had taken place between them before this moment. If she kept her mind in the present, she could believe Mayer White was, what, her new lover?

The cloth pushed in, retreated, repeated the movement. She no longer felt any soap. He must be rinsing her there now. She should thank him for his attention to detail, thank him for making her body hum. Fear that she might say things she'd regret for the rest of her life kept her silent.

When she'd stepped into the shower, her muscles had trembled in exhaustion, but strength was returning, at least enough to keep her on her feet. Although there had been many men in her life or more appropriately, involved with her body, she'd had only a handful of boyfriends. There'd been no shortage during her teen years, but they'd been as immature as she had been, for the most part jocks obsessed with their sport. She'd been caught up in the usual girl things like clothes and shopping and of course boys with the focus on being seen with the *right* ones.

High school had ended and college began. She'd discovered that the law fascinated her. But even as she excelled in debate and legal history, she'd shied away from committing to the years of study and education debts. Instead, for reasons she'd never been able to articulate, she'd eased her way into a business that put a premium price tag on a sexy body and lack of inhibition.

Whenever the *why* intruded, she'd cast it aside and remind herself of her healthy bank account.

Increasingly, she'd been asking herself what she'd do once her meal ticket started to sag and wrinkle or when the chasm between good money and self respect became too great. If she'd ever find a man who didn't think of her first, last, and always as a porn star. A man who loved her for what she was beneath the surface—whatever that was.

At the moment, none of those things mattered. Only being in this confined space with a man she knew nothing about did.

Mayer turned his attention to her breasts. Sex or the anticipation of same always caused them to swell and feel heavy. They also became more sensitive which is why she refused to let anyone whip them. The riggers or male actors could apply clips she approved of, and she liked the way her boobs looked with ropes binding them, but her *kinky* had its limits.

He'd resoaped the washcloth and was trailing it over and around her breasts. She didn't try to convince herself that he was worshipping them, not after his matter-of-fact manhandling, but she couldn't remember when she'd last experienced such gentle treatment.

"What—what's going to happen next?"

"Don't ask. Concentrate on now."

How she wanted to do that! Exhausted by the thought of facing her future, she cupped her breasts and offered them to this man who said he owned her.

Leaning down, he took her nipple in his mouth. Water sheeted over his dark hair and made it shine. He ran his teeth over her nipple, then closed down just enough to secure his grip. Her arms felt as if weights had been tied to them. Although he had to bend his knees and bow his neck, he continued to hold her. By turn he focused on her hard and sensitive nipples and sucked as much of each breast into his mouth as he could. The shower had been warm, but his saliva felt even warmer, alive.

From the moment he'd stormed into her life, everything had been about him doing things to her. Her kidnapping had been part of Philip's twisted game. The auction had been an act and no matter what anyone said, exchanging a considerable sum didn't mean she'd actually been bought. But what she'd been subjected to had imprinted itself on her. He had the key to the door. She'd remain naked until he gave her something to wear. He'd shut off her communication with the world. And most telling, he knew how to press her body's triggers.

So sit back and enjoy.

Although it was hardly that simple, her body wanted only one thing—his mouth sheltering her breasts.

And soon, please, his cock full and buried in her. Man to woman connection.

Her captured breast throbbed and grew more sensitive. If he nibbled on her nipple now, she'd cry out. Rest. She needed a break!

As if reading her splintering mind, he released her and straightened. Although she was giving away a great deal, she fingered her breast trying to ease the throbbing.

"Did I hurt you?"

What a strange thing for him to ask given everything that had gone before. She shook her head.

He backed away as far as the small enclosure allowed and studied her as if he'd never seen her before, as if she was a subject he was considering painting—or purchasing. Fine. Let him see what she had to offer, all of it. Feeling disconnected, she straightened her shoulders, showing him the breasts that had gotten her to where she was in an industry few people, she included, understood.

"They're natural. I've seen enough porn to know how rare that is."

"I don't want anyone cutting on me."

"You don't need implants."

"Not now, but maybe when I get older."

"You're willing to do that to remain employable?"

Employable? I'm more than a body, damn it. Aren't I? "What do you care?"

"Just asking. How often do you shave your pussy?"

"What?"

"How often—"

"I heard you. Usually every day."

"Pain in the ass, isn't it."

Unexpected laughter bubbled up. "In more ways than one."

He smiled, actually smiled. A shiver ran down her spine. She wanted to laugh with this man, to walk down a country path, to sit before a fireplace and sip wine, to have sex on silk sheets.

Don't! Damn it, don't let down your guard.

"We're getting out of here."

For a moment she thought he meant they'd be leaving the cabin, but when he picked her up and carried her to the bed, she understood. Still holding her, he pulled back the coverlet and lay her on soft white cotton sheets. The air attacked her wet body, causing her to shiver. Using the top sheet, he dried her. She lay passively as he tended to her arms, breasts, belly, pelvis, legs. He licked away the water on her cheeks and nose and blotted her hair as best he could.

She utterly and completely could not move.

Some of the water on him had run off onto the carpet. The rest was drying on him. She loved the way countless droplets lay nestled in his chest hair and the dark thatch over his groin.

"You turn me on," he muttered. "And unless you say no, we're going to fuck."

After everything he'd done to her, he was asking permission? Speaking to her human to human? Wanting to connect in a real way? A sudden need to cry clogged her voice. "I—I won't say no."

Watching her in that intense way of his, he flattened his hand over her mons. "You aren't too sensitive?"

If anything, the enforced climaxes had left her even hungrier for the feel of a real cock in her, his cock. "I'm tough."

"A byproduct of the job?"

Noting his harsh tone, she scrambled for a way to defuse his negative opinion of her career, but she'd tried before with men and hadn't succeeded. She struggled to keep her thoughts off where his hand lay. "Some women envy me."

"Is that what you're going to tell your children, that you were a porn actress because it made you feel superior to other women?"

Fury coursed through her. She surged upward and would have slapped him if he hadn't grabbed her wrists and forced her onto her back again, her hands now pinned over her head. She tried to kick him, but he easily stayed out of reach.

You can't win this fight. He'll just tie you up again. And what the two of you started will die.

"I don't have to answer to you." She couldn't bring herself to return his stare. "Just as I don't expect you to justify why you did what you did to me. We're—hell, who knows what we are to each other."

He nodded. Although he stopped pressing down on her wrists, he didn't free her. "Do you ever want to talk to anyone?"

"What?"

He crossed one wrist over the other so he could control them with one hand. That freed him to stroke the valley between her breasts which loosened her muscles and blunted her anger. "Do you and other subs talk about what turns you on about the lifestyle?"

"I'm not a submissive!"

"You look like one."

At the moment she felt like one, thanks to him. "Just like you look like a Dom? Is that what you want me to say?"

Something akin to regret settled in his expressive eyes. At first she'd been afraid of the his intensity, but she'd become accustomed to his determination to pull emotion out of her. She wished she understood.

She seldom had the opportunity or desire to try to comprehend what went on beneath the surface of the men she worked with. Despite the inarguable mutual pleasure gained from each scene, in the end, everyone was driven by money and self-pleasure. Just as the riggers did, she played to the camera. Afterward, they all went their own way and kept their own thoughts.

This was different. This was about two unlikely people brought together by something she didn't understand and frightened and fascinated her. Did he feel the same way? Did the heart of a Dom beat beneath his surface? Did she want it to?

Belatedly realizing he hadn't answered her question, she repeated it.

"I'm who I am," he replied. "Don't try to read anything else into it."

"But I don't know who you are." Her wrists were becoming numb, prompting her to flex them. He released her. Bringing her arms back by her side, she again studied him, looking for pieces of information, hints as to the real man. The hand once again covering her mons clearly said he knew how to keep her awareness of her sex on high.

What if the tables were turned?

"Why don't you talk about yourself?" she challenged.

"Why do you give a damn?"

There, nearly hidden in his depths, lurked a child, a boy. She could only grasp at that child and try to keep him from retreating into whatever cave he'd come from, but she'd try. God, would she!

"I care because you're a human being." If only she could dismiss the pressure low on her belly and the promise beneath that weight. "A man willing to turn a modern woman into a sex slave."

She thought he might repeat what he'd said about giving her what she wanted. Instead, he crawled onto the bed, spread her legs, and positioned himself on his knees between them. When he rested his hands on her knees and lightly kneaded them, heated currents raced up her legs to nestle in her cunt. She couldn't keep her buttocks still. Shifting slightly, she gripped his forearms. He was here, truly here. Determined to make good on his promise to fuck her.

"We're down to basics, aren't we?" He pressed his thumbs into the flesh at the top of her thigh. "No casual chatter, no 'how nice to meet you'."

She pressed back. The veins on the insides of his wrists throbbed under her fingers. "No."

"And because I've already touched every part of you, I'm not asking permission now."

"I—I didn't expect you to."

She tensed when he slid back and lowered his head until his mouth was scant inches from her core. His warm breath both calmed her and fed her inner fire. She ran her fingers into his hair but stared at the ceiling because that was safer.

He was coming closer, closer, his breath dampening her labia. She squirmed.

"Don't try to get away."

"I'm not." Her throat burned.

"Good. Because I'm going to make up for what happened earlier."

His intentions should be important to her, shouldn't they? But all she could think was that he was going to perform cunnilingus on her. She'd experimented with oral sex in her private life but never on the job since Cages was about the BDSM lifestyle.

All thoughts of what she'd experienced or missed on the job fled the instant Mayer's tongue touched her clit. Jumping, she mewed like a kitten. When she bent her legs, he slid his hands under her buttocks and lifted her. Took over.

Featherweight tongue strokes began at her perineum and worked up and over her clitoris. Shaking, she rocked from side to side. By turn she gripped the sheet and his hair. Try as she did, she couldn't relax her grip. Couldn't stay on top of the sensations.

His experienced tongue stroked first one lip and then the other, keeping her off balance and on the edge. Wet heat boiled throughout her. Relief waited just out of reach, but although she moaned and lifted herself toward him in a wordless plea, he knew how far to take her.

Countless vibrators had been used on her, but none had come close to this—this incredible intimacy. Despite the way she used hers, there was something sacred about a woman's vagina. Fully stimulated, its response turned her from civilized to primitive animal—out of control. She felt that way now, a puppet being pulled by his strings.

Lightning-like strokes inflamed not just her clitoris but her whole body. She'd caught fire, the flames deep red or ice blue by turn, beautiful and powerful. Needing something she with all her experience couldn't put a name to, she caressed her breast. When her nipple pressed against her palm, she released his hair and began massaging her other breast. Within seconds, both nipples were equally hard.

He tongue-bathed her, patient and tireless, filling her with heat and need. By pressing down with her heels, she repeatedly lifted her ass off the bed. He responded by sliding his tip inside her and driving her crazy. In her mind, his tongue became his cock. Except it was softer, more mobile, maybe more intimate.

Yes, intimate! Cocks were designed to fit inside vaginas. It was the natural order of things. Fucking brought pleasure and kept the human race going.

But surely no other creatures had discovered that pleasure came from more than one source, that the pure intimacy of a man's tongue dancing over a woman's cunt spoke of trust.

Trust? At this moment at least, she trusted Mayer.

"Thank you. Thank you," she chanted. "Oh damn, thank you."

He stopped and looked at her, putting her in mind of an animal interrupted from drinking. "From the first I wanted to do you this way."

Because this is an act for lovers, not master and slave?

Sliding his hands out from under her buttocks, he started stroking her inner thighs. Heat again slammed into her, and she cried out. Although she needed a moment of relief, he refused to grant it. Instead, his fingers inched toward her opening.

"Ahh."

"Relax."

"I can't." She tried to scoot away, but he followed her. "Oh shit, I can't!"

"Good." Fingers closed over her labial lips and held them together, sealing her core, imprisoning her. "Easy, easy."

"I've never . . ."

"No man has ever performed cunnilingus on you?"

"I didn't—it didn't . . ." Tears clogged her throat.

"Then I've taken your virginity."

A virgin. A precious gift a woman gives only once.

She was afraid he'd press her for details about why her sex life had been devoid of this special intimacy, but he didn't. Maybe he knew how hard the explanation would be, and maybe he already understood that her career separated her from true and deep personal relationships.

It was too complicated! Too much to think about while he claimed so much of her with no more than two fingers.

"I'd love to watch you dance to my tongue, but I have to get something out of this."

Of course he did. He'd had a nearly perpetual hard-on since she'd first seen him. "I, ah, I give good head."

"I know. I've watched you."

Bile rose in her throat, distracting her from the way he was sliding her lips against each other and creating heated friction. Giving head on camera was part of her job, one of her techniques. She couldn't blame him if he didn't want to become another of her subjects. Hadn't she heard that demeaning comment from men she thought she might care for. Her eyes burned, forcing her to briefly close them to keep her tears hidden.

Her life had been short-range, one role-playing session bleeding into the next, the pleasure of coming, working out and watching her diet, bills easily paid and a growing portfolio.

Now those givens had been taken from her. In their place was confinement and nearly endless sexual stimulation. Contemplation and questioning.

A man like no other.

11

Instead of probing for the source of Ferren's tears, Mayer slid up and over her so he could brace his arms on either side of her shoulders. His knees supported his lower body with her bent knees brushing his butt and thighs. He slowly, cautiously lowered himself until his cock found her, then stopped. Not forcing himself into her took incredible self restraint, but damn it, he needed her to tell him she wanted this. Needed time to make his peace with his conflicting emotions. Fucking her would change things between them. Almost as much as it would change him.

Why hadn't he put on a rubber?

Her gaze locked on his and pulled him deep. *Dive into her. Risk everything.*

No! Don't be an idiot.

Giving himself a mental shake, he searched for wisdom. He could only guess at the message in her eyes but read acceptance in the way she'd placed her arms over her head.

Trust? She trusted him?

The question of protection again came to mind. While doing

his research, he'd learned that she didn't allow penis penetration. How much would she have to give up before she fully embraced what Philip insisted she wanted?

Damn it, hadn't he'd already wrestled with the question enough? He'd do so again but not now, not with her soft and warm body under him.

Something animal-like crawled over and then attacked him. He'd fought his arousal for too damn long, his sense that he was about to dive into fire. He'd taken pride in his self-control while exacting total surrender from her, but it had come at a price.

Now was reward time.

Leaning forward, he brushed his chest against her breasts, then reared back and again studied her expression. "One question."

"What?"

"Do you want this?"

Calm followed by an instant of joy lit her features. Then she regained control, sobered, calmed. "Yes." She spoke slowly. "I'm on the pill. And . . ."

"What?"

"All right. All right. I have myself periodically checked for—you know."

"I do the same."

"Then we're both clean."

Shit! He didn't want to be having this discussion. And yet it made things easier. Freer. Safer.

More emotionally dangerous.

Rolling her knees to the outside, she opened herself. That done, she lifted her buttocks off the bed and positioned herself for him. His cock knotted, demanded. Bending toward her, he pushed forward. His tip found her soft, moist flesh. Holding himself there, he rocked, introducing his cock to her cave.

Perched at the edge of sanity.

Damn it, he hadn't turned off the camera! He'd have to

delete this part before sending the video to Philip. Maybe he wouldn't send anything to him today. Maybe he'd return the check and take Ferren home with him.

No good! Despite his attempts to distance himself from his hunger, its teeth were sharp and the grip strong. He hadn't been this horny since his teens. Instinct kicked in. His body knew what to do. Down, up, down again. Each time finding her ready and waiting, lifting her pelvis to him, her wet, hot pussy closing down as if it loved his cock. Liquid friction slid over his hard length. Nerve endings sparked.

Fast. So damn fast. Pressure building, taking him to the edge of the waterfall.

His mind spluttered and spun out. Perhaps conditioned by videos of her, perhaps fueled by his own animal nature, an image formed. He was sitting in a comfortable chair and well-dressed. Except for the swollen cock thrusting out of his unzipped slacks, he appeared the ultimate professional.

Ferren crouched before him. Her blouse had been torn off; maybe he'd been responsible. She still wore a bra, but it had been pushed up, exposing her incredible breasts. Her short skirt bunched around her waist. Her panties and shoes were gone. He'd tied her wrists behind her, then completed the image by tightly binding her elbows until they nearly touched.

She was on her knees and bent low, her luscious mouth inches from his cock. Her spun gold hair had fallen forward, making him think of angels. He brushed it back and captured the thick length behind her head. She looked up at him, eyes swimming with lust.

"Suck me," he ordered. "Suck me until I come."

Nodding, she leaned forward. Parting her full lips, she drew in his tip. She lightly raked her teeth over him; he shuddered. On its tail, another tremor hit him. Forced to face the fact that right now his *captive* held the upper hand, he strained toward her. She took him easily, fully, expertly.

Anger over something unfathomable driving him, he pushed. As he did, his knees slipped on the sheet and pulled him back to reality. The woman in the real world had fisted her fingers in her hair, back tightly arched and breasts reaching for his chest.

"Easy, easy," she chanted. "Don't rush."

Because he couldn't tell her of the thoughts that had fueled him, he forced a smile. "You want to be along for the ride?"

"I deserve it."

No sex slave or submissive would say that, would they? Before he could answer his question, she tightened her pussy around him. He became the prisoner, the one compelled to obey. But damn, he wanted to.

Slow. Easy. The chant nearly drove him to distraction, but he made it his mantra. They might never fuck again. Hell, if Philip had his way, they certainly wouldn't. He needed this to be good and right and memorable. The memorable was already a given. Good he might be able to give her. As for the right?

Don't think. Don't think.

Ferren's back was burning, and her thigh muscles had started to shake. She couldn't keep up her end of things much longer but didn't want to rush. Still, if she wasn't going to wind up too exhausted to be an equal partner, she'd have to move things along.

Shouldn't she be lost in that elusive thing called ecstasy, become a creature that cared about nothing except the silken abrasions in her cunt?

Obviously not.

"Wait," she gasped. "Please, stop."

"What?"

"I can't—" Sinking down until the bottom sheet absorbed her sweat, she rested her arms inside his. Taking a deep breath, she gripped his elbows, lifted her legs, and tucked them against her body. Mayer arched back; his cock slipped out of her.

Empty and wanting, she reached for his neck. He sank toward her, his cock easily finding its home.

He was deep in her now, buried to the hilt. She felt him maybe everywhere. His balls pressed against her buttocks added to the sensation of being consumed, especially when he started thrusting again.

He was working her, working both of them, pushing and retreating as they inched toward the head of the bed. If her sweat hadn't stuck her to the bed, they might already be there. Not being able to do more than clench and release his cock frustrated her, but she'd never taken a man deeper or felt a cock more fully. He couldn't possibly get more of himself in her and must be feeling the same thorough penetration.

They were in this together, him pounding at her, she open and helpless and vulnerable and panting. Her legs were useless, her fingers locking around his elbows when she wanted to feel more of him, do more.

Cheeks, breasts, and cunt on fire, she closed her eyes against the world. Another existence swam into view. In this one, she'd been placed on her back with her arms chained over her head. Her captor or master or whoever he was had tightly bent her knees and cinched straps around her thighs and calves so she couldn't straighten them. She tried to close her legs, but the man easily spread her.

Still, she tried to get away by scooting on whatever was beneath her. The dark man watched her for awhile, then grabbed a breast and squeezed, fastened a clip to it. He did the same to her other breast and then pulled them together via a short chain hooked to each clip.

She stared at what he'd done, tested the handcuffs, felt the taut leather pressing against her thighs and calves. Helpless. Beyond helpless. Her cunt dripping and sweat building between her breasts and her breath quick and ragged.

This time when he spread her legs, she didn't resist. And when he slid a pillow under her hips, she kept her gaze fixed on him. He had her where he wanted her. She loved it.

The man inside her mind pulled his shirt over his head, removed his belt, unzipped his slacks. Stepping out of the garment, he allowed her a glimpse of the great bulge pressing against his briefs. A smile touched his lips. He gripped elastic, pulled.

She saw him. All of him.

"You know you want it," her fantasy man said.

By the time he'd positioned himself between her legs, she was shaking so badly she had to clench her teeth to keep from biting her tongue. Something pressed against her throat. Cool air brushed over her labia, and she lifted her head to try to look at herself there.

"Be patient. I'm coming."

There, finally, his flesh kissing hers. Hot width and length penetrating and spreading her, skewering her. She forgot her chained arms and cinched legs. The nipple clamps became an aphrodisiac, pain morphing into desire.

"Now, now!"

Mayer's voice pulled her back into the real world. The drawing sensation along the back of her thighs grounded her. Her neck ached from thrashing back and forth. Mayer was staring at some point beyond them, his head framed inside her feet. Any other time she would have laughed, but laughter had no place in her existence.

"Hit me!" she screamed. "Please, do me!"

He pounded into her and lifted her. His straining muscles held them both. His come filled her. The hot, pure sensation nearly made her weep. How long had it been since she'd drunk fully, cleanly of what a man had to offer?

Although her own climax crouched, she fought it off, determined to absorb as much of his as she could. He continued to strain against her, legs and arms shuddering, sucking in air through his open mouth. God, she loved the sound!

When he sank back, her legs came with him. His pelvis clenched, then clenched again. "Hit me!" she begged.

He did, rising up and rocking forward, threatening to push her over. She no longer simply had his cock in her. It had become part of her, reaching for her belly and housed deep inside her pelvis. More come swam through her.

The sensation was her undoing. Throwing back her head, she let go. Her climax rose over her, gripped and shook, melted her down. She reached the pinnacle and clung there, muscles cramping, releasing, cramping again.

She bellowed.

12

When the phone rang, Mayer rolled over and faced away from it. Next to him, Ferren walked her fingers over his limp cock. He couldn't say how long it had been since they'd fucked. As a randy teenager, he'd been ready to go again in less than an hour, but with age had come the need for time to recover. But not too much time. His cock twitched and sent a heated message to his belly.

The phone rang again.

"Answer it," she said. "He'll just keep calling unless you do."

"I don't want to listen to him."

"He doesn't know what we've been doing."

"I should have sent the footage to him by now."

"All of it?"

Her tone hadn't changed, but he knew how much his answer meant to her. He didn't try.

Sitting up, he reached for the phone, but when he punched send, he heard only a dial tone. "He's hung up."

"Mayer?"

Tense, he turned toward her.

"Philip really is behind this, isn't he?"

He stared at her sex-satiated body. Her hair was damp and tangled, and their shared come had dried on her inner thighs. He'd paid for this woman, not he really, but he'd been paid to accomplish a single task—to bring her down into the world of submission and mastery. In exchange for his work, he'd have what he needed to forge the life he wanted, the career he needed. He, who couldn't remember when or if he'd ever truly cared for another human being, had taken the job because that's what it had been—a job.

It no longer was.

"Yeah, it's him."

"Did he say why he wanted to do certain things to me? Did he tell you about our relationship?"

Damn it. She was sitting there looking like a living, breathing sex doll with a body made for fucking. How could she expect him to carry on a conversation?

"Of course he didn't," she continued. "He probably gave you some damn lie about wanting to play a trick on me. Never mind." She waved her hand which caused her breasts to jiggle. "His site is successful. A lot of girls who want to get into the industry knock at his door hoping to be given a chance—at least they do at first."

"At first?"

"Before they learn what he's really like. I've told as many as I can. No one deserves to get sucked into his sick game."

He was still trying to decide whether to risk lying down next to her again when she scooted to the edge of the bed and stood up. She stalked to the door to the main room, spun and walked back. Her every move drove needles into him.

Surrender Island existed for one reason, to fulfill fantasies of submission and mastery. Even if he severed his relationship with Philip, maybe he could keep her here. He who occasionally entertained fantasies of dominating women, had been granted the opportunity of a lifetime.

Here was a woman with no sexual inhibitions, one accustomed to being handled and manipulated. It wouldn't take much to make her crave the real thing, would it? Already she'd given out hints that BDSM had a certain appeal to her.

He could chain her in here, secure that remarkable bullet inside her and keep it running until—until what?

"It's my word against his, isn't it?" She settled on the edge of the bed but remained tense. "I don't know how to make you believe me."

"Try."

Try? Ferren opened her mouth but then closed it. The way she made her living placed her on the fringe. What she did was considered legal within vague boundaries although there were many who would argue otherwise. Hadn't her mother told her that law enforcement would be unlikely to take anything she said at face value? Most important, thanks to Philip, she had undeniable proof of her career's underbelly.

"I worked for him because the exposure was incredible. At the time, his site was the most successful. It bothered me that he pushed things, but I didn't know what to do about it. It's not like porn models belong to a union."

"What do you mean by push?"

"He didn't always verify models' ages. I know he had some underage girls working for him. Sanitary conditions are vital given what—what happens. He was slipshod about that. That's what I tried to tell new models about."

"How did he get away with it? The porn industry's regulated, right?"

Porn industry. The words made her feel dirty. "There's incredible money involved. New sites appear all the time, both straight sex and the kinkier stuff. It's impossible for the law or morality groups or whatever to keep up with it. Besides . . ."

"Besides what?"

She'd been staring at the carpet. Now she looked up and into the eyes of a man unlike any she'd ever met. His aura of strength and power might come from what he'd done to her and not his ability to protect her, but she didn't have the time to find the truth. She could only tell him what she knew, and pray he'd believe her.

"Philip intimidates. If anyone steps out of line, he knows how to bring them back in."

Mayer stood. Grabbing her arms, he hauled her to her feet. Helplessness washed over her, and she had to force herself not to fight him. They were both naked and smelling of the sex they'd had. But he was the one with the muscles, the key to the door.

"How?"

She stared at his solid chest. "When I went to work for him, he had two experienced models working for him. They had their own Web sites and did independent stuff. Although he wanted it, he didn't have an exclusive contract from them. He kept after them, insisting they give up their other work. Otherwise, he said, he'd make sure they regretted it."

Locked in Mayer's grip, she told him about the time one of the girls hadn't shown up for a scheduled shoot. Philip had informed her she was taking the other model's place. Thinking this was her chance to star, she'd jumped at the opportunity. The session had been stressful with Philip insisting the rigger take her past her declared limits. By the time things were over, she was exhausted and more than a little frightened. As soon as she could, she'd driven to where the other model was living.

"Candy didn't come to the door when I rang the bell, but I'd seen her convertible so I knew she was there. The door wasn't locked. I walked in, calling out to let her know it was me. She— she was—"

"Go on."

How long had she been silent as she mentally replayed what she'd seen? "Candy was in bed. She'd been beaten, badly. She wouldn't say who was responsible, but I knew. I couldn't get her to go to the hospital or talk to the police. She was terrified."

"Did she recover?"

Tears formed, blurring her vision. She stared at the hazy outline of Mayer's chest. "Yes, although she missed a couple of weeks of work. I only saw her on the set once more. She told me this was the last time she'd work for Philip because she was breaking her contract and going out on her own." She sucked in air. "She did, but she'd just gotten things up and running when she disappeared."

Mayer's grip increased and then relaxed. He started massaging her shoulders. Although she felt his touch throughout her, she didn't dare let his impact distract her. "I guess the police looked for her. I didn't hear much about that. They probably figured she got what she deserved. Either that or they didn't take her disappearance seriously."

"You didn't try to find her?"

"How? We weren't close. I didn't know anything about her private life. Besides . . ."

"Don't stop now."

Her throat tightened. Bombarded by the past and old nightmares, she rested her head on his chest. "All of us models talked about Candy, wondering what had happened to her, wondering if Philip had had something to do with it. Then another model, the other successful one I mentioned—I was there the day she stood up to Philip."

"How?"

"Like Candy, Violet had had it with the way he pushed. There'd been some breath play during her session, and she had marks on her throat. She swore that she'd call the cops if he ever ordered something like that again. He called her a bunch of names. She slapped him, hard. And then she quit."

"Where is she now?"

Leaning back, she looked up at Mayer. "No one has seen her for nearly a year."

"Shit. Has anyone looked for her?"

"Me. Other girls. Mayer, I can't make you believe me. My mother always said my decisions were my own and she'd support me no matter what I did, but she warned that I was placing myself outside *normal* society. The rules are different there."

"Yeah, they are."

He'd given her a vivid demonstration of the unique standards on the island. If he wanted to, he could easily begin another lesson. Although her body hummed at the thought of being under his control, under him, she refused to be distracted.

"After Violet—that wasn't her real name of course—disappeared, I knew I had to separate myself from Philip. I'd criticized some of his practices and tried to let newcomers know what they'd be getting into. But I didn't dare make the break it the way Violet and Candy had tried, not if I was going to live."

He stiffened. "What did you do?"

"I let him know who my mother is."

"Who is she?"

"A prosecuting attorney for the D.A.'s office over in Lincoln County."

"A what? Shit. He didn't know that before?"

"No one did. Mom and I agreed that, professionally speaking, our relationship could backfire on both of us." *And I don't want to embarrass her.*

"But if something happened to you—"

"She'd raise heaven and hell looking for me. I told her about my concerns regarding Cindy and Violet. Unfortunately, I had no proof that Philip was involved. That's when, for the first time, Mom asked me to quit."

Mayer stopped massaging her arms and held up her hands. Although she sometimes wore artificial nails for shoots, she preferred keeping them natural. Right now she needed a manicure. And clothes. And something to eat. And sleep. Most of all, she needed to connect with Mayer.

"What about your father?"

"My father?"

"He can't be crazy about his daughter the porn star."

Confused and upset, she pulled free and walked to the window. It was truly beautiful out there. Late afternoon shadows spread over the lush vegetation, and a breeze caused tree branches and shrubs to look as if they were dancing. She wanted to be out there—almost as much as she needed Mayer's arms around her. His belief in her.

"My parents met while they were in college. When she realized she was pregnant, she wanted them to become a family. He didn't. End of story."

"No, not the end."

"All right, damn it! My mother didn't press him because even back then she was independent. And determined. She made sure he paid child support which he could because his father owned a chain of automobile sales businesses. He's taken over the business." Raking her fingers through her tangled hair failed to distance herself from the telling. "He's been married and divorced several times and has other children. I've seen him three times, once right after I was born although I don't remember that."

"The bastard."

"No, I'm the bastard. I—I was such a fool. As a child, I'd call and write him. Try to get him to love me. I'd send him pictures of myself and tell myself he had them framed and kept near his bed. Hell, I even made copies of my grades and mailed those to him. But . . ."

"What?"

"He never acknowledged my birthday. I got nothing at Christmas."

"Bastard."

"When—when, at seventeen, I bought my first car, I drove to where he lived. He reluctantly let me in but didn't tell his then wife who I was. I—I asked him to take me on a tour of his house. There were no pictures of me. He asked me to leave before his children got home from school. *His* children."

Although it nearly killed him, Mayer remained where he was, his nails digging into his palms. Her naked and spent body called to him as no woman's ever had before. He didn't like the feeling—didn't know what to do with it. Neither could he handle the image of a lonely girl desperately seeking one thing from her father, love.

How much of her life had been impacted by that lack?

Like he hadn't been down the same road.

"So you intimidated Philip." He deliberately changed the subject. "And he let you out of your contract?"

Her stare nearly ripped him apart. "I thought so. Obviously I was wrong."

"Do you know Candy and Violet's real names?"

"What?"

Don't look at her breasts and legs, her hollow and hurting eyes. Don't think about throwing her on the bed and ramming your cock in her so far you'll never find your way out. Don't tell her you're sorry her old man's a bastard and she has to stop looking for something from him. Most of all, don't let her know she's gotten to you.

"Their names. I want to check some things on the Internet."

"And when you have, what happens then?"

Between us or about what I do or don't learn? "It depends on what I find. Do you want another shower?"

"Yes. And something to eat."

An hour later, Mayer closed down his laptop. He'd taken a quick shower once Ferren was through and slipped into a clean pair of shorts but had been too intent on the task he'd given himself to do more than that. Because he had his P.I. license, he had access to several sites off-limits to the public. Up until now, he'd thought he'd be using them for such distasteful but economically necessary things as checking on people's personal habits and activities for disgruntled spouses or employers. But digging into Candy and Violet's lives had been both fascinating and chilling. He'd also done some research on Ferren's mother. Not only was she a senior lawyer, she also had a reputation as a political and personal liberal. Nothing, it seemed, shocked her.

He wondered if she truly supported her daughter's career or regretted passing on those liberal views.

Still thinking about the older woman, he accepted the tuna sandwich Ferren had made, but although his stomach rumbled, he didn't start eating. There was nothing here for her to wear so she'd wrapped a towel around herself. She smelled of soap and shampoo. The scents were far different from the aroma of sex that had clung to her, but his nerves approved. So did his cock.

Ignoring her impact wouldn't be easy, but he had to try. He had to think about his options and make plans.

Sighing, she dropped to the floor near his chair. Sitting cross-legged with her crotch covered by the towel, she took a bite of her own sandwich. Her gaze locked on him. Her expression spoke of a woman both free and captive. "Did you find out anything?"

"Yeah. I learned both 'Candy' and 'Violet's' social security numbers and from there tapped into bank and credit card accounts."

"And?"

"And neither woman has touched her checking or savings in months. There have been no credit purchases or payments. Candy has been turned over to a collection agency for nonpayment of her car loan, but because her condo is in default and her phone service has been cut off, the record shows that their attempts to contact her have failed."

He could tell her more, but there was no need. The way her mouth trembled, he knew she'd come to the same conclusion he had.

"What about the police?"

"There are open missing persons cases on them but no recent activity."

She glanced at her sandwich but didn't take another bite. "Do—do you believe me now?"

13

Ferren could only watch as Mayer reached for his cell phone.

"It's me," he said. It seemed as if he was deliberately avoiding looking at her. "I was occupied when you called earlier. Give me a few minutes. I'll send the pictures and latest footage." He listened, then laughed. "Hell of a damn good job is right. No, I'm not in any hurry. In fact the longer this takes, the better I like it." Another pause. "Yeah, of course she's been trying to bribe me, but you're the one who paid for my loyalty, if you get my drift. By the way, I appreciate the bonus. I think today's video will serve as proof that I got the message."

Feeling nauseous, she scooted away. Thick carpet rubbed her buttocks.

"No, not until morning. She's pretty out of it, and I need to get some rest too." He listened again. "No shit. It's damn past time to sample this piece of ass myself. That's why I'm going to take a nap. What? Fuck you! How are you going to stop me?" His harsh laugh grated her nerves. "Next time hire a eunuch. I'm giving myself another bonus."

The urge to jump to her feet and run was nearly more than she could control, but she didn't trust her legs to hold her. Even more, she couldn't believe what he was saying. This had to be an act on his part, it had to be!

He hung up and went to the video camera. After working with it for a few moments, he plugged a USB cable into it and then the laptop.

Her throat tightened. "Did you delete the last part?"

"He's not going to see it."

A few keystrokes had him back online. He studied the monitor, then nodded. She had no doubt the transfer was taking place.

Silence spread through the room, trapping her. Once she'd believed Philip when he said he was going to make her into a star. Even when he pressured her to go beyond her comfort zone, she'd stayed with him because he'd been so convincing, so supportive of her damnable goals or compulsion or whatever drove her. It was a tough business, he'd told her. But she had what it took to be a success, and the members loved her. She'd seen enough e-mails from those members to know that many considered her hot. For too long she'd bought into the compliments. Her father might wish she'd never been born, but a man about his age had given her all the attention she'd craved.

And then she'd learned the truth about Philip. He didn't personally care any more about her than her father had.

Was Mayer any different?

What made her think she'd be safe with him simply because he made her feel alive in a way she never had? Because she'd told him about the holes her father's absence had carved in her? Was he playing her along, taking Philip's money and preparing her for a life she could barely fathom but might never escape?

Might he kill her?

Fighting fears, she struggled to her feet and walked back to the window. The light was fading. All too soon night would capture the island—just as she was Mayer's captive.

"Who are you?" she asked with her back to him. "What are you?"

"A man who spent too damn long before deciding what to do with his life."

The unexpected response held layers of meaning. She just wished she could find her way through them. "Why did it take so long?"

"Lots of reasons, mostly lack of direction. Come here."

Mesmerized by his tone, she obeyed. Now that she was dry, the towel no longer clung to her. She needed to fasten it more securely but couldn't concentrate on the task. All too soon she stood before him, vulnerable in ways she could barely fathom.

His gaze held on her face. "You told me some things about yourself. They weren't easy."

"No, they weren't." *And they might have been dangerous.* "What—what about you? Surely you've—"

"Yeah, I have."

His body pulled at hers. Even stronger was the need to hear and embrace whatever he chose to share with her, if anything. Still, when he stood, she took an instinctive step back.

"I'm not going to hurt you, not now." Without bothering to ask permission, he took her arm and led her into the bedroom. She perched on the edge of the bed. Her heartbeat picked up, and the words *not now* hummed inside her.

"You're my world." She couldn't speak above a whisper. "You dominate it. And I don't know anything about you."

"Not many people do."

"I'm not *many people!*"

After a silent, still moment, he nodded. "You're one step up on me in a certain regard because at least you know who your old man is."

"You don't—"

"From what I learned about my mother, the list of sperm donors is nearly limitless."

"I'm sorry."

"Don't be." He sat beside her, his greater weight pulling her off balance so her shoulder rested against his. "It's an old song. Besides, it gets even better. I was born while my mother was in jail—for theft. At least I think that's what the charge was that time."

"She's been jailed more than once?"

"Damn near made a career out of it. One thing I have to hand her. As far as I know, she wasn't on drugs when she was pregnant with me. Or if she was, she didn't pass that little gift onto me."

"Oh. I—I'm glad she . . ."

"I don't know much about the three others she pushed out after me except that one of the two girls and the other boy have disabilities associated with drug-affected parents. Damn pretty picture, isn't it?"

What he'd told her nearly made her weep. She would have if she didn't need to concentrate on him, not her reaction. "Did she raise you?"

"Fortunately, only infrequently. And when I was with her, *raising* wasn't a term I'd use."

Thanks to her mother's career, she'd learned more than she wanted to know about the lot of children born into dysfunctional families. Too many grew up to be as screwed up as their parents. And as her mother said, criminal behavior was all too often passed from one generation to the next. "Where did you live when you weren't with her?"

"Damn near everywhere." His sharp shrug jolted her. A glance told her that he was staring at the floor, his jaw tight. "I stopped counting foster homes at six. Then because I was an

264 / *Vonna Harper*

idiot, I started doing what's called running afoul of the law. Acting out. Not giving a shit. Various juvenile justice systems and facilities started paying for my keep."

"You were in prison?"

"If by *prison* you mean an adult correctional facility, no. But juve, yes."

Locked up. Behind bars. Worse than what he'd put her through.

"Eventually a simple fact sank in. If I didn't want to spend my life looking out at the world through bars, I had to get my act together."

Much as she longed to push him for more information, she knew to go at his pace. Despite his short, no-nonsense telling, she sensed how scared and confused he'd been as a child, how unloved he'd felt. He'd become a survivor but at what cost? Was he incapable of trusting, of giving or accepting love?

"I'd dropped out of school but eventually went back for my GED. I picked up some college courses but didn't see the point of much of what's offered. Besides," his laugh was harsh. "Besides, I was making what I considered decent money working in construction. I'm good with my hands."

I know. "Why aren't you doing that any more?"

"Because I'm no longer a young buck. I've seen too many older men who stayed in the industry with bad backs and knees, or worse. And I wanted to be my own boss, to use my brain."

By letting someone like Philip pay you to treat me like a piece of property? But didn't she love some of the aspects of being under his command? Confused, she rolled her shoulders trying to relax.

Suddenly he planted his hands on her collarbone and shoved. She landed on her back, legs dangling over the edge of the bed. "What—"

He loomed over her, his bulk warning her not to move. His stare went on and on, digging through her layers. Unnerved, she closed down. *Leave me alone! I won't let you get closer. I don't dare.*

Neither do I, his eyes said. *I've already gone too far.*

"I'm in this for myself." His eyes darkened, warned, and she saw the tough kid who hadn't flinched, at least on the outside, when steel doors slammed shut behind him. "If you get something out of this, fine. But like I told Philip, I'd be a fool not to sample the goodies."

Nausea rose in her throat. Who had he become? "What— what are you going to do?"

"What I need to." Leaning down, he braced his arms on either side of her. "You can play along and share in the fun if you want. Or you can resist. Either way, the outcome's going to be the same."

She punched him in the chest. "Damn you! I'm not—"

"Yeah, you are." Straightening, he grabbed the towel at the top of her breasts and yanked it loose. "You make a living as a cock tease. In some places what you do is illegal. A lot of people consider it immoral. Why do you think the cops have better things to do that looking for those two broads? They're hardly pillars of the community. Kind of gives me free rein, doesn't it?"

Fighting emotions she couldn't put a name to, she dug her nails into his wrists. "What the hell is this about?"

"Isn't that clear?"

No, damn it, no!

He seemed oblivious to the pain she was inflicting. She could no longer read anything about his emotions. *Calm. Stay calm.* "You don't have to do it this way. We had sex once. I—"

"The last time I seduced you. Now I'm not bothering."

"Why?"

Something deep and complex flickered through him. For an instant she caught a glimpse of the small child he'd once been, then that lonely and unloved boy was gone, replaced by a man she didn't know. "Because I can."

Before she could react, he rotated his wrists and jerked his arms upward, freeing himself. She tried to sit up. Grabbing her arms, he forced them over her head. Then he flipped her over onto her stomach. The towel remained under her, her back and buttocks once again naked. He pressed against her shoulder blades and the small of her back. Although she tried to kick him, her feet found only air.

"Stop it!"

"I don't think you want me to. And if you do right now, in a few minutes you won't."

Although she squirmed, he easily planted a hand between her legs and leveraged her further onto the bed. She brought her hands down but couldn't reach behind her. Kneeling beside her, he pressed against her shoulder blades. His other hand remained against her crotch.

Leaning low, he raked his teeth over her buttocks.

"Ah! No." Her squirming accomplished nothing.

"Ah, yes."

Pinpricks of electricity attacked her as he continued to run his teeth over her ass, distracting her from her pitiful attempts at freedom. He worked his way lower, reached the back of her thigh where it connected with her buttocks. Then he sucked her flesh into his mouth and held on, his hot breath spilling over her ass. Moist heat leaked to her crack.

"Ah, ah." She thrashed her head from side to side but managed to keep her pelvis still.

He started nibbling, sampling her unbelievably sensitive upper thigh followed by the base of her spine where her buttocks was fullest. Her face felt on fire. She breathed like a spent racehorse. Her hip bones dug into the bed.

A particularly sharp nip on her right flank caused her to cry out. He immediately bathed the spot with his tongue and lips.

"Oh shit. Shit."

A chuckle sent more hot air skittering over her sensitized flesh. Reaching back, she found his knee and tried to grab hold. By twisting to the side, she managed to lift her head but couldn't see him. He closed a hand over her shoulder, holding her in place.

Countless nibbles, nips, tongue-licking, and sucking drove her nearly insane. She was melting and in danger of oozing into nothing. Her cunt throbbed. She fought the hard ache by grinding her pelvis against the mattress. Somehow her legs had separated, increasing his access to her. His fingers caressed her labia, teased at her entrance, entered but retreated. Making a point that needed no words, he wiped his wet fingers on her ass, then returned for more.

His back must be aching, his neck burning from maintaining his hunched over position. Try as she did, she couldn't extend her hand enough to reach his cock so she could inflict as much *damage* as he was. Damn his shorts, his superior strength, his everything.

Releasing her shoulder, he pressed the heel of his hand against her tailbone with a rotating motion that forced out another heated cry.

Suddenly he straightened. Before she could guess what he had in mind, he forced her up onto her knees with her arms outstretched on the bed and her face buried in the sheet. She managed to turn her head enough to breathe but remained where he'd positioned her, waited. Strong fingers separated her legs. Everything about her sex was now accessible to him.

Oh yes, accessible.

He cupped his hand over her dangling labia and cradled it. His thumb stroked her anus.

"Hhaa. Oh my God."

"This is new? I thought you'd experienced everything."

Nothing like this. And no one like you.

Hunger latched onto her. The longer he held her, the more famished she became. Lifting her buttocks as high as she could, she offered herself to him. The next time, damn it, the next time she'd tie him spread-eagle to the bed and sexually tease him until he ripped his arms out of their sockets.

This time as before, however, he was running the show, demonstrating his knowledge of her by alternatingly stroking and finger-fucking her. In her mind she became a hot puddle, a squirming, helpless, turned-on bitch. "No more. Please I can't—no more."

Powerful hands latched onto her shoulders. Limp and willing, she didn't so much as think of resisting when he maneuvered her onto her back again. She turned apprehensive when he positioned her so her head dangled over the edge, then dismissed the blood rushing to her temple because he'd again bent her knees and was pressing on her inner thighs. Obeying, she lifted her ass off the bed. Then she watched as he shucked off his shorts.

His cock! Oh damn, his cock!

When he knelt between her splayed legs, she grabbed his shoulders and held on. Eyes smoldering with unspoken command, he held himself in place over her, his arms outside hers. Again she lifted her buttocks in wordless welcome. He came hard and insistent, asking nothing, taking everything.

Home! Buried deep. Filling and stretching her.

Before she could prepare, he shoved. She slid. Friction burned her back. Her shoulders were now at the edge of the bed, forcing her to grip his to prevent him from knocking her off.

Every thrust rocked her, reminding her of her precarious perch. Then he let up, and she eased back onto the bed a few precious inches. They were fuck-dancing, sweat-slippery bodies sealed together but in danger of losing connection. By digging her heels into the mattress, she managed some control, but her thighs were on fire. Instinct took over, and she looped her legs up and over his.

Now his every movement became hers. His straining muscles transmitted their effort to her. They shared the same heat, the same sweat. They breathed with the same quick rhythm.

His muscles seemed tireless as he repeatedly thrust into her. His cock sliding along her pussy walls ignited them. Was that his tip she felt in her throat? Faster and faster he pumped. Mindless, she found a pattern that increased the friction of cock against pussy.

Familiar hunger and intensity clamped down on her. She could fight it and show him—show him what, that she didn't like being treated like a cunt? But she did!

"Feel it," he barked. "Feel me!"

"I do. Damn you to hell, I do."

He chuckled. The sound was deep and rough, rumbling out from his core and accompanied by yet another slick retreat. Feeling his cock start to slide out of her, she clenched her muscles so he couldn't escape. He laughed again, only this time a groan accompanied the sound.

Another thrust, longer and even stronger. She snarled and closed her eyes and concentrated on the hunger tearing at her. One way to silence it, only one way. Clamping her legs around his, she arched her back and stood her ground, forcing him to come at her with all his strength.

She snapped inside, flew off into ragged pieces. Straining, she met him muscle for muscle.

"Fuck. Fuck."

"Feel me. Eat me."

Her muscles jerked and trembled. If this had been her first

climax, it would have terrified her. Instead, she dove into the heat. Welcomed it with a long, low cry. Light flashed behind her closed lids. She couldn't pull enough air into her lungs. Her heart slammed in her chest.

What did he matter?

Nothing. For this moment, nothing.

14

When Ferren woke up, the morning sun slanting through the window was aimed at her face. She turned away from it and tried to bury herself in sleep. The muscles in her arms and legs ached, and her neck felt stiff. She could only imagine how sore she'd be if Mayer hadn't ordered her back into the shower after they'd had sex.

Ordered.

Teeth clenched against a groan, she lay there and pulled her world back together. When she'd stumbled into the shower, she'd been so out of it that she hadn't been able to put her mind to anything except standing under the warm, soothing spray. She'd stayed there until the hot water ran out. Forced out of the steamy enclosure, she'd reached for yet another towel.

He hadn't said a word when she returned to the bedroom that had become her world. He was already in bed with the blanket thrown back in a silent command. Her mind still resolutely on neutral, she'd slipped in beside him. She'd tried to turn her back to him, but he'd positioned her on her side facing him and slid his hand between her legs.

Somehow she'd fallen asleep with his fingers resting on her cunt.

"Get up."

Startled, she looked around. He was already dressed, loose sweats obscuring his hips and thighs, short-sleeved black pullover looking like a second skin. The shirt's color was reflected in his eyes. Unnerved, she obeyed.

Once on her feet, she stood with her hands clasped in front of her in a pitiful attempt at modesty.

"It's time to get ready."

"For—for what?"

Instead of answering, he jerked his head at the bathroom door. By the time she came out wrapped in yet another towel, he had breakfast ready. They ate cereal in silence because she couldn't bring herself to ask why he was so remote and somber. She just wanted out of here. Wanted back, not her old life, but her ability to have some say about her world.

Why the hell did he have to look so imposing? He was strong, damn it. Couldn't he just let her acknowledge his physical superiority? They'd shake hands, promise to stay in touch, and go their own ways.

Like you'll ever be able to free yourself from his impact on you.

Leaving her to wallow in turmoil, he went to the refrigerator and poured a couple of glasses of orange juice. She gulped hers down, grateful for the quick sugar jolt.

"We're going to have company," he said. "There are things I need to do to get ready."

A surge of panic brought her to her feet. "Philip. It has to be him."

His silence gave her the answer she feared, and her hand went to her throat in a self-protective gesture. He stood between her and the front door, not that reaching it would do her any good.

"Why?" she demanded. "Why are you doing this?"

Midnight housed itself in its eyes. She couldn't so much as glimpse him through the dense curtain. "You'll find out in due time."

"Due time? Damn it, tell me now."

"No."

The second wave of panic was greater than the first. Unable to stop herself, she slapped him as hard as she could. "You bastard! You damn bastard."

"Yeah, I am," he agreed and caught her hand. He squeezed, mashing her fingers together until she cried out.

He let up on the pressure, but before the pain subsided, he yanked off the towel, grabbed her around the waist, and threw her over his shoulder. She pounded his back and tried to kick him despite the restraining grip on her buttocks. Throwing her on the bed, he swiftly and easily rolled her over onto her belly. She struggled to get her arms and legs under her, but before she could complete the act, he straddled her and sat on her hips.

"Stop it! No, please. Don't do this!"

"I have to."

The question of what he meant evaporated the instant she realized he'd placed several ropes on the bed while she was in the bathroom. The first went, not around her wrists, but at her elbows. He worked with the speed and efficiency of a calf roper. Leaving her to contemplate what she could accomplish without use of her arms, he turned his attention to her ankles. Despite her struggles, he soon tethered them.

When he stood her on her feet, she discovered he'd left just enough play so she didn't lose her balance. She might be able to shuffle, might.

"Mayer, please! I don't understand what—"

"You don't have to."

She stiffened when he pressed rope against her teeth but opened her mouth because experience had taught her that he'd win the battle. Besides, not being able to talk saved her from begging for an explanation.

What a fool she'd been to believe he had an ounce of humanity in him! Money made the world go around. At least it ruled his. Money and being able to do whatever he wanted to her, his helpless victim.

"Don't move." A hard squeeze on her breasts accompanied his order.

When she nodded, he released her and walked over to the damnable camera. Accustomed to seeing him work with it, she paid scant attention to what he was doing. He then turned on his laptop, making her think he was going to send a live feed to Philip.

But hadn't he said Philip was coming here?

After pulling something out of the desk drawer, he returned to her. He held up a series of shots of a naked, gagged, and blindfolded woman with her arms and ankles tethered the way hers were. But there were differences, additions, more ropes on the nearly faceless woman.

"This is my script," he told her. "Damn near everything I've done to you has been because that's what he dictated. I want you to see what he has in mind for today."

She thought she recognized the woman in the photographs as a sometimes bondage model who was using her earnings at Leather 'n Chains to pay off an old IRS bill. Ginger admitted she got off on pain and loved having whips used on her.

To her surprise, he returned to the camera and held the photographs up to the lens. Then he dropped them onto the floor.

Although she couldn't hear his footsteps, she sensed them. He was coming closer, ropes slung over his shoulders. Looking up, she spotted a hook and chain dangling over her.

No, she said with her eyes. *Please, no!*

Stepping behind her, he deftly circled several loops around her wrists, leaving a long length dangling. Then, although she tried to twist away, he ran the loose rope between her legs. Standing on his toes, he secured the end to the overhead hook. He'd left enough play that the rope didn't press against her pussy but that could—would—change.

Her head dropped forward. Wild animals fought their ropes, but she knew how useless struggling would be. She'd husband her strength in a desperate attempt to keep from losing her sanity. And to feed her sense of betrayal.

Crack!

Gasping into the gag, she struggled to comprehend the sound. Someone had thrown open the door and was stalking in.

Philip!

"Guess what? This place came with more than one key!" The tall, overweight, balding man with perpetual stubble waved a key at Mayer. "Didn't expect me so early, did you?"

"Checking up on your investment are you?" Mayer asked. If he was shocked to see Philip, he didn't show it.

"Damn right I am." Philip turned his attention from Mayer to her. "Aren't you going to welcome me, bitch? Oh, guess you can't." He stalked toward her, his measured steps putting her in mind of a hunting lion. "A little wrapped up in your work at the moment, aren't you?"

"I was just getting started," Mayer said. "Up late last night."

Philip spun toward Mayer. As he did, the generous belly under his too-tight designer shirt jiggled. "You were fucking her, right? I told you, keep your hands off her."

"It was hard to do."

That's all their sex had been, a horny man taking advantage of the free offering?

"I should have hired someone else."

"Who?" Mayer hadn't so much as twitched since Philip burst in. "It's not as if people willing to kidnap and torture a woman are crawling out of the woodwork."

To her disgust, Philip grinned. "So you figured it out did

you? Our little porn queen here isn't a sub in need of an education after all."

"Hell, no. You going to tell her what this is really about?"

Dismissing Mayer, Philip shifted so he faced her again. Months ago she'd conditioned herself not to feel disgust at the sight of the man who had little regard for his physical health or appearance. But the way he studied her made her shudder.

"It will be my pleasure." Smiling the demeaning smile she knew and hated, Philip lumbered closer. He reached for a breast. She back-stepped and lost her balance. If not for his beefy fingers on her hips, she would have fallen.

"Don't want you hurting yourself, tight ass." He pressed his fingertips against her buttocks. "Not yet anyway. As for what this is about—no, I'm not quite ready to tell you after all. Not until I'm sure I have the bitch's full attention. I want both of you to get the whole picture." He laughed at what he obviously considered a joke. "You want to help me here?"

Mayer folded his arms across his chest and regarded Philip from under lids at half-mast. "This is your show. Maybe I'll just stand and watch."

"Yeah? Yeah, all right."

When Philip sidled around her and stepped to the wall behind her, her heart hammered. Because she'd seen the pictures with Ginger in them she knew what was coming. Still—

Looking over her shoulder at the man who used to be her employer, she watched him trail his hands over the chain fastened to the wall. The other end connected to the hook overhead. Philip tugged on the chain. Instantly the rope between her legs snugged against her. Desperate to escape the pressure, she stood on her toes. Chuckling, Philip re-secured the chain.

"There. Now you're not going anywhere."

He was more than right. Mayer had left considerable slack in the rope, but it now held her firmly in place. Between the two men, she couldn't decide which represented the greatest threat—maybe Mayer because she'd once trusted him, and he knew too much about her strengths and weaknesses.

"Spell things out for me." Mayer spoke so softly she had to strain to hear him. "What brought you here?"

"Her. And you."

"That's not telling me anything."

"You're one to be talking. What the hell was that you told me right before we shook hands? That you had no interest in banging a cheap piece of ass."

Shame, shock, and fury warred for attention. How insanely stupid she'd been to think Mayer cared about her as a human being! He wasn't looking at her. Would he once Philip started in on her and she couldn't think of anything else?

A new and even more frightening thought slammed into her. Philip had let her see him. Clearly he had no intention of freeing her—of letting her live.

"Where're the whips?" Philip's voice held no more emotion than if he'd been asking for a soft drink.

"There." Mayer pointed at a built-in drawer.

"Get them."

Hoping against hope that Mayer wouldn't obey, she held her breath. Instead, sighing as if he resented being put out, he sauntered over to the drawer and pulled out a half dozen whips of different lengths and materials. Try as she did, she couldn't suppress a shudder.

Philip made a show of coming to a decision but finally selected one with a short base and a multitude of long, thin strands. He snapped it, chuckling when she tried to back away.

"I've been dreaming about this for a long time, bitch. Getting back at you. I'm going to enjoy this."

"What are you saying?" Mayer asked. He sounded bored. "This kidnapping and buying crap you dreamed up, getting us on Surrender Island, the whole time you planned on getting personally involved?"

The way Philip studied her made her feel like a netted fish. "You want to know what the initial plan was do you? Hell. Might as well tell you 'cause you sure as hell aren't going to the police. Not with your mug on those films." His cruel grin chilled her. "Maybe you've already put one and one together, but I'll spell things out anyway. I've made copies of everything you sent me. One set's going to my lawyer. Another is addressed to the police, but as long as you play ball, there's no need to waste money on postage is there?"

"Blackmail."

"Let's call it insurance. A simple and effective way of buying your silence."

"And her?" Mayer flicked a glance in her direction that it revealed nothing of what he was thinking.

"You ever hear of white slavery?"

It took all she had not to throw up. Her calves burned from having to stay on her toes. Her pussy too felt as if it were on fire.

"You intended to sell her?"

"That was the plan, once you'd broken her down. I can get fifty grand for her, fifty. Not a bad return on my investment. A sex slave's nothing more than a lap dog—a dog kept on a chain or in a cage when she's not being put to use. Her master, or masters, wouldn't have given a damn what she said. Trying to stay alive would have been a hell of a lot more important than making my life more miserable than she already had." He stepped closer. "You got that, bitch? You brought this on yourself." He flicked the whip at her belly. Although it didn't hurt much more than a bee sting, anticipation of the next blow made her grind her teeth into the rope gag. "Thought you could blow the whistle on me, cut into my profit, and I'd let you get away with it, did you? Guess you were wrong." He struck her again, lower.

"But you can't sell her now," Mayer observed. "Not now that she can finger you. You don't dare take the chance."

Philip cocked his arm, let fly. "Like they say, change of plans."

None of the blows had cut her flesh. Only the last left a mark. Still, her flesh quivered.

"Change to what?" Mayer asked.

"Nosy bastard, aren't you? What are you doing, writing a book?"

"Like you said, my mug's on film. I've got a vested interest in this."

"More than vested. The second segment you sent me yesterday, the one of the two of you fucking did it for me."

Horrified, she willed Mayer to meet her stare. He'd promised, reassured her that Philip wouldn't see that footage!

"I thought you'd like to see what you were paying for."

Philip snorted. "The hell you did! You think I'm stupid? You wanted to make sure I understood that, not only were you getting paid to make her life hell, you were also dumping your load in her."

"Got to you did it?"

Philip's glare made her think he'd like nothing better than to see Mayer dead. Then, to her surprise, he laughed. "Got me thinking I was missing all the fun. So what if I don't make any money from selling her." The way he swiped his hand down her belly made her feel less than human. "Helping her see the error of her ways—and letting certain other bitches get the message via the films—is worth the tradeoff. She fucks like a whore. Thanks for giving me a demonstration. How about it, bitch? Ready for your lessons, are you?"

"Kill her and those in charge on Surrender Island are going to get involved."

"Good point." His grin revealed a mouthful of too-white caps. "But I didn't intend to bury the corpse here. You ever been to the Everglades? I go fishing there sometimes. A person can travel for miles and never see another human being. And the crocs—damn efficient."

"Is that what you did with the others?"

Something dark and cold settled over Philip's features. Even as he turned to face Mayer, she knew she'd seen into the eyes of pure evil.

"She tell you about that, did she?"

"Some. Then I did my own research."

"And?"

"And I came up with nothing that would connect you to their deaths."

"Damn brilliant of me wouldn't you say?" Philip tapped the whip handle against his teeth. "I'm done talking. Got more important things to do. Stay and watch or get the hell out of here. I don't care."

Don't leave. Oh, God, please don't.

"That's not my thing." Mayer shoved his hands in the front pockets of his sweats as if looking for his keys.

An instant later, he pulled out the small pistol she'd seen before and pointed it at Philip's crotch. "This is."

"What the hell—"

"Game's up."

"You're going to shoot me? What for?"

"If necessary, to keep you from harming her."

"Shit. Shit. You goddamn bastard, I—"

"Watch your language. You don't know who all's going to hear." Mayer stepped to her side. Keeping the pistol aimed where it would do a great deal of damage, he again reached into his pocket. This time he pulled out a knife and snapped it open. "Don't move, honey. I don't want to hurt you."

Honey.

The word swirled through her as he cut through her ropes. Sighing, she settled back down on her feet and removed her gag.

"What the hell are you doing?" Philip insisted. The whip dangled from his fat fingers.

"Shut up," Mayer ordered. "Honey, can you use your hands?"

"Yes." Much as she needed to embrace him, she knew not to distract him.

"Good. How would you like the job of putting cuffs on him?"

"What?" Philip demanded. "Are you an idiot? I've got those films. They're—"

"Take a look." Mayer pointed at the camera. "It's been running since before you got here. Some of the pictures might be out of focus, but the sound quality is great. Hon, are you ready?"

Yes. Yes! Taking the knife from him, she freed her ankles.

Then, at Mayer's prompting, she walked over to the drawer where the whips had been and selected a pair of handcuffs. After thinking about it for a moment, she picked up a second set. "I don't think one pair will be enough. Big as his belly and ass are, he won't be able to get his hands behind him."

"That's my girl. Always thinking."

She had to force herself to get close to Philip and was careful not to place herself between the two men. Mayer had to cock the gun to get Philip to move, and because her fingers were still a little numb, she had trouble operating the cuffs. Finally though, she heard a satisfying snap. Before leaving Philip, she yanked the whip out of his hand.

Instead of joining Mayer, she waited.

"High tech's an amazing thing." Mayer spoke to Philip. "Just as I sent you the earlier videos, this time I was able to send a live feed to where I wanted it to go."

"Live feed?" Philip looked sick. "What—if you're bluffing—"

"I don't bluff. Honey, do you want to call your mother?"

"My—my mother?"

"The feed's going to her office. She might be watching." Smiling one of his rare and utterly disarming smiles, he held out his hand.

Naked and disheveled, she rushed to his side and wrapped her arms around him. He squeezed back, his attention divided between her and their prisoner. God, but he felt good! Everything about this moment was right. Wonderful!

And she'd just fallen in love.

"You bastard!" Philip hissed. "You bastard."

"Coming from you, that's a compliment," Mayer said. "You want to take bets on how determinedly Ferren's lawyer of a mother is going to prosecute you? Thanks to what you said in front of the camera today, my guess is she'll have all the proof she needs to put you in prison for the rest of your life."

Holding onto Mayer with all her strength, she tried to order herself to let go, to pick up his cell phone, and call her mother.

But it would have to wait.

Everything would until she'd lifted her head and parted her lips, until he'd lowered his head and pressed his mouth against hers.

Long.

Hard.

Strong.

Epilogue

A breeze generated by the fan in the screened-in porch fanned her hair and cheeks. The jungle air was midmorning warm, prompting her to lift Mayer's shirt off her breasts. The fabric smelled of him.

"Would you rather go back inside?"

"No." She rolled her head toward Mayer who sat in the lounge chair next to her. Gone were his bulky and weapon-hiding sweats. He'd put on a pair of shorts that would have been a perfect fit if not for his muscled thighs. The shorts had crept up, teasing her with thoughts of what waited just above the hem. He hadn't bothered to put on another shirt after giving her his. "I'd rather stay out here until they come for him."

By *them*, she meant those responsible for the island's operation. Once they'd spirited him back to the mainland—or should she say the real world—police dispatched by her mother would be waiting for him. She wasn't sure how Mayer had convinced Surrender Island's management of Philip's horrifying plans for her because she'd been thinking about her conversation with her mother when he placed his call. She'd ask him about that, later.

"It's beautiful out there. Peaceful." As if to prove her point, a large white bird with long lacy tail feathers landed on a bush only a few feet from the porch. The growth just beyond the screened enclosure was lush and nearly as dense as it was in the Everglades.

Thoughts of the Everglades made her shiver.

"What is it?" Mayer reached for her hand.

She looked at his large, strong fingers, then placed hers in his for safekeeping. "Nothing. Really, nothing. I was letting my thoughts get away with me."

"It's going to happen for a while. Ferren?" He squeezed her hand. "I'm sorry."

For what she asked with her eyes as she squeezed back.

"The way I handled you. The things I did and forced you to endure. There at the end, I felt I needed to demonstrate Philip's sick demands for the camera. I needed to set things—you—up so he'd walk into my trap. I didn't dare tell you; it had to look authentic."

The bondage she'd experienced under Mayer's direction hadn't been all bad, far from it. In truth, she missed the caress of leather and rope against her skin—almost as much as she craved his hands on her, ruling her, knowing everything about her sexuality. That was part of what she was still trying to wrap her mind around. Although she'd long resisted her *employers'* attempts to push her limits, she'd embraced the real thing.

If it had been anyone except Mayer exploring her body, pushing her buttons, and sending her deep into the most explosive climaxes she'd ever had—

"Honey?"

Sighing, she forced carnal thoughts aside. At least she thought she'd succeeded until she acknowledged the moist heat between her legs.

"I'm sorry." Realizing she'd just repeated his words, she chuckled. "I was thinking about something my mother said." *At least I was until I got distracted.*

"Does she want me drawn and quartered? She might prosecute me too, you know."

"Oh, no. No. I won't let her."

He'd been studying the motionless white bird. Now he turned his attention back to her. "A power shift," he said softly. "You're the one in control."

Of your future. Your life.

Knowing how much of a chance he'd taken by sending the damning video to her mother, she swung her legs over to the side of the lounge. She felt like the proverbial rag doll but managed to lean over him, her hands on his sun-warmed shoulders.

"That's right, I am in charge. And I'm hungry, slave. I order you to go hunting. Bring me back a porterhouse steak. And a ham. And a turkey."

Laughing, he drew her onto his lap. Snuggled against his chest, she felt safer than she'd ever been in her life. Safe, cherished, and challenged.

"What did your mother say?"

"A lot of things like was I all right, questions about you." She took a steadying breath. "When that was over, she asked if I was done letting my father rule my life."

"Did she?"

"She's right. Absolutely right." Feeling overwhelmed by the simple truth of what she'd finally faced, she straightened. "Mayer, my old man didn't care about me. I've spent too much of my life supplying him with proof that he was right—that I was a marketable commodity, a piece of flesh, the next thing to a whore, not a daughter worthy of her father's love."

"No. Damn it, that's not you!"

Thank you. Thank you. You'll never know how much I needed to hear that. "I—I realize that, finally. What I did was legal, mostly. But it skated close to the edge. It's hardly what most modern, intelligent, reasonably educated women would choose for a career."

"Did? Past tense?"

It had come down to that, hadn't it? In a matter of moments, he'd cut through all the layers and touched the most important thing.

"Yes." She trailed light kisses over his chest, then rested her cheek against him. "I don't want strangers staring at me while I'm, you know, any more. I'd distanced myself from reality, convinced myself that I was some damn actress instead of providing more people than I want to think about with fodder for their sexual fantasies—violent fantasies."

"It's a world into itself."

"Yes, it is. Thanks to the man in there, I can no longer deny what's sordid about what I do—did." Closing her eyes, she drew on the image of a young girl running full out while the wind whipped her hair and grass stained her bare feet. Her laughter back then had been so joyous. "I need to be proud of what I do, to feel free."

"Free? All the time?" He slid a hand under the shirt hem and settled his fingers over her flank.

Your ropes. Your body teasing and igniting mine.

"I don't want to say good-by to you once we leave the island," he continued. "I want to be part of your life. I need..."

"What do you need?" she prompted after a too-long silence.

"I think I went through pretty much the same thing you did, only with me it happened awhile ago. I used to believe those who said I was my mother's son—a screw-up. A loser. Then I spent a couple of months behind bars looking out at some hills I'd never paid attention to before. I desperately needed to climb those hills, to never look at anything through bars again."

"I—I feel the same way."

"I'm glad."

"I need a life no longer dictated by a man who doesn't know how to be a father." Her throat tightened.

"You're going to need to testify."

"We both are."

"Yes. But this will eventually be behind us."

"And when it is, I—we—can get on with our lives."

"What will you do then?"

I can't think about anything except your hand on me, the beat of your heart, how much I need you inside me. "I want to finish college. And then—maybe I'll go into law. Become a lawyer like my mother, if my past doesn't haunt me."

"Your past." He wrapped both arms around her and held her so tight she could barely breathe. "That's what it is, honey. Something we can bury."

We. "You mean it?"

"With all my heart."

Sizzling romance. *Scorching* sex. Get it all in HOT IN HERE by Susan Lyons. Available now from Aphrodisia . . .

easiest thing to do, but once he'd made it, he got right down to business. It had been a while since he'd gone parking, but if there was anything a farm-raised boy knew, it was how to do a girl in a truck.

In a few seconds he'd reclined the passenger seat part way and was sitting with her facing him, straddling his thighs. She leaned forward and touched her lips to his.

His hands found their way through that midnight wash of hair and gripped her head, holding it as his tongue thrust into her mouth.

She met it with hers, and what he'd intended to be a slow kiss quickly went fiery.

And his cock was three steps ahead. He groaned. Damn! He needed her, and he needed her right now.

She was lifting her skirt higher and he realized she'd taken off her panties. He stared, fascinated, at the shiny wisps of pubic hair, so few and so fine they accented rather than hid the pale skin below.

Man, that was the sexiest bush he'd ever seen.

He was reaching out to touch when her own fingers attacked the waistband of his pants, and then he couldn't think of anything but getting out of his clothes and into Jenny. She slid down the zipper and he raised up off the seat so she could slide his pants and boxers down his legs.

His cock sprang free.

She paused and stared at it.

He'd never realized just how big it was. Now, beside tiny Jenny, his first thought was, man, she'd fit his cock as snug as a glove. A warm, wet, throbbing glove.

But what if he was too big for her?

No matter how horny he might be, he sure the hell wasn't going to hurt a girl, getting his rocks off.

But then she purred, "Very, very nice," and reached out one of those graceful hands.

Hand in hand—man, was she tiny—they walked down the alley to the open-air lot where he'd parked. The other firefighters who'd attended the competition had gone. Scott could tell because his Ford F-150 was the only truck in the lot. The few other vehicles were definitely not firefighter wheels.

He took her by the waist and lifted her into the passenger seat. No way could she have climbed up there herself without a struggle, she was such a shorty.

Short, and small. Perfectly proportioned, but miniature.

She held out a hand. "Come on up." Her fingers were small, slim and graceful, tipped with long nails painted pink, a couple of them with glittering stones embedded in them. It was the most girlie hand he'd ever seen.

She leaned toward him and her hair swung forward, gleaming, silky, alive. He had a vision of a Hawaiian woman under a waterfall, washing her hair.

Sexy hand, sexy hair. Could he get any harder without bursting?

Scrambling into a truck sporting a fire-pole boner wasn't the

"No!" He grabbed her hand. "You do that and it'll all be over."

"I'd have thought a firefighter would have better control over his . . ." she paused, ran her tongue around her lips and then finished, "hose."

Normally he did. "Depends how strong the fire is."

She was still staring at his cock, like she was fascinated by it. Or maybe scared?

He had to ask. "Are you, uh, going to be okay? I mean, you're a small girl and . . ."

She looked up, her eyes smoldering. "I think we're both going to be more than okay, big boy. You have a condom, or d'you want to use one of mine?"

Condom. Of course. He really wasn't thinking tonight. "Wallet. Pants pocket."

She fumbled for it, which had her squirming on his lap, which had him clenching his muscles again. Somehow, each time she squirmed, she ended up closer to his cock until finally her sweet pussy was pressed right against him, all hot and wet and swollen.

She stopped, condom package in hand, and moaned, "That feels so good."

It sure as hell did.

He grabbed the package from her, ripped it open and started to sheath himself.

"I'll do that," she said.

"The hell you will."

All the things he loved having women do, and he couldn't let this girl—the hottest of them all—do any of them or he'd lose control like a thirteen-year-old.

With a shaking hand, he managed to get the condom on.

He should touch her, get her warmed up and ready, and his fingers longed to explore her seductive body, to tweak those pearled nipples, but he didn't have that much self-control.

Besides, she was giving out signals that said she too was at the point just before flashover. When everything was so hot it was ready to ignite.

She lifted herself and used the fingers of one hand to spread herself open. Then she gripped him and brought his tip to her opening. And lowered herself slowly.

He fought to sit still, not daring to move for fear he would hurt her, as her sheath gripped him inch by inch. She was tight, deliciously tight, but wet, thank God, and she was taking him in.

All the way.

She rocked her hips, front and back, and moaned, "You feel so good."

No, he felt fucking incredible. His cock had never had it so good, and it was making its demands known.

Now she was rocking in circles and—oh, crap, he couldn't control this any longer.

He thrust up and Jenny gave a gasp, rocked harder against him, and she was moaning and he was gasping and their bodies were finding a frenzied rhythm of their own. No way could he last another minute but then she cried out, "Now, Scott, now!" and began to spasm around him.

And everything he'd felt all that long evening—the sexiness of the saxophone, the turn-on of the crowd's approval, this girl's lovely hands and silky hair, that pretty little pussy—it all poured through him and Scott was exploding. Coming harder and longer than ever before.

Coming like he wanted to reach her center and never find his way back again.